"AN ASTONISHING TALENT."
—*Suspense Magazine*

Haven operative Luther Brinkman has been sent into the wilderness of the Appalachian Mountains to locate escaped bank robber Cole Jacoby—an assignment that leaves Brinkman severely injured, alone, and with no way to convey his location to Haven.

Luckily, Agent Callie Davis of the FBI's Special Crimes Unit is already closing in. But when she finds the wounded Brinkman, the rescue mission is far from over. What neither Luther nor Callie knows is that their quarry is more than an escaped felon.

In hunting him, they will find themselves being hunted *by* him—deep in the unfamiliar wilds of Tennessee—and will discover the worst monster either of them has ever known.

continued . . .

Praise for Kay Hooper and her novels

Titles by Kay Hooper

Bishop/Special Crimes Unit Novels

HAVEN

HOSTAGE

Bishop Files Novels

THE FIRST PROPHET

HOSTAGE

KAY HOOPER

JOVE BOOKS, NEW YORK

THE BERKLEY PUBLISHING GROUP
Published by the Penguin Group
Penguin Group (USA) LLC
375 Hudson Street, New York, New York 10014

USA • Canada • UK • Ireland • Australia • New Zealand • India • South Africa • China

penguin.com

A Penguin Random House Company

HOSTAGE

A Jove Book / published by arrangement with the author

For information, address: The Berkley Publishing Group,
a division of Penguin Group (USA) LLC,
375 Hudson Street, New York, New York 10014.

ISBN: 978-0-515-15373-6

PUBLISHING HISTORY
Berkley hardcover edition / December 2013
Jove premium edition / August 2014

PRINTED IN THE UNITED STATES OF AMERICA

10   9   8   7   6   5   4   3   2   1

Cover design by Rita Frangie.
Cover photo of "Woods" © Guillermo Rodriguez Carballa / Trevillion Images;
"Man" by Haveseen / Shutterstock Images.
Text design by Kristin del Rosario.

AUTHOR'S NOTE

Once again, and at the request of many readers, I have chosen to place this note at the beginning of the book rather than after the story, so as to better inform you of the additional material I am providing for both new readers and those who have been with the series from the beginning. You'll find some brief character bios, as well as SCU definitions of various psychic abilities, at the end of the book, information that will hopefully enhance your enjoyment of this story and of the series.

HOSTAGE

PROLOGUE

Shayna Freeman woke with a throbbing headache and the groggy realization that she must have really tied one on the previous night. Not that she could remember, but that had to be it because she never felt this bad unless alcohol was involved.

Stupid. Stupid. When will you learn to ignore a dare?

That was usually how she got in trouble.

She just lay there for a while, eyes closed because she knew from experience that the room would be spinning dizzily if she dared open them. Gradually, though, things started to nag at her. The bed beneath her felt oddly lumpy and . . . damp. The air she breathed had a stale, faintly sour odor. Even through the headache, she was aware that the room felt weirdly hollow somehow. And cold. She didn't feel covers over her. Why not?

Little things.

Lying there, eyes closed, feeling more and more cold, she kept telling herself nothing was wrong. Again and again, she told herself that. Because if she believed it, then . . . well, then, nothing was wrong.

Nothing.

Shayna didn't know how long she lay there with her eyes squeezed shut, the mantra of nothing being wrong on a continuous loop in her mind, before she finally forced herself to open her eyes.

Dark.

But not . . . completely dark.

She thought she could make out heavy timbers above her, the sort she imagined would be used to hold up tons of earth to allow a passage into a mountain. For a mine of some kind, maybe.

She was in a mine?

How on earth—

She tried to move her arms, to lever herself into a sitting position. And that was when she heard the loud rattle and felt the heavy constriction on her wrists. Both wrists.

Instinctively, she tried to reach one hand to check the other and discovered it to be impossible. Whatever she was lying on, the chains, the . . . manacles . . . were fastened from her wrists to either side. She couldn't even push herself up to her elbows, because there wasn't enough play in the chains. Couldn't lift either hand high enough to confirm what she felt.

Not handcuffs. The bands around her wrists were wide

and heavy. The chain was—sounded—thick. Old. Rusty. She could smell the rust.

And when she tried to move her feet . . .

She lay there for some unmeasurable time, staring up at the heavy beams and trying not to think about why someone would have chained her, wrists and ankles, to an old, smelly, lumpy cot in what might have been a mine somewhere in the mountains.

Because that was surreal.

Something like that didn't happen, not to her. Not to anybody she knew. Because it was just . . . crazy. She didn't have a rich family, so nobody would consider kidnapping her for ransom. And if she hadn't been kidnapped for ransom, then . . . then . . .

Young women were snatched every day. She saw it on the news. Snatched out of their lives without warning, sometimes never to be seen again. And sometimes . . .

Sometimes seen, found, as bodies buried or floating in rivers or just left somewhere like garbage.

Bodies showing the evidence of the horrible things that had been done to them, unspeakable things.

She could hear herself breathing in shallow little gasps, the only sounds in the cold, dank, hollow space all around her. The chill was seeping into her, into her very bones, a kind of cold she'd never felt before.

A terror that took hold of her and squeezed and squeezed until it forced out a sound, a name she hadn't uttered since she was very, very young.

"Mommy . . ."

HIS DOGS WERE well trained, well fed, and well housed. In fact, if he was inside the cabin, so were they.

He didn't approve of chaining dogs. Besides, they were more likely to be protective of what they perceived as the pack's territory, and he wanted that to be wherever he was.

It had cost him valuable time and effort to make the necessary detour to pick up his dogs from the friend who had taken them in when he'd been positive he was going to be arrested.

It had also cost him a chunk of money from his stash, but he didn't begrudge that. His friend had clearly taken good care of the dogs, and the money was not only compensation but also strong incentive not to talk if the police managed to locate him.

Not that Jacoby expected them to be able to do that. He had been warned before his capture, and in time to make his preparations. And everything since then had gone very much according to plan. After his escape, he had switched cars half a dozen times, *and* he'd destroyed GPS units before moving the cars an inch. Still, paying his friend well for his care of the dogs just made good sense.

Not a lot in Jacoby's life made good sense.

The voices in his head, for instance. The ones telling him to do Bad Things. That didn't make good sense. It didn't make any sense at all. It never had.

You have to go after him.

Some of the voices were soft and whispery, and some

were distinct, but they almost always spoke in concert, their words identical.

"No, I don't." He brushed the largest of his three dogs, gently removing twigs and dried leaves from her thick coat. "He'll go away. They always go away and leave me alone."

They caught you before.

"That was a mistake. I was careless. The target was too big and drew the wrong kind of attention. You made me do that."

You had to push your boundaries, Cole.

"Not that far. There was no reason to go that far. To take that much. It won't happen again, not like that. And I told you. They always leave me alone when I hide in these mountains."

Not this one. He's different. You know he is. You felt it.

"He ran, didn't he? They all run. They all leave me alone once I run them off. Besides, I shot this one. Hit him. There was blood."

You have to go after him. You have to be sure.

"I'm sure. He's dead."

Then why does your head hurt, Cole? Why did the nightmares wake you up again last night?

"You. It's your fault. You won't leave me alone."

Because the job isn't finished. It was never about the money, Cole. We all know that. It was just the next step. The money was just bait to draw the right kind of attention.

"I didn't want attention. I never want attention. I just want to be left alone."

When it's all finished, Cole. You agreed. And now you have to finish what you started.

"But I—"

Right now, you have to change the game. You have to hunt the hunters. Because they're coming for you. He's just the first.

"No. They'll leave me alone."

Not this time. There's already someone else. Someone you need to take care of.

"It's just him. Nobody else found me."

Someone did, Cole. Someone who can hurt you.

"No, I'm safe here. Safe. I've made sure of that. Nobody is coming to get me. Nobody is taking me back."

Do you really believe you can hold them off alone?

"I can. I will. If they come. But they won't. They won't come after me. Because all I did was steal some money, and after a while they just stop looking for it." His head was pounding, and it was becoming more and more difficult to think straight.

Not that his thoughts had been normal for a long time. Not since he was hardly more than a kid. Not since his cellmate all those years ago had slammed him against the metal corner of his cot.

Jacoby wondered if that son of a bitch was dead yet.

Concentrate, Cole.

There had been so much blood, surely he was dead.

Cole—

"Leave me alone! Why can't you leave me alone?" He felt the dog tense, then tremble, and forced his hands to gentle her. "It's okay, girl. It's okay. Just ignore them, all right? Just ignore them."

We're not going away, Cole. Not until you keep your promise. Not until you do what you agreed to do. You have to stop him. Stop them. And you have to take care of the girl.

"I—"

You have to do what we taught you to do. Don't forget, Cole. Don't forget who we are.

He felt the distinctly unpleasant sensation of something cold touching him, like an icy hand stroking his back. Up and down, up and down, making him shiver.

"I remember," he whispered.

Then don't fail us.

"No. No, I won't. I promise I won't."

ONE

Luther Brinkman could see his breath misting before his face in the moonlight; mid-October was cold this year, even in the South. Many hardwood trees that normally showed off colorful foliage that drew tourists to the Blue Ridge were already bare-limbed and glittering with frost, and the rest boasted only dead brown leaves clinging stubbornly.

"Shit." He paused and leaned against a big oak, grimacing as he adjusted the makeshift bandage around his upper thigh.

Would have been nice if it was at least a through-and-through. But no. I have to have a bullet grinding against bone every time I move.

Painfully against bone.

That was the way it felt, at least; he hadn't exactly gone digging around in the wound to find out for sure. Slowing the bleeding was the best he'd been able to do. Ignoring the throbbing pain, he concentrated on controlling his breathing so he could better listen.

He couldn't hear the dogs any longer. That was something. Whether it signaled an end to the pursuit or only a pause was the question uppermost in his mind. It was well past midnight; the bastard might well have decided that his wounded quarry wouldn't get far, that waiting for daylight to resume the chase was his best bet.

Or to look for a carcass. Even way out here, it wouldn't be smart to leave a dead body just lying around for the wrong person to stumble across, and he wouldn't have been able to know just how badly he'd wounded his quarry. Not for sure.

God knew Luther was out in the middle of nowhere, in a dense wilderness that had swallowed up more than one careless hiker and quite a few federal fugitives, never to be seen again. Even with dogs and daylight, tracking someone across this treacherous terrain would be difficult; making the attempt at night was something even the locals would consider suicidal.

But he wouldn't want to leave a body lying around.

Grim, Luther pushed himself away from the tree and continued on, using a thick broken limb he had found as a rough crutch. The terrain didn't exactly lend itself to hobbling along with a nice, steady rhythm. Or any rhythm at all. Just keeping himself upright was taking more effort and energy than he liked, given the distance he had to cover in order to reach safety: the tiny mountain town he had skirted on his way up here. He had judged it to be about five miles from Jacoby's cabin as the crow flew.

He wasn't a crow and couldn't even begin to travel in a straight line, not with the treacherous terrain and all the obstacles of the dense forest. It wasn't like it was just a gentle slope downward. There were ridges and switchbacks and deep gullies gouged out of the mountain by spring and summer rains. There were boulders taller than he was, taller than a house, and dense thickets of briars and other foliage.

Working his way past or over or around took time, and it ate up distance. The ground he'd have to cover probably included an extra mile or two at least, and that was assuming he could even last long enough to make the journey.

His mind instinctively calculated, and he tried to ignore the odds it offered him for success.

Never mind the odds. Take stock. You're wounded, but it isn't mortal and you can still use the leg. For now, at least. Dawn is hours away, so even if you can't reach the town, you have time to put more distance between you and the maniac with the gun and every reason to want you dead.

Okay. Not too bad.

Except that safety is . . . not close. You've lost a lot of blood and need medical attention. And you lost most of your gear, including the water, in that first bad fall, which was stupid, but let's not dwell on it. You have your weapon but maybe . . . what? . . . four rounds left in the clip?

The bastard would probably come after him loaded for bear.

Bears. Don't think about bears.

They could smell blood. And hadn't he heard something about an attempt to repopulate the area with once-threatened-with-extinction wolves? Or was that farther west?

Much farther. No wolves around here. Maybe wild dogs. Even cougars have been reported. I think. Bobcats. Certainly bears. Too early to be hibernating. I think. Damn bears.

He paused again to rest, leaning against another tree, and mentally took himself to task for letting his mind linger on things there was no sense worrying about unless and until he had to.

He had the uneasy feeling that he'd lost more blood than he had originally thought, and that was why he was having trouble focusing. Why he was light-headed and his breathing was more like panting.

Why he had to fight the urge to slide down the tree and take a real break. Maybe even a nap.

Oh, man, you are so screwed—

"Taking the scenic route?"

Haven

Maggie Garrett rubbed the nape of her neck absently, then sighed when her husband's fingers replaced her own. "Careful, or you'll put me to sleep," she told him wryly.

"You need to sleep," John Garrett replied. "By my count, you've been up forty-eight hours at least."

"I took a nap."

"Twenty minutes maybe. Not nearly enough."

"I'm okay."

"No, you aren't. You're never okay when one of your chicks is out of the nest."

A little laugh escaped her. "One of my chicks? I think there's a better nickname for a six-foot-four-inch former Marine. And I think he'd think so too."

John came around the desk and rested a hip on the corner so he could face her. They were in Maggie's office rather than the central work area of the sprawling building that was both home and business for them, and they were alone. "Haven operatives are all your chicks, especially when one comes up missing."

"He should have checked in by now. He should have checked in hours ago."

"Given the terrain, I doubt he could get a signal out." John paused, then asked deliberately, "Not a conventional signal, at least. Have you sensed something else?"

Maggie frowned. "I don't have a very strong connection with Luther. It makes him uncomfortable. He's fine with the telepaths, but since I pick up on emotions, and he's still buttoned up tight . . ."

"He'd rather keep his feelings to himself. Okay, I get that. With all the shit he's been through, I doubt most people would be eager to open up. But you're still sensing something?"

"It's just a vague feeling that something is wrong. Sort of a ghostly echo of pain."

"Physical pain?"

"I think so. Hard to be sure, though."

"Then probably not mortal pain."

"No, probably not."

"It was a simple enough assignment," John said, in a thoughtful tone. "Granted, our information put his target deep in the middle of nowhere, but hiking in there and finding him shouldn't have been much trouble for Luther, considering his tracking and survival skills on top of his . . . psychic radar. All he had to do was get his hands on that last car we're certain Jacoby drove, however briefly. After that, it was only a matter of tracking him, then settling down to observe from a distance for long enough to make sure the guy wasn't going anywhere, then withdraw and report in. We turn the information over to Nash, and he has the location of their escaped fugitive. Our job is done. The feds can go in and get him."

"Yeah." Maggie was still frowning.

"What?"

"Well . . . didn't it strike you as a little odd that Agent Nash came to us?"

"He checked out," John reminded her.

"I know he did. I know. And it made sense that, working pretty much alone out of a small field office in Tennessee, Nash didn't have the resources to launch a manhunt when he couldn't even narrow down the area in thousands of acres of wilderness."

"Didn't have the skills to do much on his own, either. He's pretty obviously a city boy."

Maggie nodded. "And the report from the Forest Service was clear enough; without a lot more information, they couldn't narrow down the area enough to search effectively themselves, especially since the search dogs lost the scent about a hundred yards from that abandoned car. It was pretty much straight up a mountain from there, and what towns exist in the area are scattered, tiny, and have a well-deserved reputation for minding their own business and not being especially welcoming *or* forthcoming to outsiders. Especially outsiders with badges."

"Remote doesn't begin to describe them," John agreed. "In an age of instant communication, they certainly do represent almost a return to simpler times."

Shifting to betray a rare sign of unease, Maggie said, "There are reports of survivalist and militia groups in that wilderness. Very credible reports. Some of the groups have been up there for years, and they aren't just unwelcoming to visitors; they're actively hostile."

"Luther has too much experience not to be able to avoid that kind of potential trouble."

"I know, I know. But I wish now I hadn't sent him in alone."

"One man alone, skilled and accustomed to rough terrain, could cover the distance faster and get in and out with the least chance of being detected. We agreed, and so did Luther."

She nodded. "Yeah, it makes perfect tactical sense. And we had to get someone in close, since none of our operatives have the ability to pick up on Jacoby from a distance."

"It's the sort of thing our operatives do, love. And word has spread in the last few years; we have several active cases pretty much all the time."

Maggie finally voiced what had been nagging at her.

"Why didn't Nash go to Bishop? That would have been the natural thing for a federal agent to do, to keep it inside the FBI. Why turn to a civilian organization when he had to know about the SCU?"

"Bad blood?" John suggested after a moment. "Bishop has made more than his fair share of enemies, and at least a few inside the bureau have been heard expressing resentment over the relative autonomy the Special Crimes Unit enjoys. Or maybe Nash simply didn't want his superiors to know he needed outside help to complete his assignment."

With a slight grimace, Maggie said, "I'd almost rather it was the former. For a federal agent to use us and then claim the credit in locating an escaped felon is just so . . ."

"Underhanded? We always request anonymity anyway; maybe he knew that going in."

"Maybe. Still."

If there was anything John Garrett had learned in the last few years, it was to respect his wife's feelings, however vague they might seem. He leaned forward to kiss her, then said, "Well, we can't report anything to Agent Nash until Luther reports in to us. But we can call Bishop."

LUTHER FOUND HIMSELF staring down the business end of a shotgun, all too clear in the moonlight. He actually had to force himself to lift his gaze from the barrels and focus on the woman holding the weapon.

"Taking the scenic route?" she repeated, her tone calm. The angle made it impossible for him to see her face;

she wore jeans and a warm jacket with a fur-trimmed hood pulled up.

He envied her the hood; he thought his ears might be frozen.

If he'd had two solid legs under him, Luther probably would have handled the situation differently, but as it was he judged he had little choice. The light-headedness was getting worse. "Ran into a little trouble hiking," he said.

In the same calm tone, she said, "Yeah, people run into bullets all the time in these mountains. Especially miles off the hiking trails and on private land. Posted private land. Anybody comes way up here to live, they generally prefer to be left alone."

"A simple 'Go away' would have been enough."

"That's what the NO TRESPASSING signs were for. Or did you manage to miss all of them?"

He decided, after backtracking a bit mentally, that he had missed the important point, and added, "How do you know it's a bullet wound? I might have fallen or . . . something."

"Looks like you're about to fall on your ass," she said. Then added, "That gun come with a badge?"

He wondered how she could see his handgun, since it was in a shoulder holster inside his zipped jacket. "Sort of."

The barrels of the shotgun lifted until they were pointed at his face. "Either you have a badge or you don't."

"Private investigator," he said, hoping he wasn't tripping over syllables in his haste to get the words out. "Licensed. Hired to locate an escaped fugitive."

"Escaped from where?"

"Uh . . . Virginia. Federal custody in Virginia."

"And they sent a civilian after him?"

"Not at first. I mean . . . there were state cops and FBI and maybe marshals, I dunno. Bunch of people. Tracking dogs. But he gave them all the slip. And in these mountains . . . Well, fugitives have gone missing pretty much forever."

"So you were hired."

"I'm good at this sort of thing," he said, wryly aware of the irony that drove him to add, "usually."

But all she said was, "And did you locate him?"

He had to think about that for a minute, aware of the vague notion that just because she had a gun in his face it didn't mean he had to tell her everything. In fact, it actually meant he shouldn't tell her anything.

Name, rank, serial number.

He remembered the drill.

"Yeah," he heard himself say. "But I was just supposed to find him and report in, that's all. Sneaky bastard slipped around behind me when I was waiting for it to get dark enough for me to leave without being seen. After that, I was just trying to get away from him and his dogs."

"Cole Jacoby."

He had the odd, fuzzy thought that she wasn't providing information so much as probing to find out what he knew. Except . . . he also felt she didn't have to do that. For some reason. What reason? "You know that because you're neighbors?"

"That. There aren't many of us up here this time of

year. And I heard his dogs. Around here, we usually keep our dogs in at night—unless there's something we need to run off."

"Which is why you came out here?"

"I also heard shots. And the whole area is posted no hunting. Besides which, it wasn't rifle fire I heard."

Luther wondered why she was now aiming the shotgun above his head, and realized only then that he was sliding slowly down the tree at his back. His legs felt like rubber.

"Shots. Uh-huh. Those would have been him shooting at me, and me . . . returning fire. I wasn't supposed to shoot him, so . . . I didn't try to hit him. He didn't . . . grant me . . . the same . . . courtesy." He shook his head to try to clear his vision. "Jesus, you're tall."

A sigh misted in the air in front of the face he still couldn't make out, and she lowered the shotgun until the barrels pointed downward. "No, *you're* tall. And heavy. And it's going to be a bitch getting you back to my place."

"Are we going to your place? That . . . sounds like . . . a plan."

"A plan that would work better if you didn't pass out along the way."

"Me? Pass out? Nah, I'm . . . fine. Just need to rest a little . . . while. And . . . I'll be . . . good as . . . new."

She bent toward him, and he tried really hard to see her face. But all he caught was the almost eerie gleam of her eyes.

You've got a ways to go before you're as good as new, pal.

It was the last thing he remembered, wondering if that had been his thought—or hers.

TWO

Haven

"Bishop."

"You're on speaker," Maggie told him. "I'm here with John. Sorry to call so late. Although I have no idea whether it's late where you are."

Being Bishop, he didn't answer the implied question. "Let me guess. One of your operatives hasn't checked in."

Maggie exchanged looks with her husband. "That didn't sound like a guess," she said. "You have an agent in Tennessee?"

"For a while now."

This time, it was John who said, "Agent Nash led us to believe his escaped fugitive was a . . . recent problem."

"Probably was recent, to him." Noah Bishop, chief of the Special Crimes Unit, sounded as calm as usual. "The problem part, I mean. Cole Jacoby was officially in custody and halfway across Virginia two weeks ago. Neither of the agents responsible for him could quite explain how he managed to slip his leash. In fact, they had a number of unexplained gaps in their memories. Lengthy gaps."

"Both of them?" Maggie asked. "Both missing the same memories?"

"The same time gaps, at least. No physical injuries, and nothing showed up on the medical tests, including any signs of drugs or other known toxins. But they're experienced agents, and they'd never lost a prisoner during a transfer before Jacoby."

"SCU?" Maggie asked the question even knowing the answer.

"No. We wouldn't oversee or be part of the transfer of a prisoner unless he was psychic—and we knew it."

"I'm liking this less and less," John said. "You suspect Jacoby is psychic? That's why you sent an agent to Tennessee?"

"By some means we don't yet understand, the memories of two experienced agents were . . . tampered with. The vehicle was clean, no sign it was bumped or run off the road or otherwise stopped. All the prints inside and on the doors belonged to the agents or the prisoner, which is pretty strong evidence no one else was involved. And yet at some point during what should have been a routine prisoner transfer, with their prisoner safely cuffed in the backseat, two experienced agents lost that prisoner—and a chunk of time. Someone or something was responsible for that. If it was Jacoby, I need to know how he managed it."

Maggie spoke slowly. "Because we don't have an agent

or operative capable of manipulating memories or imposing their will on others, not psychically."

"Exactly."

"How did you place him in Tennessee?" John wanted to know. "Was Nash straight about that?"

"The manhunt was already under way when I was officially notified about it," Bishop said, without commenting on the second question. "Standard operating procedure, since we were expecting him. And the only thing that stuck out a bit about this particular fugitive was that he didn't seem to be in much of a hurry, lingering in the general area where he escaped, around Arlington, long enough to be spotted more than once, always in a different car. And then there's the dogs."

Maggie and John exchanged looks, and she was the one who asked, "Dogs?"

"Yeah. The last time we believe he was spotted, the witness swore he had at least three large dogs in the car with him. It was only after that, that he picked up his pace and left the area, neatly avoiding checkpoints or any law enforcement contact despite the BOLO out on him. He ditched cars a couple more times, and despite his countermeasure of removing or destroying any GPS units, the cars were found with relative speed and ease. And forensics did find dog hair as well as his prints and DNA in the abandoned cars."

"Not exactly worried about being nailed for grand theft auto," John mused. "Or escaping custody."

"If he does have a ten-million-dollar stash from his last heist, probably not."

Maggie asked, "Do we know where he got the dogs?"

"An informant who shared a prison cell with him for a short time claims he talked almost continually about his dogs, dogs he raised from pups. Said he had a trusted pal on the outside taking care of them until he got out. So far, we haven't been able to identify said pal, though he must have been within the area where Jacoby spent the most time after his escape and before he finally took off." Bishop paused a moment, then added dryly, "My guess is that once he was paid for looking after the dogs, and undoubtedly paid well, he headed straight for an island somewhere with no extradition with the U.S., there to live happily ever after."

"Do people still do that?" Maggie wondered aloud, but absently.

"I like to hope so," Bishop responded.

John kept them on track. "But Jacoby took the time to get his dogs. Even knowing every law enforcement agency in the East had to be looking for him. And then he headed for the mountains."

"So it appears. Despite changing cars a couple more times, Jacoby was traced as far as the Tennessee state line. No reports in the area of a stolen car, no dealer in the area has any record of selling a car to him. And the shady dealers were all under close observation *because* we had an escaped felon in the area. I doubt he went anywhere near them. The feeling was, he planned ahead, and planned well. He must have had a vehicle stashed and waiting for him, possibly courtesy of the same friend who kept his dogs for him while he was locked up. The vehicle had to be a Jeep or truck, maybe even a Humvee, definitely a serious four-wheel-drive. Fully gassed up and ready to go. Tracking dogs followed a trail through rough terrain to an old logging road headed up into the mountains, then lost the scent."

John said, "I gather the road was explored."

"For about a mile. Until it was blocked by several trees. Big trees, felled recently by hand, not by nature. Exploring on foot farther in, the search team found more trees blocking the way, a road growing less and less worthy of the name, and terrain so rough the rangers claimed only highly experienced and very athletic hikers could keep going."

"No sign of his vehicle, though."

"No sign."

"Decoy?"

"Maybe. Maybe he created a diversion and took another path into the mountains. In any case, as per procedure, that's when the nearest field office would have been notified."

"Nash," John said. "Was he told what you suspected?" Like Maggie, he asked a question already knowing the answer.

"No. The official report listed Jacoby as an escaped felon, a bank robber possibly armed. Which is true—as far as it goes. He's suspected of half a dozen fairly minor heists in the last ten years or so, but was never charged for lack of evidence. He was known to use a gun, but had never to our knowledge harmed anyone, or even fired the gun. But this heist was different. One, he was—rather uncharacteristically—caught on camera and easily identified. And two, the fact that he'd stolen ten million dollars still unaccounted for made him a very valuable fugitive indeed."

John mused, "Must have been some bank if they had ten million on hand."

"Yes," Bishop said. "As it happened, this bank was a hub for other banks and for various investment firms. Nine-tenths of that money was scheduled to be transferred to a Federal Reserve bank the day following that of the robbery."

Still musing, John said, "And Jacoby just happened to hit it on the right day." It was a question.

"The theory is, he had someone on the inside. Investigation of that possibility is ongoing."

"You don't believe it."

"No. Not the way Jacoby works. Which begs the question . . ."

"How did he know so much money would be there?" John finished.

"He has some computer skills. Never known as a hacker, but maybe he didn't waste his time inside. That money should have been protected by layers of electronic security, but nothing's foolproof and we all know security is usually at best an illusion; if someone wants in badly enough, and has the skills, they get in."

Realizing, Maggie said, "That's the kind of skill even more valuable than bank robbery itself. Skill the law enforcement community would want to understand. And he wouldn't give up easily. They were bringing him to you for questioning?"

"To the SCU, and, yes, because traditional means of interrogation had netted them exactly nothing. Normally, we would have gone to him for the interview, but he was being transferred near here because he'd been making noises about trading the location of the money for a reduced sentence and better accommodations. Nobody really wanted to make that deal, but judging by the security video evidence and as far as we could otherwise determine, Jacoby hadn't worked with a partner who might have talked, assuming we were able to locate him or her. The investigation into the robbery had turned up zip for leads, so he was and is still our only link to the money."

Bothered, Maggie said, "If he could manipulate someone else's mind, I'm surprised he didn't try it sooner."

"He may have tried," Bishop reminded her. "And failed. Or succeeded in some way we haven't discovered yet. That may well have been the way he was able to choose the right bank on the right day. And that could have been his first measurable success. We have no way of knowing for sure. If there's anything our experiences have taught us, it's that even with training and practice many of us can control our abilities only erratically."

Practically, John said, "Or maybe he just bided his time and used what leverage he had to manipulate the situation until the odds were more in his favor; he was alone with only a couple of agents and had a better chance of escaping."

"Maybe so," Bishop agreed. "In any case, he escaped. He didn't make the Ten Most Wanted list because he's not believed to be a violent criminal, but recapturing him could go a long way toward promoting an agent stuck in a backwater field office."

"Which," John said, "explains why Nash called us instead of the SCU. We don't need or want the public credit for that sort of success, but if another agent or unit within the FBI did the work, it would certainly be known inside the bureau."

"Yes," Bishop said.

Maggie said, "And since you've been your usual secretive self, it wouldn't be in any of the reports or alerts that you suspected Jacoby of being psychic."

Dryly, Bishop said, "I generally keep suspicion of possible psychic activity out of reports unless and until I'm certain. And sometimes even then. There are, after all, still some in—and out of—the bureau who refer to us as the Spooky Crimes Unit."

"You knew it'd be an uphill battle for respect," John reminded him with a trace of amusement.

"Yeah. And a long one. In any case, the case paperwork on Nash, the reports and stats on his crimes and on him as an escaped felon, contain nothing indicating any interest from the SCU."

"Yet you have an agent in Tennessee."

"We had reason to believe he'd head in that direction."

"Before he escaped?" Maggie asked curiously.

"When he escaped. Almost immediately," Bishop replied, unusually forthcoming with information. Maggie frowned slightly.

"He headed into a wilderness," John reminded, in the patient tone of one accustomed to dealing with the SCU's infamously enigmatic chief. "Into a state our information has him with absolutely no connection to. No family, no friends, no past job, nothing. Far as any discoverable records go, he never set foot in the state before. And you managed to place an agent close to where he'd eventually settle?"

"Within five miles, I believe. Possibly even closer. And we're reasonably sure he's hidden out in that general area before."

"Information not worth sharing?" John's voice remained patient, even as his wife smiled at him wryly.

"Not until now. Your operative needed to be there. Even more, he needed to locate Jacoby himself, at least initially."

"Some things have to happen just the way they happen," Maggie said.

"Yes."

"Life lesson or psychic lesson?" John asked, honestly curious.

"Six of one." Briskly, Bishop continued, "I have an agent in place with an excellent cover story that can be maintained almost indefinitely if necessary. An agent with specific instructions to observe for a time sufficient to reveal anything unusual, and then report back so that we'll know before he's officially approached by non-SCU law enforcement agents whether Cole Jacoby has any psychic ability."

"And if he does?" John asked slowly. "If he has enough psychic ability to affect your agent?"

Imperturbable, Bishop replied, "Then he'll be a very,

very special psychic indeed. And Nash will be stuck in that field office awhile longer."

"Because Jacoby will become an SCU target."

"He's already an SCU target. We just aren't sure— yet—what sort of threat he might pose, how much manpower it'll take to get him, and whether we need to intervene officially or leave it to Nash and his people. The initial readings on Jacoby were . . . indeterminate."

"Is that as unusual as it sounds?" John wanted to know.

"It's troubling," Bishop admitted. "Getting away from the agents transporting him, and then making it into a wilderness where it was virtually impossible to follow him, took careful planning and considerable coolheaded reasoning, but since then his observed actions have been erratic. To say the least."

"Erratic how?"

"Let's just say he hasn't been very welcoming even to innocent game hunters just passing by his place. He's called attention to himself, which I would have guessed isn't part of his original plan. Locals are talking about him. And insular though they may be, nobody wants a dangerous armed stranger up on the mountain near their town."

"Local law enforcement?" John asked.

"Not moved to intervene, so far. But that could change." Bishop paused, then added, "Wherever he hid his stash, it isn't where he is now, or at least we don't believe it is. And yet he's become aggressively protective of the remote cabin he rented up in the mountains."

John and Maggie exchanged glances, both silently

hearing the admission that whether he had known before sending his agent, Bishop most certainly knew now *exactly* where Cole Jacoby was staying. But neither of them commented on that.

"He is a wanted fugitive," Maggie pointed out. "I'd expect him to be protective of his location."

"Protective in very specific ways," Bishop said without saying much of anything at all.

John sighed. "Well, I know better than to ask. You'll tell us whatever it is you're holding back if and when you're ready to. But can you at least put Maggie's mind to rest and tell her Luther is all right?"

"He's being taken care of as we speak," Bishop replied.

"REMIND ME AGAIN why we're doing this?" Hollis Templeton's voice wasn't exactly nervous, except around the edges.

Her partner, Reese DeMarco, perfectly aware of the nerves, answered patiently. "Because you told Bishop weeks ago that you wanted to learn to interact with spirits outside our investigations, without the pressures of chasing bad guys."

"Yeah, but—"

"And our options to do so openly and without our badges are rather limited. Either you're some kind of paranormal investigator like we were in Baron Hollow in July, which would involve carting along a lot of equipment we don't need, or else you bill yourself as a medium and offer your services to allow loved ones to talk with the dead."

"But a *séance*? Seriously?"

"At least Bishop didn't ask you to wear a turban or a dozen jangling fake gold bracelets."

Hollis turned her head and glared at him. "You're not helping."

DeMarco kept his attention on his driving as he navigated a rather winding mountain country blacktop in the waning twilight. "Sorry. But you did ask, Hollis. And it's a good idea to explore the limits of your abilities whenever we have time between cases."

"In theory," she muttered.

"Well, we don't have too many ways to explore, to learn to control," he said. "We spend hours in the lab whenever the researchers come up with new tests, but we all know psychics don't do well in lab conditions, so we seldom learn anything new about ourselves or our abilities. And then we're in the field on cases where hunting down the bad guys and staying alive in the process is a little more imperative than learning how to talk to a spirit not involved in the investigation."

Hollis was silent for a moment, then said, "It was that girl in the hospital when we were waiting to see if Diana would pull through. Wandering the halls, literally a lost soul. It's been six months since that investigation, and I still can't get her out of my mind. When she asked me if there was supposed to be a light, I didn't have an answer for her. *Or* the time to try to help her find the answers she needed."

"And so, we do this," DeMarco said patiently. "You talk to spirits without the pressure of an investigation and try to help them. And if the client wants a séance as the setting, so be it."

"Easy for you to say," Hollis muttered. "Listen, I'm not going to do the candle thing, or hold hands around the table, or any of that stuff. Certainly no Ouija board; those things are dangerous. And I won't pretend to go into a trance. If I have to do a séance, it'll be *my* way."

"Suits me. Though it might disappoint the client. According to what background info we were given, she's had readings from every psychic and would-be psychic in about a dozen places in and around Tennessee. Even went all the way to California a couple of months back."

"Which hasn't made her brother-in-law very happy. Yeah, I remember from the brief. He thinks she's wasting money at best and being robbed blind at worst. Not exactly what you'd call a believer."

"Something else we've run into before and will again; might as well practice dealing with that too. In any case, our information is there were no kids and her husband's brother stands to inherit as the only Alexander left. Maybe he just wants to protect what he believes he has coming to him; some of those psychics charged pretty steep fees."

"I'm not charging anything at all."

"Yeah, but I'm betting the brother-in-law doesn't believe that. He'll be looking for the hook whatever you say, just waiting for whatever it is you intend to use to draw his sister-in-law into your con and eventually relieve her of some of her—and his—money."

Hollis frowned. "I hate it when anything is about money.

I'm also a little worried about whether I can see this spirit at all. He's been gone—what?—nearly two years?"

"Nearly."

"So maybe he's gone on to wherever most spirits go eventually. Despite popular belief, most of them don't seem to stick around very long."

"We'll find out soon enough," DeMarco said, turning the car in between two rather imposing brick pillars flanking a brick driveway that wound off into the distance.

Glum, Hollis said, "Dammit, even the driveway cost a fortune. Or was laid back when brick was relatively cheap to use and labor even cheaper. I bet this is an old house. Filled with history. And spirits."

"Family home for about a century and a half, if I remember."

"Lovely. Probably lots of feuding went on over the decades. A philandering husband or cheating wife caught and . . . dispatched. A suicide or three. An axe murderer two generations ago."

With a slight smile, DeMarco said, "Don't recall mention of an axe murderer."

"He probably got away with it," Hollis said, still gloomy. "No bodies found, right? Right. So he buried them in the rose garden or cut them up into little pieces and tossed them into that river we passed a mile or so back. Or fed them to pigs."

"Ghoulish," he noted.

"I'm going to talk to the dead. I can be ghoulish if I want to. It does cast a whole new light on bacon, though, doesn't it? I mean, that pigs are omnivores and will eat anything. It's why I eat turkey bacon. Mostly."

Ignoring the tangent, DeMarco said, "It's not as easy as most people would suppose to dismember a body, especially with an axe. Takes a lot of muscle and quite a bit of skill, never mind making a hell of a mess it'd be difficult to hide or cover up afterward—"

"All right, all right." Hollis turned her head to stare at him, frowning. "Why don't you just *tell* me when I'm being an unreasonable pain in the ass?"

"Where's the fun in that?"

Hollis couldn't help but laugh a little when he sent her one of his quick, curiously crooked smiles. "Yeah, yeah. Your idea of a nice break between cases is to babysit me."

"Not exactly the way I think of it," DeMarco replied, adding immediately, "If there are any spirits at the Alexander family home, they'll probably be waiting and ready for us. For you. You're broadcasting."

She sighed, perfectly aware that controlling that particular psychic ability was not exactly one of her strengths—and useless to even try whenever she was in the company of a telepath as powerful as DeMarco. "Emotions or thoughts?"

"A jumble of both. Hollis, you *can* do this, you know."

"Yeah? What if another spirit asks me why there's no light to guide them—wherever it is they're supposed to go? What do I tell them?"

"Follow your instincts. They're actually pretty good."

Hollis didn't want to admit out loud that she found it reassuring to hear that from him. Then again, since he *was* a telepath and she couldn't turn off her psychic Broadcast Full Wattage button, he probably knew anyway.

Dammit.

She returned her attention forward just as the car rounded a curve and their destination loomed unnervingly large and very well lit a hundred yards or so ahead.

"Jesus," she muttered. "It's a castle. It has turrets."

"Only two," DeMarco murmured.

Hollis was too busy dealing with her sense of intimidation and unease to laugh as she studied the house looming ever larger as they approached. Stone, some sections of it covered with ivy, numerous windows with the small panes that usually signaled considerable age, and a huge, grand front door that looked as if it would require a draft horse to pull it open. There were at least three floors, at least two wings in addition to the main section of the house, the two turrets DeMarco had noted—and battlements. Or, at least, what Hollis tentatively identified as battlements. Walkways high up between the turrets at roof level designed for guards to walk and scan the countryside for danger, like the threat of some army storming the place.

Which was very weird for an American structure, very few of which had experienced a threat of that kind since the Alamo.

Besides which, this was a home, not a fortress. She hoped.

"Jesus," she repeated. "Who *are* these people?"

"Old money," DeMarco replied succinctly. "And I'm guessing whoever built this place had a lengthy European trip behind them that inspired this sort of architecture."

"No kidding. Also a family that made damned sure of their privacy. They might not have a moat around the place, but it took us nearly an hour on decent blacktop roads to get here from the main highway, and thirty minutes on that from the nearest town; imagine how long it would have taken anyone a hundred years ago."

"I doubt they got many visitors," DeMarco agreed. "And those who came probably stayed a week or longer, even a month. Even a summer. It was common among people of that time—and this sort of wealth."

"Damn, you don't think they'll ask us to stay, do you? If that isn't a haunted house, I don't know spirits at all. Other than a hospital, I can't think of a place I'd feel less inclined to spend the night."

"I suppose that depends on how long the séance lasts," DeMarco said practically. "It's nearly dark, and by the time you're done it's likely to be fairly late. Depending on how pleased our hostess is with her reading, always assuming you can make contact, if you can't tell her what she wants to hear, I bet she'll want more than one reading."

"And if I *can* tell her what she wants to hear?"

"In that case, she may try to hire you to be her personal psychic."

With considerable feeling, Hollis said, "Thank God I already have a job."

DeMarco parked the car a dozen yards from the front door and said, "Well, right now your other job demands that you try your hand at contacting a spirit, probably only because his nearest and dearest wants to know that he's at peace—except for missing her as much as she misses him, of course."

"Cynic."

"Realist. Come on, let's go."

Hollis gathered herself and prepared to get out of the car but couldn't help muttering a final, "Oh, man, I know I'm going to regret this."

And it was, really, more than a hunch.

Haven

Maggie Garrett said, "So you're certain your agent can protect himself. Herself?"

"Herself," Bishop replied.

"An especially strong shield?"

"And instinctive, or at least unconscious. She doesn't have to think about it to block, maybe even repel, energy. To most of our other psychics, telepaths included, behind her shield she reads as a sort of . . . null field. As if she's not really there."

Maggie murmured, "Psychic stealth mode."

John said, "Now that sounds creepy."

"It can be," Bishop allowed, adding dryly, "Not many people can sneak up on me. She can. But that seems to be more a side effect of her shield than a separate psychic ability. Her real strength is in detecting, measuring, and possibly repelling negative energy. And when she encounters it, she does more than detect it, she becomes hyperaware."

"What about positive energy?"

"When she lets down her shield—which she has to consciously do—most of our telepaths have been able to communicate with her easily, and with complete thoughts rather than just snippets or impressions, so she's receptive to positive energy. A small percentage of our telepaths couldn't send or receive. Anything, even though her shield was down. We're not sure if it was due to their abilities or hers. Or just one of those days when one or all of them weren't able to control their abilities."

"She's also a telepath?"

"Yeah, she is a telepath, though it seems secondary to both her shielding abilities and her abilities to detect and repel negative energy. So far, at any rate."

Maggie said, "Three distinct abilities?"

"More like two," Bishop replied. "Our theory is that her mind developed the shield to protect itself from negative energy, so those two abilities are likely connected. The telepathy began as her primary ability."

"And the others developed only when she was exposed to negative energy?"

"I believe so," Bishop said.

Maggie waited a moment, then said, "You're not going to tell us when and how that happened?"

"That's her story, part of her history. Not mine to share."

John sighed, even though he was well aware, and personally grateful, that Bishop kept the secrets of many if not most of the psychics he dealt with—and that he shared such information with others only when it was absolutely necessary. "As usual, we have more questions than answers about an agent or operative's abilities."

"Some things don't change," Maggie said, then added immediately, "Bishop, did you know Nash had contacted Haven?"

"Yeah."

"But not from him."

"No."

"Have you told him you have an agent in place?"

Bishop replied, "Unless you've told him differently, he doesn't know Cole Jacoby has been located."

Maggie looked at her husband with raised brows. "Did he answer my question?"

"Not exactly."

Relenting, Bishop said, "No, I haven't told Nash—or anyone else outside the SCU—that I have an agent in Tennessee and that she located Jacoby days ago. The instant Nash is informed of Jacoby's location, he'll mount a full-scale operation to get his fugitive, with the director's blessing; everybody wants that ten million found. I'm less concerned with recovering the stolen money than I am with determining the extent of Jacoby's psychic abilities. For now, at least."

"And she doesn't know yet?" Maggie asked.

"Not as of her last report hours ago. She says the whole area around him is dark, and she didn't mean it was because he's in a cabin in the woods. Something out there, something in or around Jacoby, is producing a lot of negative energy, but so far she hasn't risked getting closer to try to figure out whether it's Jacoby—or something or someone else."

"Energy with a purpose?" Maggie asked.

"Also something we don't yet know. But negative energy is usually being channeled or otherwise controlled, especially if it's confined to one area or person."

Mildly, John said, "You might have warned us the armed felon we were hired to find was also likely to be psychic. Or was it part of your master plan to have a Haven operative on the scene?" The question wasn't as mocking as the words made it seem.

More practically, Maggie asked, "Is that why you sent only one agent instead of the usual team? Because we were sending an operative?"

Again not exactly answering the question, Bishop said, "I knew Luther would be the operative chosen to go in. And he needs to be there."

"Why?" Maggie asked.

"To save my agent's life. After she saves his, of course."

THREE

Owen Alexander scowled at the newcomers he undoubtedly didn't regard as guests, even generations of "good breeding" failing to overcome his open hostility. "Anna claims you don't charge a fee," he said the moment the door of the impressive library closed behind the equally impressive, old-world butler who had escorted them here and announced them.

Hollis was still trying to get over being announced in a private home and said almost absently, "No, I never charge fees."

"Then why do it?" he demanded.

She looked at him, momentarily startled. The literal truth, that she was an FBI agent trying to get a handle on her abilities and figure out how best to use them in investigations, wasn't something she was free to share—exactly—so she said, "I . . . want to help people."

"By lying to them?"

DeMarco shifted his weight almost imperceptibly, perfectly aware that Hollis had a temper and didn't suffer fools gladly.

Her blue eyes narrowed as she studied Alexander. "As far as I know, no spirit has ever lied to me, so I've never passed on a lie. They seem to be beyond that sort of petty human thing once they've died."

Alexander blinked, clearly startled. "Most of your sort say 'passed' or something equally euphemistic," he said.

"Kindly don't lump me into a group, Mr. Alexander. I also don't use tarot cards, crystal balls, tea leaves, read palms, go into trances, or insist anybody hold hands around a candlelit table. I don't ask for birth dates so I can use what most people know about their horoscopes to get a few easy and pseudo 'hits' without really trying. I just utilize the natural energy of my mind, which happens to be sensitive to a specific frequency, and use that tool to open a door so spirits can come through and talk to the living. Assuming they want to. I often wonder why they bother."

Like now.

She didn't say it, but it hung in the air between her narrowed gaze and Alexander's glare.

DeMarco eyed the two of them, noting the disparity in size between Hollis's slender, almost frail-looking form and Alexander's tall, bulky, just-this-side-of-corpulent self, and silently bet on Hollis to win the standoff.

In the end, there wasn't really a winner, because the door opened and a middle-aged woman hurried in. She was lovely in a slightly faded way, dressed in something rather flowing and filmy that to DeMarco's mind would have been better suited to June than October—and possibly thirty or forty years ago to boot.

But what did he know about women's fashion? Less than nothing.

"I'm so sorry I wasn't here to greet you," she said, a little breathless. "Owen, honestly, haven't you even asked them to sit down?" Before he could respond, she ushered Hollis and DeMarco to a long, elegant silk sofa and sat down in a chair at right angles and nearest to Hollis. "Thomas should be back with coffee any time now."

Thomas, DeMarco, reflected, was clearly the butler; Owen hadn't spoken a word to the man.

"I'm Anna Alexander. But, of course, you know that. Thank you so much for coming."

Owen Alexander sat down on an identical sofa facing the visitors, his scowl gone but displeasure lingering around a grim mouth. "I thought you were resting," he said to his sister-in-law. "I didn't see any reason to disturb you. They're early."

DeMarco said calmly, "The roads were better than we were led to believe. We got an early start just in case."

"You're very welcome here," Anna Alexander assured him, her gaze flitting to Hollis almost hesitantly. "Forgive me, Ms. Templeton—"

"Hollis, please. And he's Reese. We aren't very formal." She glanced around at the huge, formal library, her mouth twisting slightly.

"Then I hope you'll call me Anna. And my brother-in-law

is Owen." She didn't look at him, but kept her gaze on Hollis. "Forgive me, Hollis, but I was told your methods of summoning Spirit were somewhat unorthodox, so I wasn't certain how to prepare for the séance. I wasn't even certain which room would be best."

Hollis and DeMarco exchanged quick glances, no telepathy necessary between them to share the realization that Anna Alexander had indeed spent a great deal of time with mediums—and those who claimed to be. Enough, at least, to pick up the lingo.

Clearing her throat, Hollis said, "Well, first, you need to understand that I don't really summon anything. In my experience, mediums are simply people who have the ability to open a kind of door for . . . a certain type of energy to enter our space or dimension."

"Spiritual energy?" Anna's hands, clasped together in her lap, were twisting restlessly even though her voice was calm.

Relatively.

Hollis nodded. "There's nothing inhuman about it, nothing magical. In fact, it's based on science being seriously researched in many different reputable facilities around the world as we speak. It's an ability, the way some people have an ear for music or an uncanny flair for mathematics or physics. The theory is, some people are hardwired to . . . pick up and interpret electromagnetic energy on certain frequencies. Each medium's frequency is different, which is why we get as many misses as hits and why we tend to use our abilities differently. Some mediums see the dead, some hear them, and a relative few of us can do both. But it's perfectly natural to us. It's how the human brain works, after all, using electromagnetic energy. What I have, what I've learned to use to a certain extent, is just another sense."

A short laugh escaped Owen. "Well, you're original, I'll give you that much. So it's just a sense and not a gift, huh?"

Before Anna could offer a fluttering apology, as she showed every sign of doing, Hollis looked at Owen and answered him in a very deliberate tone.

"Believe me, most of the genuine mediums I know would never call it a gift, what we can do. At best, it's something we learn to live with, and hopefully learn to control and make some decent use of. At worst, it takes over our lives and sometimes makes us question our sanity."

"And do you question yours?" he asking mockingly.

"Only on days like this."

DeMarco spoke without haste but still managed to soothe their agitated hostess and silence her brother-in-law, to say nothing of calming Hollis—at least slightly. "I think the best thing to do right now would be for us to begin the reading."

Owen muttered, "Don't you mean 'séance'?"

"Hollis prefers the term 'reading,' since what she does involves none of the traditional trappings of a séance."

She looked at him in slight surprise but was prevented from asking him when he'd decided to toss the séance idea out the window when the butler entered the room silently, carrying a large silver tray.

Anna directed him to set it on the coffee table and said, "Thank you, Thomas. I'll pour."

"Yes, madam." He retreated as silently as he'd arrived.

"Coffee first?" Anna asked tentatively.

Knowing how cold she was likely to be after the reading, Hollis nodded, with only a glance at DeMarco. "Yes. Thank you."

They went through the curiously stilted ritual of being served coffee, both Hollis and DeMarco politely refusing little sandwiches and pastries on a tiered server.

Owen Alexander ate several of each.

Hollis thought the polite "visitor" chitchat their hostess doggedly maintained during the rather ceremonial coffee drinking was a bit ridiculous under the circumstances and wasn't very happy that her partner courteously helped it along.

Time was ticking away. It was dark now, and she was uneasily certain that they would be invited to spend the night. And Hollis didn't want to spend the night here. Because her initial guess had been right; this house was definitely what any genuine medium would term haunted. Very much so. She was already aware, on the periphery of her senses, that more than one restless spirit inhabited this old house, undoubtedly with things to communicate to the living.

It wasn't that Hollis was afraid of them; she had long ago moved past fear in dealing with spirits even if that had driven her in the beginning to block so fiercely that she had rarely seen and even more rarely been able to hear spirits. Now she wasn't even sure she *could* block; the "door" that most mediums spoke of tended by this stage of her life to be almost always open as far as Hollis was concerned.

Almost always. As with most abilities, it sometimes appeared to have a mind of its own, not subject to her will or needs.

But even with time and experience under her belt, with all the advice and counsel of other mediums in the unit, she still hadn't reached a place within herself where she found the interaction with spirits at all normal or comfortable. She couldn't be matter-of-fact about it.

And haunted houses promised sleepless nights. The dead didn't need to sleep and didn't seem to have any problem at all keeping the living up when it suited them.

She set her coffee cup down on the table and said rather abruptly, "I know you've seen quite a few mediums since your husband died, Anna. Do you feel you were ever able to communicate with him?"

Anna sent an uneasy glance toward Owen and said, "There were a few who seemed able to summon—to reach Daniel. But—"

"But Google offers more information than they did," Owen said in disgust. "Flickering candlelight, thumps and bumps, and spirit guides with low-pitched and heavily accented voices notwithstanding."

Anna looked acutely unhappy. "I'm just not sure," she confessed to Hollis. "I thought at the time . . . but Owen is right. They didn't tell me anything they couldn't have found out easily beforehand."

"What is it you expect him to tell you?" And when Owen snorted, Hollis added evenly, "I'm not asking for specifics, just wondering if you have a particular question in mind or just need to know that he's at peace."

A shaken laugh escaped Anna. "I feel a bit like Houdini's widow, but Daniel told me more than once that if there was anything beyond this life, he'd find a way to contact me and let me know. And he was an exceptionally strong and determined man, so if anyone could keep that promise, it would be him. He was . . . not as cynical as Owen, but he was a realist, and knew there was a good chance fraudulent mediums would try to take advantage of me. So we worked out a message only the two of us would know."

"And so far no medium has delivered," DeMarco murmured.

"So far, no. Then a friend of mine who sits with me on the board of a major charity told me about Hollis."

Hollis wanted to ask at least one of the questions tumbling through her mind, but DeMarco's fingers closed around her wrist, and she remained silent. Outwardly, at least.

How does Bishop manage to do *stuff like that? Arrange stuff like that? Know* when *to arrange stuff like that?*

Because she had no doubt that he had, and it was one of the few true mysteries of life in the SCU. Not many secrets in a unit peopled with psychics, except the ones Bishop kept.

Unaware, Anna said, "She said she'd heard wonderful things about your abilities, that you were genuine. And that you never took money for helping people communicate with loved ones. Even Owen had to admit he didn't know why you'd pretend to make contact if you couldn't."

"Unless you get off on delivering false hope to people," Owen said, his tone deliberately baiting.

Hollis didn't bite, though she did look at him for a moment before returning her gaze to Anna. "Just please understand, I don't channel spirits; I don't become them or anyone else other than myself. I don't have any spirit guides or, as I told Mr. Alexander, go into any kind of trance or become unconscious. I'm fully awake and aware the whole time. I just concentrate, really, try to focus." She hesitated, then added, "I can't promise anything will even happen. It doesn't always."

"What a surprise," Owen Alexander drawled.

Hollis looked at him, narrowed her eyes for a moment, then looked over his left shoulder. "You really should believe in spirits, Mr. Alexander," she said, more grim than triumphant.

"Oh? And why is that?"

"Because you've got one just behind you. And from the way she's looking at you, I'm guessing she's a former girlfriend or mistress. Did you kill her, or was it someone else?"

Haven

"I knew I felt pain," Maggie said with a sigh.

"A shot in the leg," Bishop confirmed. "Not fatal or even especially serious under normal circumstances, but he lost a lot of blood and he was in the middle of nowhere.

With a wanted fugitive on his trail, highly motivated to catch him, especially if he posed a threat."

John said, "You mean if he realized Luther is psychic."

"Yeah. If. And given Luther's tracking skills, and his ability to . . . hide in plain sight, I'm assuming that his target wouldn't have noticed his presence any other way."

"Safe assumption," Maggie murmured. "Though I'm not at all sure Jacoby's dogs wouldn't have heard or sensed somebody outside that cabin. Even somebody with the camouflage skills Luther has might not be a match for three well-trained guard dogs. By the way, how do you know he was shot in the leg?"

"Callie."

Maggie had to search her memory, but only briefly. "Callie Davis? She's your agent there?"

"She is. And she's one of the few members of the team who can reach Miranda and me without the need for a cell tower or a landline, no matter how far away she is. Whether it's because she broadcasts on a frequency right in our range or because she's capable of focusing on a particular target when she sends is something we haven't determined yet. We do know the two-way communication exists only when Callie is the one who initiates it."

"Not even you and Miranda can reach her otherwise?"

"So far, no. If her shields are up, they're impenetrable."

"But you got a message from her saying Luther had been shot in the leg."

"Not long ago," Bishop confirmed. "Miranda is in California on a case and got the same message at the same time." Miranda was his wife and partner in every sense of the word, a team primary agent in the SCU—which often meant they worked different cases far away from each other, as they obviously were doing now. But their psychic connection was rather extraordinary.

Distance between two people was one thing; being separated was something else entirely.

Not being psychic himself, and so lacking that particular mental and emotional link with his own beloved wife, John rather envied them their special closeness, even though he knew the same psychic connection that made them an amazingly strong team and solid anchor for the unit was also their Achilles' heel. No one was completely sure, but they had some evidence to suggest that because their connection was extraordinarily deep, and growing deeper as time passed, it had become a literal lifeline between them: sever it, and both could die. Injure one and at the very least incapacitate the other, physically, emotionally, and psychically.

"How's Luther?" Maggie asked. If she was aware of her husband's musings, she showed no outward sign of it.

"When Callie sent her message, he was sleeping. Out, really; she had sedated him. She dug the bullet out of his leg and took care of the wound. Don't worry; she's also one of my agents with EMS-level medical training. He's in good hands."

"And if Cole Jacoby tracks him to her place?"

"There's the thing about her being able to repel negative energy, remember. And if that doesn't work, well, she's also good with a gun. Very good, in fact."

John frowned and said, "If Jacoby was able to manipulate the minds of those agents during the transfer—"

As usual, Bishop was a step ahead. "Then why couldn't he affect Luther's mind even if he couldn't get through to Callie's? Luther does have a shield of sorts; it should protect him, or at least make him aware if someone is attempting to get into his mind or control his actions. Virtually every psychic I've ever known has been able to detect attempts such as those."

"Maybe because they're so rare," Maggie mused. "The unusual does tend to stand out."

"It does," Bishop agreed. "Which may be one reason why Jacoby's security escort never saw it coming. Remember, all Jacoby did with the agents was leave them with a few gaps in their memories. And neither one of them is psychic, so no protection, no shields, no awareness of a psychic . . . intrusion. Even so, as far as we know, he wasn't able to do anything more than . . . persuade them . . . to take a wrong turn or two, pull the car over, uncuff him, and then take a nap, forgetting what they'd done. They woke up on the outskirts of a small town where it was easy for him to boost another car."

It was Maggie's turn to frown. "You said *gaps*. That they had *gaps* in their memories."

"When they woke up, they were about a hundred miles west of where they should have been," Bishop admitted. "And somewhere along the way Jacoby must have been hungry because there were fast-food wrappers in the back, courtesy of the driver's cash."

"Surveillance cameras?" John asked.

"Yeah, the particular fast-food restaurant he chose had been robbed so many times they ramped up security.

There was a camera on the drive-through, and we got to them before they could perform the usual end-of-the-week wipe of the footage."

"Was Jacoby visible?" Maggie asked.

"No. A shadow in the backseat that must have been him, but he hid himself well. And before you ask, the agent driving as well as the one in the passenger seat seemed perfectly normal."

"Ordered food, paid for it, spoke to the employee at the window?"

"All of the above. And nothing out of the ordinary."

"You mean nothing seemed to be," Maggie murmured.

"Exactly. The agents were, to all appearances, calm and casual, and neither showed any signs of being forced to act against their wills."

John wondered aloud, "Does that creep anybody else out, or is it just me?"

"Me too," Maggie said. "Bishop, they don't remember *any* of that?"

"No."

"Did he rob them?" John asked.

"As a matter of fact, both their wallets had been cleaned out of cash, though no credit cards were taken, and both still had their credentials and cell phones."

"Weapons?"

"Still holstered, not fired recently."

"So he didn't need a gun," John said slowly. "Or knew better than to steal one registered to a fed."

"Apparently. Neither agent remembered either turning off-course or stopping anywhere. But one agent woke up before the other one did to find their car parked just off the road and out of sight of any passing traffic, and to see his partner apparently sleeping peacefully."

"And Jacoby did that," Maggie said. "All that."

"Jacoby did all that," Bishop agreed.

"HOLLIS," DEMARCO WARNED.

But she was beyond listening. The chill of gooseflesh all over her body, the fine hairs standing on end, the odd sensation of a cold breeze moving not around her but through her, all told her this was one of those times when the door between this world and whatever one chose to call the spiritual world was wide open. Barely hearing her partner, she watched instead the eerily almost-transparent spirit standing just behind Owen Alexander, concentrating hard so she could hear as well as see.

Hearing them had been more difficult for her in the beginning, and still usually required intense focus from her.

. . . was . . .

. . . was his . . .

. . . was his fault . . .

"What was his fault?" Hollis asked the very pretty and rather startlingly young spirit.

Owen glanced behind him as though against his will, scowled, and said sharply, "What're you—"

"Quiet," Hollis ordered. "I can barely hear her as it is. What was his fault? And who are you? What's your name?"

. . . No. It wasn't his fault . . . left me . . . He left me.

"Left you where?"

DeMarco, watching Owen, since he couldn't see what Hollis saw any more than anyone else in the room could, saw the older man's face whiten and a kind of dread creep into his eyes. Aside from Hollis's firm voice, the room was utterly silent.

In the car. He . . . told everyone . . . it was stolen, but . . .

"But the car wasn't stolen? What happened?"

. . . missed a curve. Went into the river. He got out. She shook her head, dark hair swirling eerily around her as though she stood even now in deep water. *He got out, and he left me.*

Hollis was concentrating intensely. "What's your name?"

Jamie. Jamie Bell. Her face changed suddenly, and she took a step sideways so she could see Owen's frozen face. *It was such a long time ago. He didn't mean to do it. Any of it. So it wasn't really his fault. He was showing off, going too fast, the way boys do. And when the car went into the water . . . he was afraid. He panicked. I . . . don't think he could have saved me anyway. The current was so strong. It was in the spring, and the river was swollen. He couldn't have saved me.*

Hollis wasn't so sure, but all she said was, "Do you need the car to be found? Your body laid to rest?"

Jamie shook her head. *That doesn't matter so much. There isn't anything left of me, really. Except this. I've been trying . . . I needed to tell him I forgive him.*

"That's what's kept you here?"

Jamie looked at Hollis pleadingly. *Tell him, please? That it wasn't his fault? That he can't let what's left of his life be ruined by that secret?*

"I'll tell him for your sake," Hollis said grudgingly.

Jamie smiled for the first time. *Thank you. He really was the only thing keeping me here. My family and friends moved on a long, long time ago. They let go. But he never could. Never could forgive himself. Tell him he can, please.*

"I'll tell him." Hollis was about to ask if there was anything else she could do for Jamie when she found herself suddenly almost flinching back as she blinked at the extraordinarily bright light that had appeared from nowhere. It seemed to have no distinct source, and yet it enveloped Jamie, leaving her in silhouette. The "floating" strands of hair that had been one indication to Hollis that she was looking at something otherworldly settled about her shoulders, and then she took a step forward, smiling at Hollis. For that moment, she looked flesh-and-blood real.

Thank you.

"You're welcome," Hollis said slowly, watching as the light brightened even more, completely enveloping Jamie—and then dimmed, shrank, and vanished within seconds.

"Well, what do you know." Hollis blinked and looked at Reese. "There is a light, after all. This time, at least."

"You reacted physically," Reese told her, calm. "Your pupils contracted."

"They did?"

"Definitely."

Hollis thought about that, then nodded. "I'm not surprised. It was a very bright light, and appeared suddenly."

"So you know something you didn't know yesterday," he responded. "Worth the trip just for that."

Anna asked eagerly, "What did you see? Who was it?"

Hollis returned her attention to her supposed client. "Not your husband, I'm afraid. I'm sorry. This spirit was here for your brother-in-law."

Owen said harshly, "I don't believe in that bullshit."

Remaining calm, Hollis said, "Suit yourself. But my job is to pass on messages, and I just got one for you. Jamie Bell says you have to forgive yourself for what happened to her."

"I don't know what you—"

"She drowned. You were driving, you lost control and missed a curve, and the car went into the river. The water was deep, the current fast. You managed to get out, but she didn't."

If Owen had been pale before, he was sheet-white now.

Anna, clearly bewildered, said, "I've never heard anything about a car accident. Owen—"

"It was a long time ago," he said slowly. "Over forty years, long before you met Daniel. I wasn't much more than a kid myself, and scared half out of my mind. When I made it back here, Dad and Daniel went back to the river with me. We tried, but . . . we couldn't even find the car. The current had already taken it. There was no rail on that curve, no visible signs of damage on or near the road."

Neutral, DeMarco said, "I gather there was no police report."

"No." He at least had the grace to look guilty, and avoid the steady gazes of the others. "No, Dad— The family decided against it. I was only eighteen, headed for college in the fall. Jamie was . . . a girl I met in Nashville.

She didn't even tell her roommate she was leaving the city with anyone."

Hollis wanted to be angry, to demand to know whether it had ever occurred to him that Jamie's family and friends had never known what had happened to her, had never been granted any sense of closure.

But then he looked at her, finally, with haunted eyes, and Hollis felt her anger dim. Whatever mistakes this man had made, whatever sins he had committed, they clearly had affected his life.

"She forgave me?" he asked, something in his voice ample evidence that he was still struggling to come up with a rational explanation as to how Hollis had known what she knew.

Owen Alexander still didn't believe in spirits.

"She needed you to know that. So she could move on. You're the only one left who even knew what happened to her."

"You're trying to tell me she's been here, in this house, all these years?"

"Not in the way you mean. Not haunting you or anything. She's been . . . nearby, waiting for an opportunity to contact you. You weren't open to that sort of experience, so she had to wait for someone who was. As to where she waited . . . We're not sure if it's another dimension the way science would define it or another plane of existence. Maybe it's even another kind of reality just out of sync with ours. We don't know."

For a moment, Hollis reflected that whatever they were, the dimensions or alternate realities or whatever had to be many and varied, since each medium's experience appeared to be unique. For instance, Diana Brisco,[1] a very powerful medium in their unit, was able to visit a gray place without even shadows, where nothing really existed in any sense, like a corridor between two worlds.

A place Hollis had visited herself, which was creepy enough; the likelihood was that having been there and being a medium, she could well be drawn there without warning and against her will. That was something she hadn't really faced and didn't want to now.

"What, she's in limbo?"

"Wherever she *was*," Hollis told him, "she's moved on now."

"On to heaven?" He was trying hard to sound mocking.

"Well, into a light place. However you choose to define it, I'm thinking better a light place than a dark one."

"You don't know?"

"You mean do I believe in heaven?" Hollis recalled an experience that had occurred months in the past and smiled without meaning to. "Let's just say I've seen convincing evidence that heaven—or something a lot like it—must exist."[2]

"And I'm supposed to just buy all this?"

"I'm not selling anything, Mr. Alexander. I'm just telling you what I saw. What Jamie Bell told me. Now you can decide it's all bullshit and go on with your life, or you

1 *Chill of Fear*
2 *Blood Ties*

can choose to accept the forgiveness offered to you and go on with your life, or you can ignore the whole thing and pretend today never even happened. Up to you. I'm just the messenger."

She hesitated for a moment, then said unwillingly, "Jamie told me that her family and friends had moved on a long time ago. So even though they never knew what happened to her, they must have known somehow that she was never coming home again, and made their peace with that. You were the one Jamie was worried about. You were the one she said needed to let go of what happened and move on."

His gaze avoided hers then, and he remained silent.

Hollis turned her attention to Anna, who she realized with a start was looking at her with desperate hope. Reluctant to disappoint the older woman, she nevertheless said, "I did tell you there was no way of knowing who might come through. Mr. Alexander was angry, and he made me angry—and sometimes strong emotions have a distinct focus. That was why Jamie came through. Well, that and the fact that she'd been waiting such a long time for someone who could open the door for her."

"And . . . and Daniel?"

Hollis rubbed one forearm absently, glancing down to see what she felt: no goose bumps or fine hairs standing on end, and no sense of that strange wave of cold sweeping through her, the three things that almost always happened whenever she was in the presence of spirits.

All had existed the whole time Jamie had been visible. She was still vaguely aware of spiritual energy around her, but it was distant, on the periphery of her senses. All of her senses.

Something new.

"I'm afraid the door's closed for the moment," she said, hoping it was because she was abruptly conscious of being very, very tired. Physically and emotionally. And cold in a different way; she was only barely able to stop herself from shivering.

DeMarco spoke up then to say, "It might not show so much, Anna, but this takes a lot out of Hollis, a lot of her own energy. She needs to rest before she tries to contact your husband."

"I'll be happy to come back tomorrow," Hollis offered, not about to argue with her partner, since she wanted to take a very hot shower and then curl up and take a nap. For about twelve hours.

Anna was clearly disappointed but spoke quickly to say, "There's absolutely no sense in you two making that long drive from town twice. You can stay the night here. In fact, you're welcome to stay as long as you feel it's necessary. It might even help," she added with more than a touch of pleading in her voice. "If you spend more time in his house, it might be easier for you to contact Daniel."

"Oh, but—"

"Please, the guest rooms are always ready, and there are two connected by a little sitting room on the second floor that I'm sure will suit you."

Which, Hollis thought, neatly resolved their hostess's potentially awkward dilemma as to whether to ask if her unmarried guests needed one bedroom or two. Before she could gather her thoughts to form a refusal, she heard her partner smoothly accepting the invitation.

"Thank you, Anna. You've saved me a long drive back to town with Hollis snoring in the passenger seat."

"I would not," Hollis said somewhat indignantly. "Snore *or* sleep. Besides, we didn't even bring luggage."

"Yes, we did. Since we hadn't unpacked at the hotel, I put both our bags in the car while you were . . . discussing . . . with the hotel manager the remarkable lack of high-speed Internet."

"His sign *said* Wi-Fi was available," Hollis said irritably. "Not just high speed, but *wireless*. The sign didn't say a thing about it being available apparently only during a blue moon that happened to fall on a Thursday. In December."

"Point made," DeMarco murmured.

"Truth in advertising. There ought to be consequences."

"Trust me, he knows that now."

Anna said brightly, "So that's settled. I'll have Thomas show you to your rooms and have your luggage brought up. You two can rest and freshen up, and we'll have dinner around eight thirty. Is that all right?"

Hollis wanted to argue, but she was just too tired. And cold. Maybe a hot shower would help, or maybe she'd take a little nap before dinner. At any rate, despite her misgivings, she admitted to herself that either was infinitely preferable to getting back into the car and heading back to that odd little town, especially since that odd little hotel in that odd little town didn't offer room service. And she had a strong hunch they rolled up the sidewalks in that town somewhere around sundown.

Supper would be out of a vending machine if they didn't stay here and take advantage of the Alexanders' hospitality.

"Thank you," she said with a little sigh. "That would be wonderful, Anna."

Whether the spirits of the mansion would disturb her was only a faint and passing thought.

FOUR

Luther Brinkman realized he was waking up even before he could force his eyelids to open, because he smelled coffee. It smelled wonderful.

He had no idea how long he'd been out, but his stomach felt empty and when he was finally able to open his eyes, the lids practically scraped across his corneas.

He'd been out a while. Quite a while.

"More than twenty-four hours. It's around dawn. On Wednesday."

He blinked several times, staring up at rough-hewn beams, turning her voice over in his mind.

Ah. The woman in the woods. The one with the shotgun.

Suddenly wary, he began to push himself up onto his elbows, biting back a sound of pain as his leg throbbed a protest. He was covered with a blanket but could feel the constriction of a bandage around his upper thigh.

A pillow was stuffed behind his head and shoulders, and a steaming cup placed in his hand. "You shouldn't move very much just yet. You'd already lost a lot of blood, and I had to dig pretty deep to get that bullet out."

She had to dig?

"You're lucky, though. The bullet was right up next to bone but hadn't damaged it as far as I could tell. And, luckily, it missed the femoral artery."

When he was able to focus, he found her back to him as she poured herself a cup of coffee. All he could tell was that she wasn't nearly as tall as he remembered but was nevertheless a tall woman, was slender in a thin, ribbed sweater and close-fitting jeans, and had long, very pale hair almost silver in color.

Tearing his gaze from her, he looked around to find himself in what appeared to be the main room of a log cabin that was less rustic than one might expect out here in these woods. He could see a hallway, so assumed a bathroom and probably a bedroom. A couple of oil lamps as well as battery-powered lights scattered around testified to the absence of electricity. This main room was on the small side and was divided by a long, narrow table into roughly two halves: cooking/dining and a comfortable living room.

Luther was on the couch. A comfortable couch.

The place was spare, but rather cheery, with a brisk fire in the big stone fireplace and thick, colorful rugs scattered on the wide-planked wood floor. Plain linen curtains covered a couple of small windows. A hunting trophy, the head of a ten-point buck, was mounted above the fireplace, but it was the only sign this might be a hunter's cabin. On other walls, innocuous prints of peaceful mountain landscapes provided the decor.

Beyond the table where his rescuer stood, he could see a compact kitchenette that looked clean and well organized. Something that smelled good enough to make his mouth water bubbled in a pot on a gas stove. Stew, maybe, or soup. Whatever it was, his stomach growled a longing.

Remembering the coffee cup in his hand, he lifted it and took a cautious sip. As he savored the strong taste he preferred, he caught a glimpse of movement from the corner of his eye and turned his head.

A dog lay on a thick rug near the door, watching him fixedly.

A very big black-and-tan dog, heavily muscled.

A Rottweiler.

"His name is Cesar," she said. "You should thank him. From here, it's an almost continuous climb to Jacoby's cabin. I never could have gotten you back down here without him. He's trained to pull a litter."

Luther thought the dog could probably have pulled a semi, but he didn't say so. Instead, he looked at the woman, now facing him.

There was something curiously . . . unreal . . . about her. The pale hair that wasn't platinum blond or gray or white but truly silver, almost metallic. The heart-shaped face with delicate features, not beautiful but somehow infinitely memorable. Dark, dark eyes. Hypnotic, those eyes.

He guessed she was in her early thirties, less because the few lines in her face hinted at maturity than because there was a curious stillness and serenity about her that could only have come with a certain amount of years and experience.

"I snooped while you were out," she said, her voice calm and as unremarkable as her face was remarkable. "Checked your ID, assuming it's real."

"It is."

"Okay, Luther Brinkman, your wallet and gun are in the drawer of that end table beside the couch. Your jeans are soaking in the washtub; I managed to get them off without doing any more damage than the bullet had already done, but they were blood-soaked all the way down to the hem."

Luther, suddenly very conscious of being in a T-shirt and shorts, tried not to think about her stripping his unconscious form. She had, after all, taken care of his wound—undoubtedly her only concern.

"With this chilly weather and without a dryer, those jeans won't be wearable anytime soon; I usually go to the Laundromat in town no more than once a week, and I went a couple of days ago. Luckily for you there's a trunk packed with an assortment of clothing kept here, and I think there are some things that'll fit you well enough.

"My name is Callie Davis. My family built this place about thirty years ago; a lot of them liked to hunt. I don't like to hunt, even though I can handle guns." She paused, studying him for a moment, then went on. "With a very stressful job, breaks are a good idea. I come up here for the solitude. The month of October is generally very peaceful and uneventful. This year, not so much."

"Sorry," he murmured.

"Well, you didn't start the trouble, as far as I can tell. It appears that Cole Jacoby started the trouble, when he took up residence in that rented cabin and promptly began going berserk whenever anyone got within a hundred yards of the place."

"So that's why . . ."

"Why I went out so late yesterday to check and see if he'd shot somebody? It seemed a wise thing to do. You're the first he's actually hit with a bullet, as far as I know, but he peppered a couple of surprised hunters with buckshot a few days ago when they were just hiking past to get where the hunting's legal. And had his dogs chase them far enough to make his point."

"Nobody called the cops?"

"Out here? We take care of our own problems. He wants to be left alone, and he's made sure everyone in the area knows it. So he'll be left alone. Future hunters will be warned to give the area a wide berth. No fuss, no bother."

"And if he's dangerous?" Luther asked.

COLE JACOBY WIPED his nose with the back of one hand and stared at the blood. "I can't do this," he muttered.

You can. You have to.

"She'll know. I'm almost sure she knew before." His head was pounding so hard he felt dizzy.

She won't know. Not if you're careful. Not if you push in just the right place.

"But I'm not sure where to push. How. There are . . . She's not alone. And I'm so tired."

Reach down deep. That's what you have to tap into.

Jacoby found a paper towel to hold to his nose and fought to control the dread sweeping over him. "There? The dark place? I don't want to go there again. Please don't make me."

That's why they want you, Cole. Why they'll hunt you. Why they won't leave you alone. Because you can go to the dark place. Because you can use the power you find there. You can use it against them, use it to defeat them. We all know that.

"Then I'll stay away. Leave the dark place alone. And they won't care about it anymore."

Cole . . . Cole. They'll care as long as you're out here. As long as you aren't under their control. Locked up in their prison. You know that. We all know that.

There was a pause. Cole wondered vaguely if his nose was still bleeding but didn't remove the paper towel to check. He was tired. He was so tired, and his head still pounded, and he just wanted to be left alone.

You know you aren't alone, Cole. You're never alone now.

"But I want to be," he whispered. "I need to rest. Can't I rest for a little while?"

A little while, Cole. But not for long. You have too much to do.

Cole was hungry and thirsty, but he was more tired than anything else. He sat down on his cot and prepared to curl up, taking a moment to reassure himself that he'd fed his dogs hours before, that they were safely in their beds for the night.

They were all looking at him, he realized dimly. In their beds but not asleep, not even resting. They were wide awake, staring at him alertly. Almost watching him. They looked tense. In fact, he thought Ace's fur was standing up all along his spine.

Cole wanted to calm them, reassure them somehow. But he was confused about why they would be tense. He'd raised them from pups, an abandoned mixed-breed litter some bastard had tied up in a burlap sack and tossed off a bridge into a river. Luckily, Cole had seen it happen. Had been able to rescue the pups before they drowned, dry their small, shivering, terrified bodies. Feed them what had seemed their first meal in days, at least.

Except for the months in jail, he had taken care of the dogs all during the three years since that day, and all three had rewarded him with their absolute devotion. He'd been a responsible pet owner: they'd been properly socialized as pups and were obedience trained. Lucy and Cleo had been spayed, Ace neutered, and all of them were current with their vaccinations and flea and heartworm prevention. The friend who had kept them for Cole while he'd been inside all those months had been well paid but was also an animal lover like Cole and had kept meticulous records detailing any necessary vet visits as well as routine care.

Cole had always wanted them to feel safe and loved. He kept them clean and well groomed, and they ate a high-quality dog food. He was good to them, kind to them. He loved them.

Why were they all looking at him like that?

Or maybe it was the others they were afraid of?

Too tired to keep wondering about it, he lay down on his cot, the paper towel still held to his nose. He didn't even take off his shoes or draw the thin blanket up around himself, just curled up on his side, drawing his knees up and huddling inside his jacket.

Tired. Just so tired.

But at least *they* were finally—

We're still here, Cole. We're always with you. And we'll never leave you. Never.

He pressed part of the paper towel to his mouth but still heard the whimper escape.

And looking across his single-room cabin in the faint, flickering light of the dying fire, he was absolutely sure that the eyes of his watching dogs all glowed red.

"IF HE'S DANGEROUS?" Luther repeated when the silence had stretched a good minute. "What then?"

In a deliberate tone, Callie Davis said, "Bears are dangerous. Snakes can be dangerous. Escaped felons—assuming he's the one you're after—are quite likely dangerous. Private investigators who carry guns are probably dangerous." Her shoulders lifted and fell in a faint shrug. "This is a dangerous place. Most of us like it that way. Living with danger can make you feel alive in a way nothing else can."

Luther happened to agree with that but wasn't quite ready to delve into the subject. Something was nagging at him, some question, but he couldn't seem to find it in the fuzziness of his mind.

Callie didn't seem to notice—or just wasn't bothered by—his silence. She merely said, "I thought it best to let you sleep, but you must be starving by now, and the stew is ready. You should eat, then probably sleep some more. Give your body time to heal. The sun will be up in a bit. Cesar and I have been out a few times to check on Jacoby, and to judge by his lack of follow-up, it would appear he's forgotten all about you."

"Seriously?"

"It would be in character, at least as I've judged it in the last week or so. As long as no one gets close to that cabin, he keeps to himself. No sign he's ventured far from it, and when I backtracked, it was clear he made no effort to get out and try to find you yesterday, in daylight; the only tracks between here and there were ours."

Luther wished that made sense to him.

"I thought he might have decided to wait until night and clear out, in case he'd killed you. So I took Cesar and went out a couple of hours ago, and got a bit closer, close enough to check on Jacoby's cabin without attracting his notice. He's still there, dogs inside and quiet, no sign of life except the dying fire in his fireplace, and his Jeep is parked in its usual spot. If he's your escaped felon, he sure isn't acting like he cares whether he's been found. Or even that he shot someone who could be dead or dying in the woods."

"He has a Jeep?"

"Yeah. You actually approached his cabin from the more difficult direction, given the terrain; over the rise behind his cabin is something that used to be an old logging road. Not on any of the maps. It's still usable—if you have a major four-wheel-drive and serious all-terrain tires. Jacoby does."

"Then he didn't come from town."

"No, not directly. In fact, I haven't talked to anyone who saw him there. Or up here, for that matter." She shrugged. "There's a series of old logging roads and mining roads all through these mountains, and most cabins built up here are within a fairly short walk to one of them. We have to bring up supplies, after all, and hiking with a propane tank or fuel for a generator isn't exactly smart, never mind awkward and exhausting. My Jeep is parked at the end of one of the logging roads only about fifty yards from here."

Luther frowned. "Do the forestry people know about the roads?"

"Of course." Her tone was patient.

"Then why couldn't they follow one to Jacoby?"

"You have to know where you're going in these mountains, or the roads just take you in circles. Assuming Jacoby was smart enough to leave the main roads miles before he got near any town, let alone ours, and then used a few tricks to throw off trackers following him from Virginia, I imagine any search parties sent after him would probably have been about two mountains north of here and wouldn't have a clue in which direction to aim their teams. There was no way in hell they were going to find him using a traditional search. Which, I gather, is why you're here."

"You think one man on foot is better than teams of forestry people and other trained searchers with dogs?"

"Well, they didn't find him, did they? You did."

"And you," Luther said.

She looked faintly surprised. "I was here before Jacoby. It was when I went down to town for supplies last week that I heard all the talk."

"About Jacoby?"

"About the renter in the Scotts' cabin. He didn't get his supplies from town—this town, anyway. That was seen as a bit odd, considering how far we are from another town. And the cabin was rented a while back, in cash, by a man who said a friend would be using it."

"This man have a name?"

"I heard it was Jones. Probably not his real name. That cabin is usually empty by now and stays that way all winter, so the rental income would have been welcome, and nobody would have wanted to screw up a cash deal with too many questions."

"So nobody in town knew Jacoby was up here?"

"Other than the run-in with hunters being a topic, I have no idea what anybody else knew. I doubt anyone down there knows his name. He hasn't exactly been visible enough to identify." Her shoulders lifted and fell slightly. "Like I said, people around here mind their own business. Talk is one thing, action something else. Mind you, if he started causing a real . . . ruckus . . . I imagine someone would get pissed off about it. The sheriff would stir himself and take a trip up here to make inquiries."

"Not a good idea," Luther muttered.

"Yeah, I'm thinking he'll need to be warned."

"He should already know something. I mean, know that a federal fugitive could be in the area. There would at least have been a BOLO for Jacoby, probably all up and down the Appalachians. By name and description, photos and fingerprints. Standard procedure. He was in federal custody, and nobody considered him just a petty thief. No sign he was armed or particularly dangerous at the time of his escape, but they want him badly, so there would have been a certain . . . urgency . . . to the requests to be on the lookout. The sheriff wouldn't be curious about who rented that cabin if all anyone knows is that he's a stranger?"

"Despite the wilderness of these mountains, there are several cabins scattered over the slopes in this general area that tend to be rented on and off through the winter. Most are cash deals, and unless the renters go down to town on a regular basis, nobody generally knows or cares who's up here. Like I said, as long as there's no serious trouble, I doubt the sheriff would suspect a fugitive being in his jurisdiction."

"The hunters being run off wouldn't have bothered him?"

"Run off posted land, like I said. They didn't file a

complaint. Formally, at least. Just generally admitted to taking a shortcut across posted land, their mistake and one they won't make again. No harm, no foul."

Getting the gist, Luther said, "So your sheriff isn't one to get all stirred up over minor issues."

"Something like that. Usually has his feet up on his desk doing the crossword. He's eyeing retirement."

"I see." Luther frowned as the question nagging at him finally settled within reach. "Wait. *You* knew the man in that cabin was Cole Jacoby."

"Yeah."

"You weren't surprised when I said he was a wanted fugitive."

She smiled faintly and waited.

"But you said all anybody in town knew was that someone rented the cabin for an unnamed friend."

"That's right."

"So how did you know the man in that cabin is Cole Jacoby?"

"Well, I saw him. Unlike my neighbors up here and down in town, I like to know who's around me. Especially when I recognize him from newspaper and TV reports as a wanted fugitive."

"But you didn't tell the sheriff?"

"Like my neighbors up here and down in town, I try to mind my own business. He hadn't come near me or caused me any trouble."

Luther was still aware of the nagging feeling of too many unanswered questions but couldn't seem to focus on what he thought he should have been asking her.

Callie waited a moment, then nodded. "The news reports I saw in town had Jacoby on the loose hardly more than a week or two ago; the Scotts . . . let it be known they rented out the cabin a couple of months back. To a stranger with good references who said his name was Jones. He paid in cash, six months' rent. Said his friend might not get up to the cabin for a few weeks, but not to send a cleaning crew, he'd take the cabin as is."

"And nothing in all that made them suspicious?"

Still almost preternaturally calm, she replied, "Not that they said. Hasn't really been a good tourist season, so the money, as I said, would have been welcome."

He brooded, then said, "Was it just the news reports that made you sure it's Cole Jacoby in that cabin?"

"I also encountered one of his dogs, when Cesar and I were hiking the other day. Friendly dog. Greeted us politely and then headed with a purpose toward the Scotts' cabin. The tags had Jacoby's name listed as owner. And a phone number. Looked like a landline."

"Up here?"

"No. Prefix isn't one used for this area. My guess, if he expected to be on the run or at least moving from place to place, is that he arranged with a veterinary clinic to be the contact if the dog—any of his dogs—went missing and turned up somewhere. There was a rabies tag, current. Virginia."

"You wouldn't happen to remember the phone number on the owner tag?"

"I remember. Prefix is Arlington."

"Close enough," Luther muttered, half under his

breath. He frowned at Callie. "And you recognized Jacoby's name. As a wanted fugitive."

"Yeah."

"And didn't think to tell the sheriff."

"Well, he's eyeing retirement. Probably deserves to get there. And it's not like Jacoby is a serial killer. Just a bank robber, right? A bank robber who never hurt anyone? Except you, of course."

"Yeah. But I was sent to find him. I should probably call and report that I did."

"It'll have to wait. No landline. No cell service up here. And you're in no shape to get down to town."

"Right," he said finally, slowly. Something was still nagging at him, but he couldn't seem to get hold of it. All Luther could really do at the moment was to acknowledge to himself that he needed to eat, possibly sleep again, and consider the puzzle that surrounded Cole Jacoby when his mind was considerably more clear.

And the puzzle that was Callie Davis as well.

He really hoped they would both make a lot more sense once he was more rested and clearheaded.

"I'll get the stew," Callie said, setting her coffee cup on the table and moving into the kitchen area.

"Did I thank you for digging that bullet out?" he asked, watching her.

Her expression remained serene when she glanced at him. "A couple of times, but you were pretty out of it, especially after I gave you something for the pain."

"What?" He was curious and not a little uneasy.

"Morphine. Out here, we have to be prepared for just

about anything; it's a long hike to my Jeep, and a longer drive to the nearest doctor or pharmacy. I have an EMS-grade first-aid kit here, and I've quite a bit of training, so I cleaned the wound and sewed you up after I got the bullet out. You shouldn't have much of a scar. I have penicillin but didn't want to give you any until you were awake and could tell me if you were allergic. An awful lot of people seem to be these days."

"True. But I'm not allergic to anything, far as I know."

"Then a shot to protect against infection would be a good idea. That bullet did a fair amount of damage, and the wound wasn't exactly clean."

He could recall falling down once or twice in his haste to get away just after being shot, escape being more vital at the time than rigging a makeshift bandage. "You're probably right."

I'm not out of it now. Thank you, Callie, for patching me up. Taking care of me.

"Don't mention it," Callie said, without turning.

Luther waited a beat, then said matter-of-factly, "So how long have you been a telepath?"

HOLLIS HADN'T EXPECTED to sleep much, but she had in fact napped at least an hour before dinner, eaten in a slightly drowsy state her hostess seemed to view with awe and her host with wavering suspicion, and then fallen into bed after a hot shower she'd expected to keep her awake rather than make her even more sleepy.

She had the vague memory of DeMarco covering her

up—even though she wasn't at all sure where in the process he had joined her—and saying he'd leave the connecting doors open in case she needed anything. She also had the uneasy suspicion she had sleepily invited him to join her.

She woke up alone, the pillow beside hers smooth and bearing no imprint of a head.

It always took a few moments to get her eyes working properly if she'd been really out; it was, according to her doctors, an aftereffect of the truly groundbreaking surgery that had given her back her sight nearly three years ago. In any case, things were always blurry in a weird, shape-shifty sort of way for several seconds. It had been disconcerting to get used to, but once she had, Hollis seldom gave it a thought.

Once she did get her eyes working on this particular morning, she realized dawn wasn't far away and that she felt amazingly rested. She was relieved to see that she had at least managed to get herself into pajamas after her shower—or, at least, she hoped she was the one who had done that. At any rate, she smothered a wry laugh when she realized they were her flannel kitty pajamas.

Very sexy.

Not.

Without turning on the lamp by her bed, she could still see the room quite well, so she elected not to turn on any light; it might wake DeMarco before he was ready, and despite the fact that he never showed it, he must have been nearly as weary as Hollis had been. Possibly more so; they'd had barely a weekend off after the last difficult, grueling case.

Besides that, ever since Bishop had partnered them—and even before then, actually—DeMarco had seemingly appointed himself her watchdog, and though he tended to be unobtrusive about it in public, she was never surprised to feel him suddenly take her arm or mildly suggest they could both use some rest.

She sat up in bed and wrapped her arms around her raised knees, not really looking at the extremely large and luxurious bedroom she'd been allotted. Instead, her gaze was on the open door that led to the equally spacious sitting room separating this bedroom from DeMarco's.

She hoped to God she wasn't broadcasting. Bad enough the man could read her most of the time when he was awake—she really didn't want her thoughts or emotions to disturb his sleep.

Do I broadcast my dreams? Damn. Note to self: Ask Reese if I broadcast my dreams. Ask like it doesn't matter.

Right.

She knew herself to be a wary woman when it came to personal relationships with men; the horrific events that had awakened her psychic abilities slightly less than three years before made that a given.[3] And it had only been back in January of this year, after all, that she had met Reese DeMarco—just as he was ending an unusually long and dangerous undercover assignment that had nearly cost him his life.

---

3 *Touching Evil*

So neither one of them was especially unburdened by emotional and psychological baggage. Or scars. The opposite, in fact; it probably would have been extremely difficult to find two people who had been in darker, more evil places conjured by the human psyche than Hollis Templeton and Reese DeMarco.

Outside the SCU, at any rate.

But after what had happened to Diana, Reese had made his interest in Hollis crystal clear. Life was short, a brutal lesson they had both learned, and DeMarco had not wanted to find himself in the position of regretting that he had not spoken up about his feelings.

After that . . . not very much had happened between them. Not, at least, of the romantic relationship variety.

He had the advantage of being a powerful telepath often able to read her emotions and thoughts—not that she could hide them, since she "broadcast," especially at stressful moments—so perhaps he simply knew she wasn't quite ready to take a lover just yet. Perhaps he knew that the ever-growing psychic abilities Hollis had been coping with left her too vulnerable to deal with anything more at this point in her life.

Perhaps.

Hollis didn't exactly resent his self-appointed watchdog status. The SCU team had become her family, a place where she felt welcome and understood, and she was well aware that DeMarco was never questioning her strength *or* her ability to take care of herself when he made sure she ate regular meals and rested when she could. He just saw or knew that she tended to get so focused on the job at hand that she forgot more mundane matters. And that, unlike some of the other team members, her reserves of strength and stamina were rather dramatically tapped and drained by her abilities, especially when she pushed herself.

And she nearly always pushed herself.

So . . . was he merely taking care of his partner? Or taking care of a woman in whom he was interested?

Hollis wasn't sure there was much of a difference when push came to shove. He was at her side, a strong presence she could count on, and that meant a lot. It was something she had never really known before in her life. And they had developed, over these last months, a kind of humorous banter that at times did a dandy job of lessening tension in a situation. He helped keep her spirits up, and called her on it when she was being gloomy or pissy for no good reason.

Hollis had a shrewd idea that he had also been asked by Bishop to keep an eye on her. She knew they were worried about her, Bishop and Miranda, because her abilities weren't just growing—they were leapfrogging. And that was unusual.

Unheard of, really.

So nobody quite knew what it meant, the way her abilities were developing. Maybe it would prove to be a good thing.

Or maybe not.

Maybe her brain would reach its breaking point, short-circuit, and she'd end up stroking out or going into a coma.

It had been known to happen.

Hollis winced, making another mental note, this one to update the living will all SCU agents kept on file back at the office. Because she didn't want to live hooked up to machines. She didn't have Diana's nightmares about that, but just the possibility made her skin crawl.

Then, realizing, Hollis frowned down at herself, ran light fingers over her forearm, and felt the gooseflesh. Felt the fine hairs standing up all over her body. And felt the chill of that cold wave sweeping through her.

"Oh, shit, not now," she muttered under her breath. But she had learned that spirits who wanted to communicate with her were remarkably stubborn, so she forced herself to look up, at the foot of her bed.

And felt a jolt. Surprise. Bafflement.

"What are you doing here?" she whispered.

CALLIE DAVIS LOOKED at her guest for a moment, then ladled stew into two bowls, picked up a couple of spoons, and brought the food into the living room. She set his bowl on the coffee table in front of him, returned to the kitchen for her own coffee, then settled herself in a comfortable-looking chair across from the couch.

"Eat it while it's hot," she said, following her own advice.

Luther set his coffee cup on the table and picked up the bowl of stew. It was good, hot and filling, and his military training told him to eat it while he had the chance, because in a soldier's life one never knew when or even if the next meal would be forthcoming.

Besides, he was starving. It took all the manners he could muster not to shovel the stew in as fast as he could chew.

"Good," he noted about halfway through his generous portion.

"Thanks. But you may get sick of it before we've finished the pot. My energy source for appliances is propane, and taking the tanks down into town to get them filled is a pain, so I use the stuff sparingly. Quick hot showers using a tankless heater. One-pot meals that last a few days when I hang them in the fireplace over to the side."

He looked briefly at the fireplace, noting two iron swing arms that would make that arrangement possible; as long as the fire burned or embers just gave off heat, the food—and probably the coffee in that pot as well—would remain at a low simmer.

Which probably explained the strong coffee.

"Am I going to be here a few days?"

"Unless you heal a lot faster than the average bear, yes. Besides, if you're going after Jacoby, this is about the only thing close to a base shelter from which to launch your offensive."

He didn't have to listen very hard to hear the faint note of mockery. "I'm not going after him. My orders were to find him, make sure he's not going anywhere, and report in."

"And what if he comes after you?"

"You mean to finish the job?" Luther asked, gesturing with a spoon toward his covered bullet wound.

"That would be one reason."

"You know of another one?"

"Oh, I don't know. Because he knows you can track him no matter where he goes?"

"Track him? You found me lost in the woods, remember?"

"I found you wounded in the woods. Whether you were lost is an arguable point."

"I pretty much was," he admitted.

"You'd lost a lot of blood. Probably that more than anything else had your sense of direction off."

Luther finished his stew and set the bowl on the table, then picked up his coffee cup and sipped, watching her. "But you believe I can track Jacoby wherever he goes."

"I know you can. That's why they sent you."

"They?"

Callie set her empty bowl on the table, shifted so she could reach into the front pocket of her jeans, and then tossed a small metallic object to land on the coffee table precisely in front of Luther.

"Haven," she said.

FIVE

He reached over and picked up the small, smoothly cast lightning bolt, stared at it for a moment, then looked at her.

"I followed a hunch," she said. "Checked your hiking boots."

"That was more than a hunch."

Callie shrugged.

The nagging question finally came within his grasp. "You know about Haven. You knew about Jacoby not because of any news reports, but because you were expecting him to be here. You're here *because* of him. You're FBI, aren't you? More than that, you're SCU."

Callie replied readily. "I am. And, yes, that's why I'm here. Because of Jacoby."

Evenly, he said, "I asked you before. How long have you been a telepath?"

Matter-of-factly, she said, "Born one. As soon as I could talk, I was freaking my parents out telling them what they were thinking." A fleeting smile crossed her face. "And learning a *lot* more about all kinds of things kids aren't supposed to know."

"How soon did they have you in therapy?"

This time, the smile lingered, a bit wry. "I was lucky. Psychic abilities run in the family, reportedly going back generations. Between my grandmother's Sight and my aunt's ability to talk to the dead, telepathy wasn't such a big deal. Once everybody got used to it. And once they taught me to begin building my shields *and* to keep it to myself whenever the odd thought from someone else slipped through, especially if they weren't family."

"Which you did. Keep it to yourself, I mean."

"Sure. Even kids know that to be different is to attract the wrong kind of attention. Especially kids. Didn't want to be considered a freak. Besides, it gave me even more motivation to build strong shields so I could shut out the mental chatter all around me at will. I've had a lifetime to make those shields very, very strong."

"So . . . what? You dropped them with me?"

"I was curious. You send and receive. Not so common."

He debated with himself for a silent moment, then said, "Far as I know, I've never sent or received with anyone else. And I've been tested, like we all are."

Callie didn't seem disturbed. "Must be right on my frequency then. Bishop and Miranda are too."

Like all Haven operatives, Luther knew who they were

talking about, even though he had not met either of the FBI agents. "Yeah, but they're both telepaths, and strong ones. I'm not."

"News for you. You're a telepath now. I'm guessing you got a little bit too close to the energy around Cole Jacoby. It's powerful stuff. Powerful enough to trigger a latent ability. Maybe even create one."

Luther also knew what all operatives and agents knew, that external energy from various sources could affect, even change, a psychic's abilities. Sometimes drastically. Such as activating what had been a completely unknown, latent ability. Like flipping a switch. But . . . creating one?

"There's energy around him?"

"Definitely."

"I didn't feel anything. When I was there."

"Didn't you?" Her gaze was steady.

Luther thought back, then sighed. "I don't know, maybe I did. It's hard to say because that sort of thing isn't normal for me. I tend not to pick up energy of any kind unless I'm touching something *and* concentrating. The only thing I touched near Jacoby were a few trees." He glanced down at his leg. "And . . . a bullet."

"Which he touched when he loaded his gun." Callie shook her head slightly. "I didn't feel anything unusual when I dug it out of you. But we both know any energy it might have held could have been discharged earlier."

"Into me?"

"I suppose it's possible. But I'm no expert when it comes to the . . . transference of energy. Not really my job to figure out the why of all this. From what I'm told, the SCU and Haven operatives are adding a hell of a lot of empirical data to scientific understanding of just how energy works. Still a lot more questions than answers, though."

Luther frowned, considered a few unsettling possible consequences to himself, then dismissed it as something to deal with later, if and when he had to. "This energy you say is around Jacoby. Is it created by him?"

"Not sure yet whether he's the source; I didn't get the chance to explore the area around that cabin before he got here, and so far I haven't caught him venturing very far away."

"So it could be coming from the area rather than from him." Luther was very carefully not thinking about any change in his own abilities. Not yet. He suspected his mind wasn't quite ready to deal with that just yet.

"Some places store energy," Callie agreed. "Some are even sources of energy; we've figured out that much. Energy the earth itself generates and the topography of a place holds on to. And these are old mountains with a lot of violent history soaked into the very ground and held there in some places. Maybe the area around Jacoby's cabin is one of those places. Maybe choosing that particular cabin was no accident or coincidence; maybe he knew what was there. Or maybe it's . . . just him."

Somewhat belatedly, Luther said, "I'm surprised Maggie didn't tell me there was an SCU agent here. Or didn't she know?"

"I have no idea whether she knew. All I know is that

I'm here because Bishop had a hunch. And before you jump on that one, I'm guessing we both know his hunches are never just that. Whatever he believes is going to happen, he didn't share with me."

"You're here alone?"

"Except for Cesar."

"I thought Bishop always sent people out in teams."

"Almost always. There are some teams with multiple agents. A few agents work solo more often than not. And a few work only with a single partner. Far as I know, I'm the only one on the team with a canine partner." She nodded toward the watchful Rottweiler.

"He's your partner?"

"Yep. Trained and certified as a law enforcement dog. I raised and trained him, going through several different programs in which we both received specialized training. And then I got him . . . Bishop-approved."

Luther was surprised, but when he considered, it did seem quite reasonable for Bishop to accept a trained dog to aid one of his agents. From what little was really known, outside the SCU, of the unit chief, he was all about giving his people whatever tools they could use to investigate crimes. And the FBI certainly employed K-9 units for a variety of purposes.

"You might have told me some of this sooner."

Her eyebrows lifted in faint surprise. "I was trained by Bishop. Never volunteer information unless and until you have no other choice or else deem it necessary. Until you asked, I really didn't see any reason to explain why I was here."

"How long have you been here?" Luther asked, deciding not to waste a glare.

"Couple weeks, like I said."

Luther swore under his breath. "Then what the hell am I doing here?"

"I gather the FBI agent in the nearest field office requested help from Haven in locating his fugitive. Since the fugitive escaped from FBI agents while in their custody, this is one of those cases where it's the FBI rather than the U.S. Marshals Service who's responsible for tracking and recapturing this guy."

"And the FBI field agent doesn't know you're here?"

"No. And my cover is solid. Anybody checking the records would find that this land and cabin belong to the Davis family, this branch of which I'm connected to through a couple of marriages and a few cousins."

"For real?"

"On paper. The current owner of this place doesn't usually come up here this time of year and was happy instead to take a nice vacation out to Vegas, cash bonus in hand. He was also happy to mention his trip and my occupancy here before he left to a few friends down in town."

"Devil's Gap?" When she nodded, he said almost as an aside, "I wonder whose bright idea *that* name was?"

"Maybe a translation of an old Native American name. There are a lot of them in these mountains, especially in areas like this with a lot more wilderness than civilization." She paused, then added wryly, "Anyway, it's the sort of town where everybody pretty much knows everybody else's business, even if they keep it among the natives. So my bona fides are established."

COLE WASN'T ENTIRELY sure he was awake. He was walking through the forest, dawn still a distant coming, and he was looking for something. But . . . he wasn't sure what he was looking for.

There were no voices in his head, and that was good, that was so good he practically sat down and cried with relief. But instead he kept walking, looking around as best he could in the moonlight.

When he thought about it, he realized that he wasn't even sure where he was. He didn't feel lost, only . . . displaced. And driven. Driven to find whatever it was he needed to find.

There was a little ravine, he thought, and a tree on its banks with roots exposed from many spring rains. That was where she was.

She?

A niggling unease stirred in his mind, but it was pushed down relentlessly, this time not by voices but by something else inside him he was briefly aware was darker and more powerful.

And . . . needful.

After that, he stopped worrying about it and just kept walking, briskly, climbing up to where he'd hidden her safely away.

Because it was time.

———

"BISHOP IS THOROUGH, I'll give him that much. And probably easier to be prepared for things when you see some of them coming." Luther shook his head, but added, "We both know what my orders were. What about yours? I gather capture of the fugitive isn't necessarily Bishop's primary goal."

It wasn't a question.

Callie smiled wryly. "My assignment is to try to figure out how Jacoby managed to escape two experienced federal agents without any apparent outside help, without being armed, and leaving them with no memory of what happened."

"Figure out psychically, I gather?"

"Yeah. One of my things is picking up on and sometimes being able to interpret negative energy."

"That's what Bishop figured Jacoby used?"

"As it was explained to me, it would take negative energy to . . . steal time . . . from someone. By definition, taking away is a negative action. The agents lost time, or the memories of time. Whichever it was, they haven't gotten it back yet. Not such a good sign, that."

The realization that his own newly created abilities as a telepath—assuming Callie was right about that—might have come from negative energy made Luther's skin crawl more than a bit.

"Right now, you're a neutral telepath," Callie said calmly. "I'm not picking up on anything either positive or negative coming from you. Not so unusual with abilities that go active suddenly or unexpectedly. They tend to just sort of sit there for a bit, letting us adjust. Usually. The thing is, you need to keep your distance from any kind of negative energy, at least until you've learned to shield this new ability."

"I have a shield," he said slowly. "Usually, I mean. It's how I . . . blend in when I'm tracking someone. How I'm not seen. That's my thing."

"I know. But that shield . . ." For the first time, she seemed to be struggling to convey something, but whether it was because she didn't have the knowledge or lacked the ability to express it was something Luther couldn't begin to guess.

"What about it?"

She was frowning. "It's . . . cracked. For want of a better word. I wasn't around you before you came here, but I can't believe that what I sense is normal for you. Not if it's always hidden you the way you describe, the way I was told your abilities work. So something must have happened. To you. To it. And I doubt it was being shot."

"I've been shot before," he said. "Nothing changed that time, not psychically."

"Okay. Then we should probably assume the damage to your shield has something to do with the energy around Jacoby's place. Which makes it especially vital that you keep your distance now. Aside from the cracked shield, new abilities tend to be affected by external energy a lot faster and more . . . drastically . . . than established ones."

"Affected how?"

"You probably know as much as I do."

"I sort of doubt it. Affected how?"

She studied him for a moment, then gave a faint shrug. "Thing is, I can't tell for certain how strong a telepath you are. I mean, my abilities don't work that way. I know you can send and receive, apparently complete thoughts— sentences—and I know that's unusual. It speaks to the strength of your abilities, especially since telepathy is a new one, but still doesn't tell me just how powerful you are."

"And that's important because?"

"The more powerful you are, the more at risk you are right now, as a new psychic, of being affected by external energy sources. Especially with that cracked shield."

Luther stared at her for a long moment, then repeated steadily, "Affected how?"

"That depends on the energy. How strong *it* is. What the source is. What's generating the energy and why. Whether that cracked shield offers you enough protection or even any at all. If you can't protect yourself at all . . . Well, energy can do all kinds of things. Psychic energy, we both know, can do amazing things, positive as well as negative. Since this is negative energy, it could have a negative effect on you. Physically. Psychically. Even emotionally. At best, it could attack you in a sense, be a drain on your own energy."

"And at worst?"

"I don't know the worst. To my knowledge, this particular situation has never happened to an SCU agent or Haven operative."

"I don't much like the sound of that," he said slowly.

"No, I imagine not. In fact, I imagine it wouldn't be

a good thing for any of us. Especially not here and now. Whatever Jacoby can or can't do, the energy all around him is dark, and though I haven't gotten close enough to be sure, I have a strong hunch it's controlling him rather than the other way around."

"Energy can do that?" It was something he'd never heard of.

"It can if he can't protect himself, or deliberately opened himself to it. If it's coming from a powerful source with an agenda—so to speak. A disembodied spirit who doesn't like being disembodied or is just plain angry or evil, for instance. An energy that wants, needs, control. An energy that wants to escape whatever's been holding it, containing it, here."

"Wants? Needs? That implies a consciousness. In fact, it damned well demands one."

"I'd agree with that."

"How can energy have a consciousness?"

"Like I said, it could be coming from a disembodied spirit or spirits. Jacoby himself could be a psychic whose abilities became active due to some event we have no way of knowing, or due to the sudden onset of mental illness of one kind or another; psychiatric patients are usually at the mercy of their illnesses, and that is one of the psychic triggers we've recently identified."

"One of the scarier ones," Luther noted dryly.

"Yeah, most of us feel a little too out of control a little too often as it is. The threat of maybe going crazy isn't exactly reassuring. One reason I'm glad I was born with my abilities and have never had a new one triggered."

Luther was wishing he could say the same on both counts.

"Anyway, the dark energy could come from Jacoby for whatever reason. Or it could be the place, the area around that cabin or the cabin itself that's somehow soaked up the negative energy of something horrific: a battle, maybe a murder or murders. Energy that's been trapped there a long time, growing darker and darker because it's been trapped there. Energy that is, in a sense, holding him hostage. Possible. Possible he's trying to deal with something he's never before had to deal with. Maybe gaining control. Or not. As I said, I know he hasn't strayed very far from the place since he got here. Not far at all, in fact."

She frowned. "I don't know how he was able to escape the agents, but all through that part of the story his actions were careful, methodical, planned, precise. Organized. And unhurried. He didn't try to run right away, he took the time—and the risk—of staying in the same area long enough to get his dogs. Maybe long enough for something else we haven't yet discovered. He had the cabin rented and waiting, probably the Jeep hidden somewhere waiting for him, maybe the other vehicles as well, and all of them turned out to be untraceable. He had supplies stashed, or got them somewhere along the way where no one recognized him and no security camera we know of recorded it."

"And I guess both likely and unlikely stores were checked."

"By some very good technical analysts, yes. Between

traffic cams and cameras at ATMs and security cams at a lot of businesses, and especially given the relatively small area, there was a good chance of catching him on security footage somewhere. At least, that was the logical thought. But he wasn't spotted anywhere on camera. No sign of him shopping. Or getting gas, for that matter. No recordings of him at all. Just a witness here or there who'd never have noticed him except that his picture was all over TV and the Internet." She smiled faintly. "Never mind the BOLO. Today it's TV and the Internet that brings more witnesses forward. And he hasn't shown up on any cellphone-captured videos on YouTube yet. We have people monitoring that too."

She drew a breath and let it out slowly, thoughtful. "He was headed this way all along, and both before and during the trip was sharp enough and careful enough to lay false trails miles away from his destination. He had a plan for his escape and it was a good one. He picked a place to hide, and it was a good one—at least on paper. It really wasn't until he got up here that his behavior became very obviously erratic."

"Which makes it at least possible he wasn't nearly so dangerous until he arrived here and became affected by something in the area. Something in that cabin or in the area around it." Luther thought about it. "But you said taking away the memories of those agents was a negative thing, something he did before he got here. The first step he took in escaping."

"The first step that we know of."

COLE JACOBY WAS in a very dark place. He felt an enormous pressure, as if something with incredible strength and will had backed him into a corner or put him inside a box or wrapped him tightly in something, and was holding him still.

He couldn't see.

Couldn't move.

Couldn't hear even his own breathing, or feel his heart beating, or sense anything in the darkness except that, except the impenetrable blackness of *nothing*.

Was he dead?

No. No, because . . . because he could smell something. Something rusty. Something metallic. Something very, very old that made him afraid in a way he could never remember being afraid. And something that smelled a lot like . . . Well, it had to be sulfur. Had to be. Even rotten eggs didn't have the bite, the sharp, eye-watering sting, of true sulfur.

There was nothing else like that. Except . . . maybe . . . brimstone.

Even as that realization surfaced, he decided to ignore it. He was just . . . sleeping, that was all. Caught in some kind of weird nightmare. That had to be it, because it couldn't be real.

Could it?

No. A nightmare. It explained why he couldn't move. Why he couldn't see. Or speak. Or feel anything except blackness and terror.

And nightmares were unpredictable, he knew that. It explained why he could smell when he couldn't use any other sense. And then . . . it explained why he could suddenly hear with a painful clarity.

It just didn't explain what he heard.

It didn't explain the screaming.

LUTHER NODDED. "TRUE, attempting to control the guards may just have been the next step for him. Maybe because he'd already tried whatever his psychic sense is and realized he could only influence one or two minds at most. Or couldn't control them long enough for his purposes. So he had to figure out a way to get out of prison, even temporarily. His actual first step may have been to offer the feds just enough information, or the promise of it, to persuade them to transfer him. He either took the chance or was reasonably sure he could exercise some kind of control over the two agents. Maybe they were all he could handle."

"Makes sense," Callie agreed.

"He had to have practiced in prison. We may know little about psychic mind control, but common sense says nobody learns how to successfully control the minds of two other people the first time they try, and he was in there for weeks waiting for his trial, and months after his conviction. He must have taken every chance to practice when he was relatively alone with someone else. His cellmate. Maybe a guard or two. Even his legal counsel. Especially his legal counsel."

"Privileged communication and so not monitored even within a highly monitored prison," she agreed. "That would have been a good chance. Except that he had no visits from his attorney."

"None at all?"

"No. A couple of phone calls, but there wasn't much chance of an appeal. The prosecution had him cold. They caught him with about a hundred grand on him, all of it from the robbery. Security footage from the bank when it was actually robbed wasn't much use because of a glitch, but they had footage of him pretty obviously casing the place the day before. They had his fingerprints. Even his DNA."

"Should I ask how they had that at the scene of a bank robbery?" Luther asked warily.

Callie smiled. "The place was busy when he got there, and he killed a little time while he was covertly studying the layout pretending to fill out a deposit envelope. Which he licked."

"Not very bright."

"Well, in fairness to him, the camera footage shows him shoving it into a pocket. His bad luck that it fell out before he left and was missed by the cleaning crew that evening. Fingerprints on the envelope matched those later discovered in the vault."

"He didn't wear gloves?"

"Latex ones. One of which he left behind in the vault; the techs got his prints from the inside of the glove."

Luther shook his head and frowned as he thought. "So he's caught, tried, convicted, sent to prison. Talks to his legal counsel only over the phone. What about visitors?"

"No visitors."

"What, none at all?"

"No." Callie was certain. "Or mail. And no Internet connection. At all. In fact, no computer access; prisoners only get that after proven good behavior. Once he was inside, and except for a couple of brief calls from his attorney, he only had contact with the people inside."

"No family?"

"A half sister, considerably older. Not so much estranged as complete strangers; her mother got total custody after a young, brief marriage, and Jacoby's father apparently never saw her again. He remarried, then started a second family when his son was born. Far as we were able to determine, Cole Jacoby never met his half sister and likely doesn't know she even exists."

Luther frowned. "Okay. So no visitors maybe makes it even more likely that Jacoby had to spend a lot of time practicing, figuring out what he could do. And maybe easier on strangers. He still could have been trying to control other minds a long time before he escaped."

"Trying, yeah. But even being semi-alone with his cellmate, or a guard or two now and then, it wouldn't have been easy even for an experienced psychic to control any abilities, especially such a specific ability, with so many violent minds all around. So much negative energy. Prison bars can hold prisoners, but their violent energy permeates the place. It . . . soaks into the walls and floors. The older the prison, especially a high-security prison, the more negative the energy. Where they kept Jacoby the energy was very dark and very bleak."

After studying her for a moment, Luther said, "You appear to speak from experience."

She nodded. "Prisons were one of the places I visited when we were trying to analyze my abilities. Square foot by square foot, they're the most negative places I've ever visited—and that includes psychiatric hospitals and trauma units. Even the federal country-club-type prisons where white-collar criminals are kept read as pretty damned negative, at least to somebody like me."

"And the most positive place you've read?"

"So far, it was a monastery in Asia."

He blinked, thought about asking her, then decided that was an undoubtedly interesting story for later.

Callie didn't seem to notice. "So if Jacoby was able to open any kind of psychic door to his own mind in that prison, it's dollars to doughnuts he let *something* in, and that was more than likely to be negative energy."

"Let something in before he was able to escape the prison."

"If he was practicing, especially something new to him, that's a virtual certainty. We all tend to leave ourselves vulnerable when we use our abilities. We're somewhat protected when we use them in a positive way. His way wasn't positive."

"And whatever he let in, he wouldn't be able to control."

"I wouldn't think so. Not then. And I still think the more minds around him, the less likely he was and is to control a specific mind with any kind of accuracy."

Luther frowned. "Negative energy. If he started trying

to control other minds there, in prison, and didn't really know what he was doing because the abilities were new, or he'd never tried to use them before, then wouldn't he have been affected *then*? I mean, wouldn't he have shown signs of erratic behavior during and right after his escape?"

Callie considered, then nodded slowly. "You'd think there would have been some sign. But I don't know; if it was recent enough, he might have been able to hide what was happening to him. Especially if he was focused on escaping. If prison is where he first tried to control other minds, he likely would have failed except maybe in some really small way. But in just trying, and trying there, unable to protect himself even if he realized he should, he still could have . . . fed off negative energy. Even then. Unconsciously. Which could have given him more power, including the power to open a door in his own mind."

"And let in something darker than he expected?"

"Maybe. Maybe he started shaping his mind, his abilities, and because he was in a negative place, that was the only energy he could use. He probably couldn't tell the difference. Strong energy is strong energy; it takes experience to tell one from the other, usually."

"And," Luther said, "however he experimented, whatever the results, there was enough to convince him he could control other minds, if the conditions were right. That he had a shot at using whatever it is to escape federal custody. Maybe he had a successful experiment or two, and the authorities just never noticed."

"Possible. Even likely. The paranormal tends to be the last possibility most people consider. Way easier to believe a sleeping guard just nodded off than that he was put to sleep by a psychic."

"Let's assume," Luther said. "That he practiced. That there was success. But maybe he realized there were too many people around, too many minds to control. He had to figure out a way to get himself alone with just one or two. He'd been inside before, he knew about prisoner transfers, about deals made. Also knew what bait was most likely to get him out of there."

"The money. No one knew where he'd hidden the rest of it. No evidence at all, and no sign of a partner."

"So just him. And feds eager to question him, maybe make a deal. They make deals with serial killers; Jacoby wasn't dangerous, never had been, and they didn't see him as a threat."

"Especially," Callie agreed, "a psychic threat. Bishop was already suspicious, though I don't think even he had any idea Jacoby was capable of escaping custody."

"Or he would have sent SCU agents?"

"That, or made sure Jacoby was knocked out for the trip." And when Luther lifted his brows, she added, "Best not to take any chances, would have been his reasoning."

"Well, events proved that probably would have been wise," Luther said dryly.

"Yeah." Callie brooded for a moment. "But what's here now, in Jacoby or around that cabin . . . I've never sensed anything that dark, even in a prison, and most certainly not at a distance. If Jacoby came up here with a . . . door open to darkness, with a latent ability suddenly gone active, or an old ability he was still learning how to control, if he didn't know how to protect himself from a darkness that powerful, or even—stupidly—welcomed it because he thought it meant more power for him . . ."

"Trouble."

"I'll say. We haven't found any psychic capable of the sort of mind control Jacoby must have used. That would take a *lot* of power. Probably a lot more than Jacoby ever had a hope of mastering, whether he realized it or not. That kind of power would have had no trouble getting inside him, and it's more than likely taken hold of him by now."

"You're saying in hardly more than two weeks, he could have gone from controlling, rather benignly, the minds of two agents to being . . . possessed . . . by some negative energy powerful enough to control *him*?"

"It's possible. Maybe even likely. His behavior up here is clear evidence something unusual is going on with him. Whether it was here or he brought it with him and it broke out once he got here, that darkness is nothing but negative. Maybe even evil."

Curiously, Luther said, "You believe in evil as an actual, physical force?"

"Oh, yeah." Her voice remained calm, her eyes serene. "And the thing is, we have more to worry about than what it's doing to Jacoby. There's also you. You have that cracked shield. You're vulnerable because you have a new ability not under your control. At all. You have an open door. The darkness, the evil, up there could be very bad for you."

SIX

"What are you doing here?" Hollis repeated, her voice a little louder but still low. "You're one of Diana's spirit guides, not mine." She frowned. "I don't even have guides."

The spirit who in life had been a young girl called Brooke shook her head. "Diana has lots of spirit guides; she needed them to get through what she had to in her life. But I was there last time because of the situation, not because of her. Your team was still fighting Samuel, and you needed my help."

"Sure that wasn't a little bit of vengeance on your part? I mean, he was directly responsible for your death."

Brooke's young face appeared thoughtful. "You know, there really isn't much of a need for revenge or even justice once you get here."

"Here?"

Brooke smiled.

Hollis didn't waste a breath for a curse. "And now?"

"You wanted to learn how to handle being a medium. I'm going to help you do that. At least for a while."

"Why?" Hollis asked, never accused of being indirect.

Brooke seemed to hesitate, then said, "Bishop and Miranda aren't wrong to be . . . concerned about you."

Hollis hugged her upraised legs a little tighter. "Too much going on inside my brain, huh?"

"Let's just say the energy is becoming . . . palpable."

"Meaning?"

Brooke said slowly, "The only time you—unconsciously— used a conduit was when you helped Diana. Reese was there, touching you, and because you were so tired, and the need was so great, you drew on his strength without being consciously aware of it."

Hollis moved uneasily. "I wish you hadn't told me that."

"You already knew."

"Okay, maybe. But not for sure. And I don't like it. Bad enough I've needed him as an anchor to escape Diana's gray time. I don't want to be someone—something—that feeds off others."

"You can't look at it that way."

"Oh, can't I?"

"No. All his life, Reese has had extra energy, at times almost too much to contain. You've noticed it yourself, that tension you've sensed in him. The hair-trigger alertness. He worked hard to contain it; it's why he has that unique double shield of his, and why the surface of him almost always seems so calm. It's also one reason he joined the military, to have a strict focus, a rigid routine, and a high degree of physical activity to help burn off excess energy."

Hollis felt almost as if she were eavesdropping, learning things about him Reese wasn't the one telling her, but somehow she couldn't ask the spirit to stop. Something inside her told her that she needed to hear this, now, and that Reese would be slow to tell her—if he told her at all.

"Bishop saw that excess energy *and* Reese's ways of dealing with it. Because of the experiences of other agents, he thought there was probably a better way. Better for Reese."

"And better for me? But if he has too much energy, and I have too much energy, then— Well . . . bang? Too much energy collides and both of us stroke out or worse?"

"If the two of you were just trying to combine energies, especially without a powerful emotional connection, that's probably what would happen."

Hollis narrowed her eyes and stared at Brooke, but the spirit remained serene.

"But Bishop believes that instead of merely combining your energies, both of you can act as conduits, channeling energy safely away from yourselves at need. You did it helping Diana—by channeling not only your energy but some of Reese's as well."

"You said it yourself: That was a onetime thing, pure instinct driven by need."

"But successful."

Hollis thought about it for a minute. "You didn't just

casually drop in that little item about a powerful emotional connection, did you?"

Brooke smiled.

"Look, whatever we—he said during a difficult and exhausting point in an investigation, the truth is that we're partners. And that's all. There isn't an emotional connection."

"In just about five minutes," Brooke said, "Reese is going to walk through that door. Not because he heard you talking, but because he feels that you're awake and upset. *That* is an emotional connection. Like it or not, the beginnings of something potentially much more powerful already exist between the two of you."

Hollis glanced toward the connecting door, then unconsciously lowered her voice even more. "He's a natural caretaker, that's all."

"Actually, he isn't." Brooke looked thoughtful. "Probably as a consequence of struggling all his life to contain all that energy, even his emotions turned inward. Oh, he's an honorable man and a responsible man, which made him an excellent officer in the military. And makes him excel at undercover work. But he could probably count on one hand the people he's truly cared for in his life—and most of those would be recent adds."

"Look, I don't know what it is you expect me to do." Hollis didn't even like having this knowledge; it made her uncomfortable. Assuming any of it was even real.

"Just . . . keep an open mind."

Hollis stared at her. "I'm a medium talking to the spirit of a girl who was murdered by an insane preacher bent on ruling the world—after he destroyed it with his very scary and evil psychic abilities. I see auras. I can bring myself pretty much back from the dead and heal others at least to a degree. My friends are telepaths and seers and other mediums, and I know about and can visit—sometimes against my will—a gray place that's probably limbo or purgatory but definitely an elsewhere, and is really, really cold and creepy. All of that can be defined as beyond normal, and I believe in it all. I've experienced it all. If I were any more open-minded, my brains would fall out."

WHEN COLE FOUGHT his way back to consciousness, it was to hear a low, rumbling sound that was at once strange and familiar. And to smell something equally both strange—and familiar.

He managed to sit up, to swing his legs off the cot. He lifted his hands to rub his eyes but stopped short of touching himself because the smell was overpowering. He blinked and tried to focus on the very dim light of dawn coming through the cabin's windows and the even fainter reddish gleam of embers in the fireplace.

That was why his hands looked red.

Wasn't it?

He fumbled for the kerosene lamp on the rustic coffee table and fumbled even more to get a match from the box beside it and light the lamp.

That low rumbling sound. What *was* it? It made the hairs on the back of his neck stand out.

And the smell made his stomach churn.

He was finally able to light the lamp and adjust the flame until its yellowish light brightened the room, managing not to actually look at his hands until it was done. Then, a wordless dread inside him, he looked.

It hadn't been the fireplace light that made his hands look red.

They were stained red. His hands, wrists, halfway up his forearms, stained red and stinking of something metallic that was familiar in an odd way and explained why his stomach churned. Flashes of memories mixed with a primal instinct.

Blood.

His hands were covered with dried blood.

Baffled, fearful, he stared at them for a long moment, until the low rumbling sound again drew his attention. He looked up, around the room.

Their eyes weren't red anymore, but his dogs were all tensely awake, staring at him.

And growling.

BROOKE WAS SMILING faintly. "Okay. Just so you . . . don't lose sight of that. Expecting the unexpected should probably be your mantra."

"I thought that was some things have to happen just the way they happen."

"The SCU mantra. And Haven's, really. I guess being ready for the unexpected should be your personal mantra."

"God knows it fits." Shaking her head, Hollis said, "Well, everything else aside, I don't know what it is you expect to happen here. Anna wants to communicate with her dead husband. Maybe I can help bring that about, or maybe I can't. Wouldn't want to tell me which it is, would you?"

"That would be—"

"Against the rules, yeah. Thought that would be your answer. Well, then, what about the bright light. Can you tell me—"

Brooke was shaking her head. "All I can tell you about that is some people see it when they cross over and some people don't."

"Why?"

"I don't know. I suppose because every experience is unique."

"Did you see it?"

"No," Brooke replied readily. "But I haven't really crossed over yet. Things to do first. Mediums to help."

Hollis sighed her disappointment but wasn't surprised. The universe, they had discovered, seldom made things easy for them. Which rather begged the question . . . "Why help me?" she demanded. "If I'm one of the things you need to do before you can move on . . . there must be a reason."

Her tone innocent, Brooke said, "I'm just following orders."

"From?"

Brooke smiled. Again.

With another sigh, Hollis said, "Not going to be *too*

helpful, huh?" Then she frowned. "Okay, if you won't tell me why me, then tell me why now. We aren't on a case. Like I said, I'm just trying to reach some poor woman's husband so she knows he still exists in some kind of life after this one."

"You really believe that's the only reason you're here?"

"Isn't it?"

"Remember the mantra. The SCU and Haven one. That bit about being taught that some things have to happen just the way they happen?"

"Well, yeah, but . . ." For the first time Hollis realized that the SCU mantra might encompass more than just investigations.

Hollis stared at Brooke for a long moment. "Diana warned me about spirit guides. How cryptic you guys can be. Usually are. And how remarkably unhelpful for, you know, guides. You might want to look up that word. Or tell your boss to." She reflected, then added, "Well, ask. Not tell."

Brooke's smile faded. "I will tell you that there's more in this house than you came here expecting. A lot more. You need to be careful. Very, very careful. Don't open the wrong door or hold any of them open for too long; you won't like what might come through. I'll be around, Hollis."

"Wait, what—"

Brooke vanished, and in almost the same moment Reese appeared in the doorway, wearing a robe and seemingly wide awake.

It occurred to Hollis that she'd only ever seen him in

two states: wide awake or dead asleep. He probably didn't even have an in-between.

"Hollis? You okay?"

"Just tell me I wasn't broadcasting my dreams."

"As far as I know, you weren't. I didn't pick up anything last night once you went out like a light after your shower. And nothing now except a . . . general unease."

She stared at him, wondering if he remembered her sleepy invitation to join her. Wondering if that had been only her imagination.

Surely it was that.

Surely.

"Then why are you awake?" she asked finally.

"I usually wake about this time in the morning."

"Before dawn?"

"Old habits."

Military habits, she thought, but all she said was, "Well, I don't think I'm up for the day. I think I'll go back to sleep until a decent hour." If she could do that, after Brooke's very unsettling warning.

Reese didn't seem surprised or disturbed. "Sounds like a good plan. I'll shower and shave, and maybe do a little exploring."

She started to warn him about all the spirits, then remembered he wouldn't be troubled by them. "Okay. If I'm still asleep when they usually serve breakfast around here, wake me up, will you?"

"No problem. I'll see you later."

He turned and retreated back into their shared sitting

room and from there, presumably, to his own bedroom and his shower.

Hollis stared after him for a long time, trying not to think because she didn't want to broadcast. It was hard, though, not thinking. When there was so much on her mind. So many questions.

And worries.

She had known for a while that Bishop and Miranda were concerned about her, about the way she kept acquiring "fun new toys" of the psychic variety seemingly with every case. And when those two worried . . . well, they didn't worry over trifles. Nobody had to tell Hollis that the human brain was both exceptionally powerful—and, conversely, fragile. Like every other organ in the human body, it had its limits.

Unfortunately, nobody really knew what those were.

Yet.

But everybody who counted was pretty damned sure that Hollis was pushing limits way, way too often.

Would she be pushing yet another limit if she—she and Reese—found a way to channel excess energy? Or would that help somehow?

No way of knowing without trying, which seemed to be very much the norm in Hollis's life.

And now here was Brooke warning her to be careful, telling her without saying very much at all that there was reason to be wary in this house, wary in doing this relatively simple exercise in being a medium that was not supposed to be dangerous.

Hollis lay back on the bed and pulled the covers up around her. She felt cold, and uneasy, and just a little bit scared.

Just a little bit.

LUTHER SAID, "WE all struggle with our abilities. We live with the potential dangers of using them. It's just . . . possibilities we accept. And I came here to do a job."

"You've done that."

"Found Jacoby, yeah. But . . . there's more to it."

"Is there?"

"You wouldn't be here otherwise."

"Well, my assignment is a bit different. I need to understand just what kind of psychic he is, assuming that's how he escaped. And I have to try to get a handle on that energy all around him."

"You know it's there. You know it's negative. What else do you need to know?"

"Everything else we've been talking about. How strong is it. Whether it's coming from him or something else. Whether he's in control—or it is. If the source is the area somehow, then there's at least an even chance its effects on Jacoby would lessen, or even disappear if we could get him away from here."

"A chance. Not a certainty."

"No. Depending on whether he was a latent, or just unusually vulnerable to the effects of energy, whether he's using it or it's using him, he may have changed permanently. I'm sure you know as well as I do that psychics rarely lose abilities or the strength of abilities once they have them, though some kind of trauma has been known to affect, even destroy, abilities. But we really don't have much data on what might happen if a psychic's abilities were created or at least strengthened by an external source. Especially an ability apparently triggered or created by negative energy."

"Like my telepathy?"

"Like your telepathy. And possibly Jacoby's abilities, whatever those really are."

Callie rose and took both their coffee cups to be refilled. Luther only half watched her, trying to think the situation through from a standpoint of tactics and resources.

He accepted the coffee from her and took a swallow, grateful for the warmth even if it did little to help the cold unease inside him. No matter which way he looked at it, which way he considered, the situation up here just seemed like a bad one to him.

He looked at her as she sat across from him, knowing better than to underestimate any of Bishop's people, but way too conscious of himself likely being more of a burden than a help.

"Every instinct tells me that could be bad a lot easier than it could be good. For both of us."

"Given that it's negative energy, you're probably right."

"I should leave." He took another swallow of his coffee, frowning. "We should both leave. Or get down to town and call for backup."

"Possibilities," she allowed. "But . . . so far the bad is

distant enough not to worry me. This being a safe spot, I'm inclined to stay, at least for the time being. And you need time to heal."

"I can't be much help while I'm healing."

"Well, there isn't all that much to be done," she reminded him.

"Yeah, right. You trying to gather information about Jacoby and his bad energy alone also sounds like a bad idea." He held up his free hand when she would have spoken. "Granted, I don't know the strength of your abilities, but the point is the going-anywhere-near-him-alone part. With all due respect to Cesar, if Jacoby's stronger than you believe, or darker, more negative, neither your abilities nor your dog might be able to protect you. What then?"

She returned his gaze steadily for a moment, sipping her coffee, then said, "Well, I'm a great one for not crossing bridges until I come to them. Right now, there's no urgent reason why I need to get close to Jacoby. Time enough in a few days, I'm thinking. Give him a chance to settle down after the encounter with you. Give him time to drop his guard, if it's up. You'll likely be on your feet by then."

He uttered a short laugh. "Yeah, but there's also the thing about me becoming an active telepath with a cracked shield. And being affected by that negative energy even more than I possibly already have been. If you're right about that, I could well be more of a hindrance than a help."

"Maybe. Or maybe we'll just have to keep you near— but at a safe distance from that cabin."

"And if it's Jacoby generating that negative energy, or

he's . . . able to carry it with him?" Luther was having a bit of trouble concentrating, and he frowned when her grave face seemed to blur a bit. He took a drink of his strong coffee, hoping it would help. It didn't.

"It's something we—I—have to find out about him. Along with other questions to be answered. Whether it's growing or getting darker. Just how far he can go in using it. If he has any control at all."

"So you have to get closer to him."

"Eventually. No real hurry."

"He's shooting at people, Callie. Those hunters weren't threatening him, and I didn't threaten him, but he shot at all of us." He rubbed his face with one hand, wondering if maybe a hot shower would clear his head somewhat. Except he didn't want to use up her propane . . .

"When the time comes, I'll be careful," she said.

"Still. Bishop should have . . . sent somebody else. With you. Or we should call. For backup." He was vaguely aware that Callie had gotten up silently and come over to take his coffee cup away from him.

"Why don't you rest a bit," she suggested. "Your leg needs time to heal, and nothing much is likely to happen in the next few hours. Sleep."

He didn't want to. In fact, he fought against it, trying mightily to keep his eyes open. But he lost the fight, and it wasn't until he was almost out that he suddenly wondered . . .

"You . . . Did you . . . ?"

"Would I do that?" she murmured, apparently understanding.

Luther thought she would. He also thought he didn't care much, and slipped into a peaceful darkness.

CALLIE CARRIED THE bowls and cups to the sink. Cesar uttered a curiously human sigh when she passed him, and she laughed under her breath. "Well, he obviously wasn't going to rest any other way, his mind was going a mile a minute. Just a little sedation, that's all. He'll sleep a few hours, and be the better for it."

Won't like you.

"He won't be happy, but I doubt he'll be angry."

Tricked him.

The easy telepathic link she had with Cesar, existing since the first time she'd picked up the wiggling black-and-tan puppy, had become an important part of Callie's life and an integral part of the professional partnership.

Also the major reason Bishop had not only okayed the partnership but had asked that she provide rather extensive reports of her communications with her dog—as well as other animals she was able to connect to.

There had been a few of those along the way, but communication with animals other than Cesar tended to be brief and not nearly so . . . human. Whether Cesar had developed better language skills over the years or they had simply become more familiar with each other through almost constant contact, their silent communications were sometimes very like human discussions.

Like now.

"I know I tricked him. But he'll forgive me. Sometimes

people have to be . . . persuaded . . . to do what's best.
Don't worry about it."

Stubborn man.

"Yes, he is."

Stubborn Callie.

She chuckled. "True enough. And since he's weakened
by loss of blood, my stubborn beats his."

With another sigh, Cesar rose from the rug and
glanced at the door, then back at her. Callie nodded
slowly. "Guess we should, and now before it gets too
light." She retrieved her weapon from a drawer of a small
table near the door and clipped it to her belt, then took
her quilted, hooded jacket from the hook also near the
door and put it on.

She automatically checked to make sure her flashlight
was in her pocket, took a last look at her guest to make
sure he was resting comfortably, then said to Cesar,
"Remind me to give him that penicillin shot when we get
back. Probably best if I do that before he wakes up."

Probably. Shots hurt. Cesar's tail, not docked as was the
case with many Rottweilers, waved once, and then he followed her from the cabin.

Callie didn't use her flashlight. She stood there on the
wide porch of the cabin for a couple of minutes to allow
her eyes to adjust, then moved out. It was dawn, but not
by any stretch of the imagination bright; the mountain
slope that hosted both her cabin and Jacoby's faced east,
but with another mountain between them and the rising
sun, every new day took its time arriving.

The air was cold and clear, only the wisp of wood

smoke from her fireplace hinting of anything not of nature's doing. Callie automatically chose a path slightly different from the one she had used the last time she had gone out to check on Jacoby; every time, she varied her way, if only by a few yards, because she was naturally cautious and because she didn't want to wear an actual path through the woods between his cabin and hers.

Despite the blanket of fallen leaves beneath her boots, it had been a wet autumn, so she didn't have to worry about making noise as she walked. Not that she generally made any noise unless she wanted to.

She was in no particular hurry, walking slowly but allowing her gaze to scan the way ahead, looking and listening for anything out of place. About fifty yards away from her cabin, she stopped and quietly released Cesar from his automatic heel position so he could do his own kind of scanning. He moved out willingly, nose to the ground and moving silently, pausing here and there to mark his territory, but keeping her within sight and at the center of a wide circle.

Clearly, since he had no comment and showed no other signs, he sensed nothing to disturb him, and after a few minutes, Callie continued on.

Depending on the path she took, it was nearly a mile between her cabin and Jacoby's, and she had covered around half that distance when she stopped suddenly, frowning. Nothing looked out of place. Nothing sounded out of place.

And yet . . . she felt an odd pressure. A reluctance to take another step forward. Still, she had to try—

Stop.

She turned her head to see that Cesar had also come to a halt, even with her but higher up the slope. He didn't make a sound but dipped his nose toward the ground, then lifted his head and looked at her.

Trouble? She communicated silently because she wasn't sure what it was Cesar was bothered by.

Not good. Come see.

Callie was wary, but not overly concerned; if there had been danger about, Cesar's behavior as well as the warning would have been quite different.

Still, as she crossed the space to join her dog, she slid her hand inside her jacket and rested it on the handle of her gun, thumb ready to unsnap the holster. When she reached Cesar, she looked at the ground just in front of him—and even in the faint dawn light, she could see a wetness that was not last week's rain or last night's dew.

She took her hand off the weapon and drew out her flashlight instead as she went down on one knee. She didn't turn the light on immediately but instead reached down and touched two fingers to the wetness. In the faint light, her fingertips looked stained. A quick check with her flashlight confirmed what she already knew.

Blood.

"But whose?" she murmured.

It wasn't Luther's, because he hadn't gotten this far and because the path she had used to bring him to her cabin was a good fifty yards farther downslope, where a narrow but relatively flat ridge had made it easier for Cesar to pull the litter.

An animal, wounded by some hunter or the attack of another animal deeper in the forest? An injured hunter?

Not animal. Human.

Cesar was both too sensitive and too well trained to be wrong about that sort of thing.

Okay. But without something to compare it to, that's all you can really tell me, right?

Yes, for sure. Human. But . . .

But what?

I think girl. Afraid.

It didn't surprise Callie that Cesar could determine the gender of a victim from blood. His senses were extraordinary; even after years she was still marveling at them.

She turned the flashlight back on and carefully examined the ground all around them. Nothing. No tracks, no pawprints or hoofprints or footprints visible anywhere except the faint marks left by her and her dog. Of course, the blanket of leaves was thick, so there would likely be clear marks only if sharp hooves had dug into the ground here, or something heavy had fallen. Or there had been a struggle of some kind.

No sign of anything like that.

A girl who had been afraid, perhaps forced or carried against her will? There could have been no other physical signs of that here, at least none that would be visible without a forensic examination.

The blood was fresh. Callie was no forensics expert, but she knew enough to be reasonably sure this blood was only a few hours old. If that. Yet she and Cesar had walked past this spot, no more than twenty yards down the slope, when they had come out to check on Jacoby earlier.

Callie was certain Cesar would have scented the blood even at that distance, had it been here.

Yes. Would have. Wasn't here then.

Do you know who she is?

Not familiar scent. But fear. Much fear.

Was she running?

No. Carried.

By Jacoby?

Not sure. Strange scent.

Strange like what?

Cesar looked at her, and for a moment Callie was certain she could discern bafflement in his calm eyes.

Strange. Old. Dark. Black. Evil.

It surprised Callie more than a little that Cesar gave her that answer; even with all their investigations over years, he had never used the word "evil," and she would have said it was a concept he didn't understand.

Clearly, she would have been wrong.

Bad. Very bad. Hungry bad. Needing bad.

Needing what?

Needing . . . power. Needing energy.

Why?

To escape. And . . .

And what?

Fight.

Fight what? Fight who?

Not sure. Fight. Escape. Dig.

Callie could feel the strain as her dog tried to sort

through impressions and concepts that were familiar to his canine mind, and others that were clearly difficult for him to understand.

"It's okay," she murmured aloud, resting her free hand briefly on his head. "This is my job too."

And that job had just become a lot more complicated.

There was darkness and evil; she felt that herself.

But there was also blood, and fear.

And a girl.

So who had passed this way in the last couple of hours, in darkness and in silence, and bleeding?

Was there another danger on this mountain, or had Cole Jacoby become much, much worse than a bank robber?

Can we help the girl? Callie had to ask.

No. Cesar's response was instant.

She's already dead?

Dead. Gone. Worse.

Callie was almost afraid to ask, but steeled herself and did.

Worse than dead?

Pain. So much pain. It needed energy. It made her afraid.

Jacoby?

The evil. Inside. Becoming.

Becoming what?

More evil.

SEVEN

Special Agent Tony Harte was frowning at a map pinned to an evidence board in the cramped room they were using here at this small police station in a little town an hour or so from Boston. He had been working on a geographical profile, marking both abduction and dump sites for a string of murders that, so far, numbered eight.

Rather unusually, all the victims were men.

Also unusually, their profile pointed to a female killer.

"Think I found her comfort zone," Tony announced. When only silence greeted that, he turned to face the only other person in the room.

Bishop had been working his way through a stack of evidence folders spread out on the small conference table, but he was motionless now, staring into space in a way that was both familiar to Tony and yet still unsettling.

Watching a premonition from the outside was like that.

Tony had a fair enough idea about what it was like from the inside to be glad precognition wasn't one of his abilities.

He waited patiently, until the pale gray eyes of his boss slowly lost the weirdly metallic sheen that always accompanied a vision, until some of the color returned to his lean face and the scar down his left cheek, almost invisible unless something had disturbed him, became less noticeable.

"Something I should worry about?" Tony asked finally, very deliberately keeping his tone light.

Bishop blinked, looked at Tony for a moment as if he didn't see him—and then he was completely back, completely normal. For him.

"Maybe something we should all worry about," he said.

That surprised Tony, since his queries at such times usually earned him no more than an evasive nonanswer that was very characteristic of the Special Crimes Unit chief. "What is it?"

"The situation in Tennessee."

Tony thought about that for a moment, then asked wryly, "Which part? You've got Callie and Cesar there in the wilds of the mountains, and Haven sent in—Brinkman, wasn't it?—as well. To go after Jacoby, figure out if he used some psychic ability to escape and, if so, what it is and how powerful. Presumably get him back into somebody's official custody before too much longer, and maybe even find all that missing money. And then you've got Hollis and Reese over in the next county so Hollis can work on her medium skills *and* take the only kind of break we all know she'd take from working active cases."

He eyed his boss, waiting.

And then Bishop said a remarkable thing.

"I may have miscalculated."

Tony gave that the silent respect it deserved, then said slowly, "So who's in the hot seat?"

"All of them."

"All of—What, for the same reason?"

"I'm not sure."

Tony wasn't sure he'd ever been rendered speechless twice in a few short moments, even by Bishop.

Seemingly unaware of the effect he was having on Tony, Bishop said, "We can't even contact Callie or Luther unless and until she reports in, they come down off the mountain and find a landline, or they find one of the very few sweet spots on that mountain with cell reception. Hollis and Reese, on the other hand, might not have decent cell service, given how far out they are, but are currently guests in a private home with a landline, so they can contact us—and we can contact them."

"And tell them what?" Tony asked slowly. "What's the danger? Is Jacoby more dangerous than you thought? And even if he is, could it affect Hollis and Reese a mountain or two away? Or is Hollis in danger of letting something really bad in, like what happened to Quentin and Diana?"[4]

"I don't know," Bishop said slowly. "I'm not even sure

---

4 *Chill of Fear*

a warning of any kind might not do more harm than good."

"Some things have to happen?"

"Maybe."

"Boss . . . not having all the facts is one thing, and a thing we're more or less used to, but not even knowing there's danger about is something else entirely. Callie and Brinkman at least know there's a potential threat; Hollis and Reese aren't on a case."

"No, but neither one is going to treat the situation lightly, Reese because he's always wired and alert and Hollis because she's wary of opening herself up too much. Even without any warning, they'll take care."

"You hope."

"It's a reasonable assumption, given their training and abilities."

"And you've spent a lot of time teaching us not to assume anything, especially if we're not in possession of all the facts." Tony barely hesitated before hammering home at least one point. "Which, working for you, is most of the time."

Bishop reached for one of the file folders on the table and opened it, saying calmly, "Well, then, no one involved will assume danger might not face them around the next corner."

Tony thought about expressing his feelings. He thought long and hard about it. But in the end, he turned back to his geographical profiling without saying another word, certain only that no matter how tangled or enigmatic they looked from the outside, or how many curve balls fate threw into the mix, Bishop's plans had a way of working out.

Most of the time.

HOLLIS REALLY HAD intended to go back to sleep, but in the minutes after Reese returned to his room to shower and get ready for the day, she found herself wide awake—and still conscious of that creeping unease.

Giving up finally, she got out of bed and got herself ready for the day, a routine that took very little time; she wasn't a woman who fussed about her appearance, and since she'd showered the night before, that was a step easily skipped. She washed her face and brushed her teeth quickly, as usual, and even after years avoided her reflection in the mirror.

And those blue eyes that still looked . . . alien . . . in her face.

Stupid. She should be used to them by now. But she wasn't. And she didn't know if she ever would be.

Pushing that thought aside for maybe the thousandth time, she ran a brush through her short hair and got dressed in jeans and a loose sweater and slid her feet into comfortable flats.

She paused at the doorway to the shared sitting room and could dimly hear the shower in Reese's room. And then heard it shut off.

There was no clear plan in Hollis's mind, no intent to explore or sense that she should. Just that general unease that Reese had picked up on, something she tried very hard, now, to tamp down inside herself. Even if she did tend to broadcast under stress, there was no reason she couldn't practice at least a bit of self-control and maybe even build a shield for . . . most of the time.

Bishop had told her she could do it, and if anybody would know about that sort of thing, it would be him.

Of course, he hadn't told her *how*.

Typical.

Hollis slipped out of her room, closing the door quietly behind her. She wasn't surprised to find, in the dark old house, scattered lamps burning on tables and chests in the wide hallway. Maybe on timers. Or maybe left on all night. It was still very early, and she seriously doubted that either Owen or Anna was up. They didn't seem the up-with-the-chickens sort. Just the staff, probably.

Not that she had any idea who or how many made up the staff that cared for this huge house. She had seen only the butler, Thomas, and a silent youngish maid who had helped serve dinner the night before.

There had to be more, if only daily help. A cook, maids. Maybe a housekeeper to oversee everything. Just keeping up with the main part of the house would take a small army, never mind the two wings of assorted rooms and bedroom suites.

Their rooms were in the East Wing, which also housed the family "apartments" that were on the ground floor.

Hollis vaguely remembered some of the conversation going on around her sleepy self at dinner, and she was almost sure Anna had made the comment that the West

Wing of the house was closed most of the year and opened up only during the weeks in spring and summer when the public was admitted.

During those weeks, Owen and Anna were . . . "not in residence" was the term Hollis thought she remembered. An estate manager was in charge of the place, plus other administrative staff, and the family was gone, presumably visiting elsewhere, like maybe a city or the beach or somewhere that wasn't to hell and gone in the mountains of Tennessee.

And while they were gone, the Alexander mansion was turned into a very exclusive hotel. Alexander House. Full service, Owen had said, glum rather than boasting. He'd have preferred a bed-and-breakfast, but given how far they were from anything resembling a good restaurant, it was full service or don't bother.

Apparently, they bothered to the point that the place was booked up for all of the coming season, with a few reservations already made for next year. To hell and gone as a vacation spot clearly held attractions Hollis couldn't appreciate.

Somebody had mentioned extensive gardens the night before, she thought. Said to be gorgeous spring through summer. Tennis courts, a swimming pool. And horses. She remembered mention of a stable and horses, with miles of mountain trails. All of which added numerous employees to the growing number of staff Hollis had been compiling in her head. Not just staff working in the house, but gardeners or landscapers, people who cared for horses and tack, and probably a *lot* of purely maintenance people inside and out, to keep this place in tiptop shape and running smoothly.

Most employees would be full time and year-round in order to keep this place at its best. Even during the off-season, Alexander House was probably the major employer for that little town with its odd name of Devil's Gap and its apparent lack of amenities to attract visitors.

Offering plenty of amenities plus the opulence of an earlier era, Hollis supposed, would attract to Alexander House plenty of visitors looking for quiet and luxury and excellent service. She supposed all that could offset the almost eerie isolation of the place.

Or maybe that was just her take, the eeriness of this place. She was, after all and even trying her best to shield, fully conscious of spiritual energy hovering at the fringes of her awareness. A lot of it. She was, in fact, surprised that Alexander House was not one of the places frequented by paranormal investigators. But it wasn't, at least according to their briefing.

The briefing given by Bishop.

And when has he ever told any of us the whole truth?

The thought was more resigned than angry or even irritated; by now, it was a character trait in the unit chief familiar to if not expected by all who worked with him.

Hollis began moving down the hall toward the main part of the house, frowning. She was reasonably sure she would have remembered if either Owen or Anna had mentioned the house being haunted. In fact, she was sure one of them would have said something about it the evening before when she had seen the spirit of Jamie Bell.

And later, talking about hotel visitors, surely someone would have mentioned the draw of a reputedly haunted Alexander House?

Then again, between Owen's scorn for the paranormal and the business sense that undoubtedly told him he could charge visitors more for luxury and service than for ghosts, perhaps it was not something discussed.

Or even . . . known?

Jamie Bell had waited a long time, after all, for help in passing on her message to Owen; if any genuine medium had visited here in all the years since that tragic death, Hollis had to believe Jamie would have come through, and if not her then certainly someone else—because there were others. Surely at least one genuine medium would have tuned in to the right frequency to let *someone* come through.

Or maybe Anna Alexander really was the first family member to actually consider the paranormal, was driven to do so, and she was so focused on trying to contact her husband—and had clearly had little luck either in finding genuine mediums or one able to tune in to this place— that Hollis doubted she'd given any thought at all to contact beyond reaching Daniel.

Probably one reason she'd been so surprised when Hollis had made contact with Jamie. The idea that there might have been other spirits waiting about had clearly never occurred to her.

So . . . no family stories of hauntings, or if there were,

certainly no recent ones. It was a surprise, that realization. Granted, Hollis was considered a strong medium, but she would have thought *someone* either living in or visiting this house over decades would have experienced something paranormal. That was almost always the case in haunted places; sooner or later, someone saw or heard something eerie to tell someone else about the experience.

Or just bolted out the door without looking back.

But there were doors—and then there were *doors*.

"Don't open the door too wide or leave it open too long," Hollis muttered, mostly under her breath. "Thanks, Brooke, that's swell—except that I don't seem to have a whole hell of a lot of control right now."

"May I help you, ma'am?"

Hollis nearly jumped out of her skin and tried not to look embarrassed when she realized she was being addressed by a maid in a neat uniform, apparently carrying folded linen.

"Oh. No, thanks. That is . . . I was just exploring a bit. If that's okay?" she added tentatively.

"Certainly, ma'am." The maid was serene. "If you need it, there's a map of the house and grounds downstairs, in the top drawer of the foyer table by the front door; it's printed up for the hotel guests, but private guests have found it useful as well."

"Thank you."

"You're welcome, ma'am. Breakfast is served at eight thirty, but if you wish something before then there's a bell in the dining room. Anyone will be happy to serve you."

Hollis could only imagine the consternation an order

for breakfast was likely to cause in the kitchen, given that it was barely six A.M., but she merely nodded and silently told her growling stomach to shut up.

"Okay, thanks. Thanks very much."

The maid nodded, smiled, and then bobbed a curtsy, turned toward what Hollis assumed was another bedroom door, a closed door—and vanished through the solid oak.

Hollis slowly looked down at her arm, pushing back the sleeve of her sweater. No gooseflesh. No sensation of the hairs stirring on the back of her neck. No cold wave washing through her. No oddly muffling quality of the normal sounds around her.

None of the signs she had grown used to, signs telling her that the door between this world and the next was open or opening, and that she was able to communicate with spirits.

No signs. No warning.

"Oh, shit," Hollis said rather numbly. "It's worse than I thought. If I can't tell the living from the dead here . . ."

Then something new had been added to her bag of psychic tricks.

Either that . . . or something very, very strange was going on here in Alexander House.

And neither possibility was at all reassuring.

COLE JACOBY TRIED to shake off that dark pressure he could feel inside him, even as he stood in the tiny shower stall and washed himself head to toe, in cold well water with strong soap, to get rid of the blood.

He refused to think about where it had come from beyond the fleeting hope that *when* he thought about it he'd realize that he had simply killed a game animal even now hanging outside in the cold somewhere near the cabin.

That was it. That had to be it.

And never mind that the dogs had never growled about that.

Never mind.

He washed himself and got dressed in clean clothes, tossing the dirty ones into his washtub with more cold water and double the detergent and bleach he usually used, then returned to the cabin's main room and stirred up the embers in the fireplace. There was just enough heat left to catch when he tossed in some kindling, and when that was burning, a couple of logs.

They were still watching him from their beds. Ace's fur was standing up all the way down his spine, and both Lucy and Cleo were visibly trembling.

"You need to go out," he said to them, holding his voice calm. "That's what's wrong with you. I should have taken you out first thing, instead of . . . Come on, guys, let's go out and do your business before breakfast."

He opened the front door of the cabin and waited for the dogs, clearly reluctant, to leave their beds and approach. He stood to one side, trying not to flinch at the way they sidled past, avoiding any contact with him. Half afraid they'd run if given the chance, he stood on the porch and waited, again giving them the command to do their business, the command they'd been raised to obey. Answer the morning call of nature and then come back inside for breakfast. That was the established routine, and dogs were very much creatures of routine.

All three eyed him, clearly uneasy, but they did as commanded, going no more than a few yards from the cabin. Ace found a tree to lift his leg against and the two girls squatted. There was no joyous running about, no hint of the morning playfulness that was usual for them. There was just obeying his command and relieving themselves, none of them wasting time for anything else before returning to the cabin and their beds, again almost sidling through the doorway, rubbing against the door frame rather than come close.

Close to him.

He felt a pang about that.

"Probably just hungry," he murmured as he closed the door behind them. "I know I am." More than that, he felt . . . hollowed out inside. Empty of everything except that dark pressure he was so starkly aware of. But he ignored that, and tried not to raise his voice when he said to the dogs, "I know I'm hungry. Starved. So we'll eat. We'll eat, and everything will be okay."

Never mind that they'd never acted like this before.

Never mind the dark pressure.

Never mind.

The voices were silent, which made him feel grateful for a while as he briskly prepared the dogs' breakfast and got eggs and sausage for himself from the ancient cold-storage box just outside the cabin's back door.

He put the dogs' bowls down as he usually did, spread out a couple of feet apart between the kitchen and living/

sleeping area of his cabin, called them to eat with a cheery voice that sounded unnatural even to him, and went to start his own breakfast.

As he added fuel to the embers still burning in the old iron stove provided to cook on, he told himself he wasn't looking to make sure the dogs were eating because of course they were.

Of course they were.

He waited until sausage was crackling and popping in his single frying pan and eggs were broken into a bowl ready for cooking before he finally forced himself to look.

The dogs were eating.

But the animals he had raised to healthy, happy, affectionate adulthood were almost hunched over their bowls, gobbling their food as if to just get it down quickly, their tails tucked tightly and ears flat—and their eyes fixed on him.

Fearful eyes.

He wanted to cry. But he turned back to his cooking, facing the realization only then that perhaps the dark pressure he felt inside himself might actually be worse than the voices.

He didn't know how. He didn't know what it meant. Where it had come from. All he knew, all he was really certain of, was that he was afraid.

And that he was changing.

"WHAT DO YOU mean, you don't know what it means?" Hollis demanded, keeping her voice low as she used the house phone in the foyer.

"I mean I don't know," Bishop replied, patient. "You've always been able to tell the dead from the living before. Obviously something has changed."

"I know that much. But what? And why?"

"I don't know. I can't see the situation for myself, or sense it firsthand. I'm not there, Hollis."

"No, but you're our Yoda," she said with something of a snap. "You're *supposed* to know this stuff."

She was the only member of the SCU who dared call him a rather mocking nickname, and other team members had speculated as to why Bishop seemed more amused than annoyed by it.

Still patient, he said, "You said yourself you're in what appears to be a very haunted house, filled with a great deal of spiritual energy. Aside from the hospital when Diana was injured, you probably haven't been exposed to so much spiritual energy since your own abilities became so powerful."

"So?"

"So . . . another psychic tool, perhaps."

Striving mightily to hold her own voice calm, Hollis said, "I don't see how on earth an *in*ability to tell the living from the dead could possibly be of any use to me. The opposite, in fact, since it's bound to add confusion to a situation. Besides, don't you always say that our abilities come about because we have a use for them?"

"I have always said that."

Hollis waited a few beats, then snapped, "Well?"

"I'm not there, Hollis," he repeated. "And you know very well we don't deal in absolutes. Energy changes us, often in unpredictable ways. Perhaps the energy there is changing you. Or perhaps you're experiencing a . . . temporary glitch caused by that energy."

"I'd rather this were temporary," she announced. "It's unsettling."

"I imagine so."

She let out a sigh. "And you haven't seen anything in the future that might help me understand what's going on here?"

"I'm afraid not."

Hollis silently counted to ten, taking her time about it. "You didn't just send us here so I could practice being a medium, did you?"

"You said yourself it's a place with a great deal of spiritual energy, and what better location to use your abilities?"

"Bishop."

"Just . . . carry on, Hollis. Try to make contact with Mrs. Alexander's husband. Deal with what's in front of you, with . . . whatever comes up. Follow your instincts. And talk to Reese about this."

"I don't have to talk to him, dammit, I broadcast, remember?"

"That's not the same as having a conversation, Hollis, and you know it. Talk to Reese. Get his take on what's happening. He may be able to help more than you realize."

"You know, I don't have to be precognitive to know that one of these days there's going to be a real situation, and you're going to be too damned enigmatic and uninformative for our good—and for your own. And very bad things are going to happen."

"I've never asked for anything except that you do your best, Hollis. And you've never delivered less than that."

She was caught off guard by the unexpected compliment—and not at all sure he hadn't deliberately done it to stop questions he wasn't ready to answer, something of which he was most certainly capable.

"Uh . . . thanks. I think."

"Just keep going," Bishop repeated. "Call if you need to. I'll be here."

"Where's here this time?" she wondered.

"Outside Boston."

Reminding herself that it was still very early, Hollis said, "I woke you up, didn't I?"

"No. Serial killers don't keep regular hours as a rule. Call if you need to, Hollis."

"Okay. Thanks. I think. Be safe." She cradled the phone slowly, absently wondering if places that served as hotels and inns clung to corded telephones simply because if they didn't, handsets would be lost by guests more often than TV remotes.

"Probably," Reese said, joining her in the foyer.

"I would say stop reading me, but I guess that's fairly useless." Without pausing for a reply, she added, "Did you just come from the dining room? And do they have food in there yet? And coffee? I need both."

He took her hand and led her back the way he'd come. "They have both. I gather we were heard stirring around, and the excellent staff here threw together breakfast more than two hours earlier than normal. A very nice buffet is waiting for us."

"How did you get past me?" she wondered. "I was in the foyer and didn't see you come down the stairs."

"Rear staircase. One of several, I think. Found it while exploring. Although I think I'm going to study one of the maps a maid told me they have in that table back there in the foyer before I go exploring again. The staircase took me to the servants' quarters, I believe, and from the reaction, that was a social faux pas even in these modern times."

"Yeah? You catch somebody coming out of the shower naked or something?"

"No, just a maid still tying on her apron as she came out of her room. Which was awkward enough."

"Wish I'd been there."

"Sadist."

"I like my entertainment twisted. Sue me."

"You just want to see me . . . at a loss."

"Well, it happens so rarely," she explained, grave.

"I'd rather it never happened. I don't like losing control."

"No, really?"

"Smart-ass."

Hollis was distracted a bit then by the enticing aroma of coffee and bacon as they entered the cavernous formal dining room, and inhaled thankfully. "Ahhh . . ."

"Sideboard's over there."

"They don't have a little breakfast room somewhere?" Hollis wondered, looking around the huge room as they crossed it. "Maybe something too cozy for, I don't know, more than thirty or forty people?"

"Breakfast tables are set up in the conservatory, according to Thomas. But it's only used for breakfasts when the place is a hotel. When the family is in residence, meals are served here—or on a tray in the bedrooms."

"Room service?"

"He didn't call it that, but yes. I gather most meals are expected to be taken here, but breakfast on a tray is the norm for family and a large percentage of guests. Which also means I doubt we'll see our host or hostess before lunchtime."

"I'd already figured that much out. Neither of them struck me as early risers, and if they get breakfast in bed, there's even less reason to stir themselves before they have to."

"I didn't know people still lived this way," DeMarco said. Then he added, "Here, grab a plate."

Food and coffee were kept hot on a long sideboard, and in the covered servers Hollis found a breakfast substantial enough to satisfy even her rather unusually strong appetite.

She didn't really think about that until some time later, when she and DeMarco sat in lonely splendor at one end of the very long dining table and finished their meal, enjoying the really excellent food and coffee.

"Um," she said, sipping the latter.

DeMarco sipped his own, eyed her for a moment, then said, "I could be a gentleman and not comment on the fact that you ate enough to feed three people, but I gather that's on your mind."

"Well, it's unusual," she pointed out. "You're always trying to feed me, so you know I don't generally have much of an appetite."

"No, you don't. Something new here, maybe. Or a gradual evolution; you've developed more abilities just in recent months, and abilities require energy. Physical energy, stamina. Maybe your body has finally figured that out."

"Maybe. I just hope I don't end up like Riley and have to keep those energy bars in my back pocket all the time."[5]

"She only has to do that when Ash isn't around," DeMarco pointed out. "Which is almost never."

Hollis's mind shied away from the possibilities Brooke had mentioned and spoke hastily, hoping to deflect DeMarco at least from picking up on the discomfort she felt about that. "Well, if I can eat like a pig and burn it all off, I'm not going to complain."

"You didn't eat like a pig. You just ate with an appetite."

"I won't quibble." Hollis drank more coffee, frowning. "The thing is, if a need for more energy is new, it's not the only new thing."

"What's the other new thing?"

Surprised, she said, "You don't know already?"

He looked at her with slightly lifted brows. "I assume it has something to do with you being a medium. You haven't realized? Hollis, the only time I literally can't read you even when I try is when you're using your mediumistic abilities."

---

5 *Sleeping with Fear*

"Seriously?"

"Entirely. I may well feel there's something wrong if you're in trouble, but no actual thoughts. I assume it's because the energy of your thoughts is different, on a different frequency, when you're using those abilities. And it's not a frequency I pick up."

Thinking back only then, Hollis realized that DeMarco had indeed always behaved as if he had no specific awareness of information or knowledge she gleaned from her contacts with the spirit world unless it was something she discussed out loud or thought about later.

She looked toward the sideboard, watching as the same maid she had encountered earlier checked several dishes, apparently to make sure nothing required replenishing, and casually said to DeMarco, "So I'm guessing you don't see her over there by the sideboard."

The maid turned, smiled at Hollis, and bobbed a curtsy.

"See who?" DeMarco had turned his head and frowned toward the sideboard.

Hollis watched as the spirit walked the length of the sideboard, turned, and again vanished, this time through what was clearly a solid wall.

"Although I suppose there could have been a door there once," she mused out loud. "Had to be, I guess. When the place was first built and parties were huge, there were probably two places servants could enter the room. Carrying stuff in one door and out the other, so as to avoid traffic jams and a lot of broken china. Judging by the size of this table, there must have been some hellaciously big parties."

"Hollis?"

She looked at him.

"What're you talking about?"

"The maid you didn't see. Just now."

"A spirit?"

"Forgive a bad pun, but so it would appear. I saw her earlier upstairs. And thought she was alive. Spoke to her and everything."

"You mean—"

"I mean I can't seem to tell the living from the dead right now, or here in this place. Not sure which." She drew a breath and looked at him. "It's . . . unsettling. Bishop said I should talk to you about it. But you probably already knew that part."

"That you were going to talk to me about something. Not about what."

Hollis absently folded her linen napkin and placed it beside her coffee cup on the table. "Well, why don't we do a bit of exploring outside while we talk? I need air. And to get out of here for a while. Because I can sense the others all around me."

"Close the door."

"Yeah, well, that's the third new thing," Hollis replied somewhat grimly. "I can't seem to close the door. At all. And I've already been warned that that isn't exactly a good thing."

EIGHT

Luther Brinkman shifted slightly on the couch, adjusting his leg, which was propped on the coffee table and resting on a pillow, and trying to find a comfortable position.

"I told you it was too soon to get dressed," Callie said.

"If you hadn't given me that shot while I was unconscious, I'd be fine," he retorted.

"If I hadn't given you that shot, the wound would likely have gotten infected. Is it my fault penicillin needs to go in the hip?"

He ignored that question. "Look, we both know I need to get on my feet and mobile as soon as possible. Especially after you found that blood."

It was early afternoon, and Luther was more than a little disgruntled that he'd slept through the morning totally against his will, waking only when Callie had roused him for lunch. Already, he was itching to be up and doing things. Like his job.

"I told you, the only blood test kit I have is unreliable. Even testing positive for human blood doesn't necessarily mean that's what it was because of the high percentage of false positives. Could have been animal blood. And even if it was human, it could easily have been from a hunter careless enough with his tools to hurt himself. It happens."

Callie told herself that there was no sense in telling Luther what she was sure of, that the blood was indeed human and the person who had shed it beyond their help. She told herself it was for his own good, that he didn't need to be agitated more than he was, not when he was recovering from the wound and not when there was nothing he could do about it anyway.

She told herself all that.

And she knew she wasn't being fair to him, or even just professional. He needed to know what she knew.

But . . . not now. Not yet.

"We need to know for sure, Callie. In case it has anything at all to do with Jacoby."

"Yes. But it was more than half a mile from Jacoby's cabin, and he's shown no signs to date of venturing that far out."

"Maybe he got curious about me."

"Maybe. But if so, he wasn't tracking you. That blood was nowhere near the path you took going to his cabin or the path I took getting you back down here after you were shot."

"Look, you said Cesar didn't pick up a trail from the point where you found the blood; if it was just a hunter, wouldn't he have headed for town? Or for one of the cabins up here?"

"Not necessarily. Hunters often camp up on the mountain, and some would consider it completely unnecessary to have a minor cut looked at by a doctor. Could be, he realized he was bleeding and just went back to his camp to take care of it himself."

Okay, now she'd gone beyond lying by omission; now she was posing a possibility she knew very well hadn't happened.

"So why didn't Cesar lead you in that direction?"

Because he knew what was there. Because he knew we couldn't help her, that no one could.

Luther knew she didn't want to answer, and that was one of the reasons he was pressing the matter. That and a certain evasiveness he had heard in her voice when she had first told him about finding the blood. She was holding back, and he didn't like it. Granted she barely knew him, and granted she could be following orders, but, dammit, they were both in this now, and he needed to know what she knew.

Plus, he was feeling generally irritable because he was a grown man and not accustomed to needing help getting his damned pants on, a procedure made more annoying (for some reason) because she had been utterly matter-of-fact and efficient getting him into the borrowed jeans and flannel shirt while he was barely able to stand upright.

After a long moment and a thoughtful stare, Callie

said, "Cesar didn't want to go in any direction except back here. He made that very clear. Not up or down the mountain, and not toward Jacoby's cabin."

"I gather that's unusual?"

"First time he's done it here. At other times in other places . . . it was always his way of protecting either me or someone else. Sensing something potentially bad and guiding us away from it."

"He wouldn't have had a reason to protect me; you were the one out there with the blood."

"True enough." She went to top off her coffee, sent him an inquiring look, and then hung the pot back on its hook in the fireplace. She didn't sit down, but wandered rather aimlessly toward the kitchen and leaned against the counter, frowning.

"What?" Luther asked.

"I could feel it too," she said finally. "Out there with Cesar. Pushing at me, like wind but . . . not. Pressure. I felt the edge of that darkness, that energy, that I felt before around Jacoby's cabin."

"Why does that surprise you?"

"Because," Callie said, "the last time I felt it, it was weaker, less defined—and it was much closer to Jacoby's cabin. A good three or even four hundred yards closer."

"What?"

"I can't be sure, because my instincts as well as Cesar's were telling us to get back here and not stop to probe, but that feeling, that sensation of dark energy, isn't something easily forgotten. It was the same thing. Stronger, darker, but the same thing."

"Then . . . it's what? Expanding?"

"Maybe. Or maybe he was close out there and we just couldn't see him. Maybe he carries it with him. Maybe he always did."

Luther watched her, absently rubbing his wounded thigh. "I have a strong hunch your background info on Jacoby is a lot more extensive than mine, especially when it comes to possible psychic abilities. Was he ever examined by anyone in the SCU? Before he escaped?"

Callie shook her head slowly. "There was never a reason. The SCU generally doesn't deal with bank robbers. Until Jacoby escaped the way he did, there was no reported indication he might have a paranormal ability."

"He was given psych evals, right?"

"Several times, as a juvenile and as an adult. This most recent robbery wasn't his first rodeo; he has quite the rap sheet. Starting with petty theft and boosting cars when he was around twelve and ending up eventually with both armed and unarmed robbery by his late teens. But no real sign of violence. His psych evaluations were pretty standard. Not a psychopath or a sociopath, just on the antisocial end of the scale, like a lot of small-time criminals. He could make casual friends, he could hold down a job, he could talk to people with fair ease and even charm when he wanted, but most considered him a loner. Good with puzzles, with numbers, tested a bit above average in intelligence.

"He came from an abusive background, but he was removed from the home before his teens, and since there were no other relatives located, he went into the system. Decent foster home, from all accounts; he was in the same one until the judge got tired of making allowances for a troubled kid who couldn't stay out of trouble and sent him to a juvenile facility when he was fifteen."

"And he was on his way."

"Yeah. Not so much rehabilitated as educated; he pulled his first successful major robbery not six months after he got out. Managed to stay ahead of the cops for a couple of years before they got their hands on him again, and that judge in that particular jurisdiction was dealing with homicides, gang wars, drug crimes. Wasn't much concerned by a young thief who hadn't used a gun in that particular robbery and who promised with great sincerity to go straight."

"So . . . time served?"

Callie nodded. "Time served. After that, he got more careful, and he got good at robbery, good at getting away with it. He got very good, and for years. Never did time again until they caught him after he pulled this last heist. Probably wouldn't have caught him then if he'd stuck to his usual type of robbery, netting himself a few hundred grand at most and then laying low and living simply."

"But ten million draws a lot of attention," Luther finished. "A lot of resources."

"Yeah. Bishop believes Jacoby had no idea that payrolls for several major corporations were sitting in that vault. From the tools he left behind, he was going after the lockboxes—which were *supposed* to be in a secondary vault, not one connected to the cash safe. He shouldn't have been able to get that safe open, and nobody is sure even now how he managed it. Maybe he had time to spare and was curious to try his skills. The alarm was down, though no one seems to be sure how he managed that *or* how he disabled it in such a way as to avoid an automatic secondary alarm. No way to be sure. But once that safe was open, with millions in cash just sitting there . . ."

"Who'd blame him for taking the easy route."

Callie nodded again. "He dumped his tools and presumably filled the bag that had held them. Everybody was surprised that he managed the break-in alone, but there was never a shred of evidence to suggest he had an accomplice, or that anyone on the inside helped. It was almost as if . . . everything just fell into place for him. A glitch in the security system of the building itself that made access a lot easier than it should have been; a security guard who was supposed to be watching the monitors happened to be taking cold medicine and fell asleep—"

"Or maybe was put to sleep," Luther offered.

Callie nodded slowly. "I hadn't thought, but maybe so. Maybe even then he could do that much."

"The cold medicine could have made it easier," Luther said thoughtfully. "Unless the guard lied about that to cover his ass."

"Yeah. But either way, Jacoby got in with amazing ease. The disk storing the camera feeds was faulty and nobody knew until afterward. Even the vault lock itself was just days away from being upgraded because there was some kind of issue with the electronics of the locking mechanism. Just a whole string of glitches that helped Jacoby get in and out way too easily."

Luther frowned. "Does Bishop think Jacoby might have used some paranormal ability? Even then?"

"I'm not sure what Bishop knew or suspected about the robbery; he didn't say. But, looking back, it's certainly possible. At the time, the SCU wasn't called and knew nothing about it, which means we were never able to inspect the actual vault and safe or talk to employees, when it might have mattered, right after, with a secured crime scene. I think Bishop knew or suspected something before Jacoby was transferred months later, but, well, it's Bishop. Whatever he knew or suspected, he didn't say."

Luther glanced absently toward Cesar, then said to Callie, "Maybe it's time to report in and talk to Bishop about the situation. I know there's no cell service here, but is there service anywhere nearby?"

"Five hundred yards higher up the mountain is a sweet spot where cell reception is crystal clear because of the tower on the next mountain to the north. There are a few spots like that one, scattered around, but none are close and the terrain is hellish."

Luther realized he was looking at Cesar again, frowned, and returned his gaze to Callie. "You're saying you'll have to hike up the mountain to make a call?"

"No, actually, I don't need to do that. As I said, Bishop and Miranda are right on my frequency, so I can communicate with them telepathically and as clearly as I can talk to you here."

"Dammit, why didn't you tell me that sooner?"

Honest, she said, "I wasn't ready to report in. You were

okay, we were safe here, and I hadn't yet done my job. Still haven't."

Luther sighed but wasn't angry because he completely understood her attitude. It was typical of those who were accustomed to working alone, or virtually so. "Are they close by?"

"No. Bishop is outside Boston, and Miranda is in California. Distance doesn't seem to matter, as long as I can focus. Luther, do you realize you keep looking at Cesar?"

"Just realized," he admitted. Then added slowly, "Also just realized I'm feeling profoundly uneasy."

That was when Cesar suddenly got up—and they heard the frantic scratching at the cabin's door.

Outside.

COLE JACOBY THOUGHT breakfast would make him feel better. And then he thought lunch would.

Neither helped.

But what really bothered him was that he had no memory of the time *between* breakfast and lunch. It was just . . . blank. When he tried to remember, there was only a dark nothing.

At first, realizing that, he was grateful at least that he didn't have blood on him. But then he realized that he was not wearing the same clothes he had dressed himself in that morning.

He found those in the washtub with the other set he had stripped off that morning. Soaking in reddish water that smelled strongly of bleach.

He was almost afraid to look at the dogs, and when he did, he was surprised at first. Ace's bed was empty. Cleo's. Lucy's. But if they weren't in their beds . . .

It nearly broke his heart when he found them huddled against the back door, all three trembling. And as he watched, Cleo began frantically scratching at the floor while the other two stared at him fearfully.

They wanted nothing but to get away from him.

"You know, don't you?" he murmured. "You know what's happening. You know I'm not . . . safe anymore."

He could feel the darkness then, not just at the edge of his awareness, but creeping inward, like some smothering black sludge that would swallow everything in his path.

Even him.

Especially him.

Cole didn't know how much time he had left, but he knew he had to use it to save the only beings in the world he had ever truly loved.

He went to the front door of the cabin and opened it wide, then stepped back. "Here," he called to them, holding his voice steady and calm with what he suspected was the last of his control. "Let's go, guys. Out."

They hesitated for only a moment, and then all three scrambled for the door, and out.

This time, Jacoby gave them no command—except one. He stood in the doorway and watched the dogs race away, calling after them in a voice that wasn't steady anymore, "Stay away from me. *Away*. Find somebody to take care of you. And don't come back. Don't ever come back . . ."

LUTHER WAS STARTLED by how fast Callie moved, setting her coffee cup down, getting her weapon from the table near the door—and then halting suddenly and for a long moment to look at Cesar.

The Rottweiler, still on his feet, was looking at the door but didn't seem at all disturbed. He lifted his gaze to Callie, and if a dog designed by nature to look fearsome could look serene, he did.

"Huh," Callie murmured. She kept her gun in her hand but didn't hesitate to open the cabin's door.

They pushed it wider open, the three large dogs, rushing inside so close together they nearly tangled in the doorway, and they would have run over Cesar if he hadn't backed up several quick steps. And they didn't stop until they had wedged themselves into the farthest corner of the main room of the cabin, beside the couch where Luther sat. All three were shaking visibly.

"What the hell?" he said.

"They're terrified."

"Yeah, I can see that. You don't have to know much about dogs to see that. But terrified of what?"

Callie looked outside for only a moment, then closed the door and returned her weapon to its accustomed place. She came over to where Luther was and sat down on the end of the coffee table near his propped foot, facing the dogs. She didn't say anything for a moment, just leaned forward with her elbows on her knees and hands linked loosely between them.

"Hey, Cleo," she said quietly. "Remember me?"

All three of the dogs had been avoiding eye contact, but when Callie spoke, the largest of them finally looked at her and gradually stopped trembling.

"The one you met out hiking?" Luther guessed, keeping his voice low and casual.

"Yeah. Her name's on her tag. I'm guessing the other two as well. It's okay, Cleo. It's okay now." Her voice was, somehow, infinitely reassuring, something even Luther felt.

The dog took a step toward her, then another. And finally laid her head on Callie's knee. The other two dogs watched, their trembling finally easing as Callie stroked Cleo's head.

"Think Jacoby drove them away?" Luther asked.

"Maybe. Or maybe they ran away."

"Because he was cruel?"

Callie frowned, then shook her head a little and said, "Wait."

She continued to stroke Cleo, gradually working her way over the big dog until she'd completed a pretty thorough examination. By then, the other dogs had ventured closer, and she went through the same routine with each. Calm and gentle, but thorough. By the time she was done, the dogs were relaxed, two of them lying on a rug near the fireplace and the one male sitting at the end of the coffee table having his ears gently rubbed by Callie.

"This is Ace," she told Luther after examining the tag

on the dog's collar. "The one beside Cleo is Lucy. I'm guessing they're littermates, obviously mixed breeds. And I can't find a single sign that any one of them has ever been abused."

"Could be verbal," he noted.

But Callie was shaking her head. "These dogs have been cared for, and I mean *really* cared for. They've been well fed, well groomed, and obviously socialized. What-ever terrified them, it didn't have anything to do with people. At least . . . nothing to do with how people have treated them in the past."

"Then what?"

"Maybe . . . the negative energy. Cesar was sensitive to it. If they are too, and they've been with Jacoby since he got here . . ."

"Would negative energy affect dogs? I mean—negatively?"

"No idea. Their brainwaves are different, so I'm guessing if there was an effect, it wouldn't be the same as with us."

"You said the dog—Cleo—acted friendly and normal when you and Cesar met her before."

"So what's happened since then?" Callie finished slowly. "What's different now? Just that energy that we know of. Stronger. Darker. Maybe the dogs were okay as long as Jacoby was. As long as he was able to fight off whatever the negative effects have been."

"Like shooting at people?"

"You said the dogs chased you for a bit, and I heard them; when did he send them after you? While he was still shooting?"

Thinking back, Luther said, "No. I'd managed to get at least a hundred yards away before I heard the dogs barking. Now that I think about it, they didn't come very far after me. I think—I remember a whistle. He must have called them back."

Callie nodded. "The hunters said he did that, whistled his dogs back before they were out of sight of the cabin."

"So he was just making a point."

"Probably. But my point is that the dogs were still obeying him then, still willing to return to him. I'd bet next year's pay they won't go anywhere near him now."

"You're basing that on the idea that the energy you sense is strong enough, you believe, to completely over-power him?"

"I think it's a reasonable assumption. My only ques-tion, still, is whether the energy is centered around that cabin—or around Jacoby. Until today, I was hoping it was the cabin, the area."

"Because we could have gotten him away from it."

Callie nodded. "But if it's centered around the cabin, and that's what I felt hundreds of yards away from the cabin, then it's way the hell too big to be anything we could deal with, so now I'm hoping Jacoby is at the center, that rather than find it here, he somehow brought it here with him."

"And lost control?"

"That fits his behavior. Okay at first, not social but not violent. Puts his fed handlers to sleep and escapes. Takes his time, gets his beloved dogs, makes his way to the cabin he's made arrangements for earlier, the cabin he believes is safe, losing almost everyone trying to track him in the process. Settling in. Then the fairly rapid escalation, shooting at hunters, at you—and finally scaring off his own dogs. Everything changed, and in less than two weeks."

Luther let that sink in for a few moments, then said, "Do you think he'll come after his dogs?"

"No. I think he let them go or drove them off to save them. From himself. And if I'm right about that, then some part of Cole Jacoby realized he was becoming dangerous, that there was something in him he could no longer control, or couldn't control for much longer."

"And now it's got him."

"Probably."

"Negative energy?"

"I know how it sounds, believe me. But . . . I felt it, Luther. Some energy is just power. Force. But some energy is more than that. I can't explain it. I don't know if anyone could. But I know what I felt."

He waited, looking at her.

"Purpose. Strength contained and intensifying, for a reason. Building up to something. Whatever that energy is, wherever it came from, it has a purpose, an end game, a goal. And I can guarantee you we won't like whatever it wants to do."

"Okay," he said finally. "In that case, I think we have two options. We call in major backup, or we get the hell out of here." He held up a hand when she would have spoken. "I know, your job was to figure out the energy. But I can't help you do that and, no offense, I don't think you can do it alone. Not if this stuff is as deadly as you feel it is. Shield or not, you may be even more vulnerable to the energy because you're a born psychic."

"It's a point," she conceded. "Though I've been able to deflect negative energy in the past."

"But you can't be sure about this negative energy. That you'd be able to do the same thing. Every energy has a unique signature. And this one could very easily be one that could punch a hole through your shield or otherwise disable or hurt you."

"It's possible," she agreed.

Luther nodded. "The other point is a lot more positive. Jacoby has, so far, shown no signs of wanting to leave the area. Hunters have been warned to avoid him. The area is practically deserted otherwise. So we can be fairly certain no one else is in immediate danger. We can alert the sheriff down in Devil's Gap, if you think we should, especially after finding that blood. But Jacoby's here, relatively contained, if only by the isolation and geography of this place. We have no reason to believe he's going to move out of the area, at least in the short term, so we have no reason to believe we'd be putting anyone else in danger by getting out of here until we can get some help. We need backup, Callie. At the very least, I say you contact Bishop and let him know what's going on."

She chewed on her lower lip for a moment, then said, "Well, there's a danger in that. Up here, I can only reach out to contact Bishop if I drop my shields. Completely. You may not have noticed, but they've been up since this morning."

He was a bit surprised that he hadn't noticed.

And a bit worried about that, even though he reminded himself that he was new at this telepathic stuff.

"I don't feel that energy now, here, Cesar doesn't feel it, and Jacoby's dogs are calm now, so they don't feel it either. That tells me that Jacoby isn't close, and/or that the energy field around him isn't expanding."

"Or hasn't expanded this far."

She nodded. "But if I drop my shields and reach out to Bishop, no matter how narrow my focus is, I'm not only opening myself up to attack, but sending out positive energy. And positive energy can attract negative energy."

"He'd know you were here."

"Oh, I'm pretty sure he already knows I'm here. What he may not know so far is that I'm here because of him and that I'm psychic. Not that I'm certain my shields have kept him out, especially since I haven't kept them up consistently while I've been here. But I think I would have known if that negativity touched my mind, and I think Jacoby simply hasn't been paying enough attention to consider who or what I am."

"Seriously?"

"He's had a lot to deal with, remember. I'd bet he fought as hard as he could to maintain control, and probably lost it a few times for minutes or hours. Until, finally, he lost it for good. Which probably happened just about the time he got his dogs away from the cabin."

"*What* happened when he lost control?"

"I don't know. But my guess is something bad. Negative energy needs something to feed off if it's to grow more intense. The darkest energy comes from evil acts."

I should tell him. I really should.

"That blood."

"No way to know for sure. I doubt Jacoby could have caught himself a hunter, and there aren't many other people up here. Usually hikers, but the weather's been colder this season, so that's less likely."

"But possible. He could have killed someone."

Why does it seem so wrong to tell him the truth? Because I'm afraid he won't believe me if I tell him we can't help her now?

"That's a big leap to take from a few drops of blood we don't even know is human."

"Blood plus increased negative energy I say makes it less of a leap."

"Point," she conceded. "If and when he lost control, he could have done almost anything. If the energy has taken or is about to take him over completely, then he's likely capable of evil acts, even if he isn't aware of committing them and doesn't remember them afterward."

"So you believe whatever personality made Jacoby who and what he was is . . . gone."

"For good? I don't know. I'd probably know if I met him face-to-face, but given all the negative energy surrounding him, possibly controlling him, I'm considering that a last-resort confrontation. Until we know what the ultimate agenda is, what's driving that negative energy and whether it's feeding off Jacoby or is actually dictating his actions, I don't think we can be sure of much of anything."

Luther nodded slowly. "Okay. Well, I made my suggestions. What are yours?"

"Given just the possibilities we know of, pretty much the same. Starting with contacting Bishop."

"In spite of the risks?"

"I'd rather risk it up here than get down to town first. I don't want to come down off this mountain without letting Bishop know what the situation is. The potential for danger to the public might be low, but that's been an assumption based on his past actions, not the current state of Jacoby's mind. Too many variables now for me even to make an educated guess about what level of threat he poses. To the public. And to us. At the very least, Bishop needs to know for sure that we're dealing with a hell of a lot more than a bank robber."

"Agreed. Anything I can do to help?"

To his surprise, Callie nodded. She went over to a cabinet where she kept her first-aid kit and carried it to the kitchen island. She had her back to Luther, and he was surprised again when she returned to sit again on the coffee table and hand him a syringe. There was a clear liquid inside.

"What the hell?"

Soberly, she said, "I want you to watch Cesar. If you see him start to react in any negative way, give me that shot."

"Callie—"

"If he growls, if the hair stands up along his spine, if he's staring at me as if I pose a threat, give me the shot. He'll react before the other dogs will, because he knows me."

Keep a close eye on me, boy.

Yes. Always.

Luther looked at the syringe in his hand and once again felt a profound sense of unease. "Is this a sedative?"

"No. The last thing I want to do if that negative energy finds mine is go to sleep. That's leaving a door wide open for it to come in."

"Then what is this?"

Callie pushed up the loose sleeve of her sweater to expose her upper arm, and pointed to a specific spot. "Just pop it in right here, and hit the plunger. Full dose."

"Callie—"

"It's a . . . stimulant. It'll break the connection with Bishop, slam my shields back into place."

Surprised, Luther said, "There's a med that'll do that? First I've ever heard of it."

"Experimental. The lab people have been testing it, and so far I'm one of the few showing a . . . useful . . . reaction."

Uneasy, he said, "Are you sure it won't hurt you?"

"I'm sure that negative energy could hurt me a lot more. I'm trusting you, Luther. If Cesar reacts, give me the shot."

"Listen, can't we talk about this?"

"We already have." She closed her eyes. "Watch Cesar. You'll know if something bad is happening."

"Are you sure?"

Callie was silent. And so Luther fixed his gaze on her attentive Rottweiler.

And hoped to hell nothing bad would happen.

YOU KNOW WHAT to do. What you have to do. You under-stand, Luther, don't you?

"Luther."

Something was growling. It sounded mean.

It's very simple. And easy. You've done it before, during your tours of duty. Just one quick movement, and it's done.

"Luther. Listen to me. To *me*."

Don't. Don't let her stop you. Stop us. We have to do this. You know we do. It feels right, doesn't it? All the strength? All the power surging through you? Making you invincible? And it's all yours. You'll be able to do amazing things, Luther. You'll be able to do anything you want. Anything.

"Luther, you have to listen to me."

Growling. What was growling?

"Luther, concentrate. Listen to me. Ignore everything else."

No, don't listen to the bitch. She doesn't know you. She doesn't know us. Doesn't know what we're capable of. Do it, Luther. Kill her.

Kill the bitch.

"Luther!"

He snapped out of it with something between a gasp and a grunt, his mind abruptly clear, that dark, dark voice gone, shoved out of him with a strength he hadn't known he possessed and wasn't even sure had been entirely his own.

And found himself in another kind of nightmare.

They were outside. In the woods.

He had her pinned up against a tree, his greater size and weight holding her there. That—and the big hunting knife he usually carried while in the outdoors pressed to her throat. A thin line of red showed that he had already cut her.

Luther realized that in an instant. He also realized that she had her weapon in hand, and that it was between them, snugged up just below his rib cage, pressing hard upward, inward. Aimed at his heart.

She could have killed him at any time.

As he stumbled backward, he saw as well that her free hand was extended down and to her left, fingers wide in a holding gesture. Holding in place the exceptionally well-trained Rottweiler standing about three feet from them. A hundred and twenty pounds of straining, trembling muscle desperate to leap to the defense of his mistress, Cesar kept his eyes fixed on Luther. And both the exposed and gleaming fangs and the deep, guttural growl promised that if he was given the command or even the chance, he could and would tear the throat out of the man threatening Callie.

Quietly, as though nothing had happened, she said, "It's okay, Cesar. Break. Sit."

The Rottweiler stopped snarling and sat down, but he was still trembling visibly and never took his eyes off Luther.

For his part, Luther took another stumbling step backward until he came up hard against another tree. He stared at the knife in his hand, then let it fall to the ground.

"Jesus Christ," he muttered hoarsely. "What the hell happened?"

Callie drew a deep breath, and let it out slowly. "The dark energy got in. Into you."

NINE

Hollis said, "Okay, I'm beginning to see the appeal of this place as a vacation spot. It's a little quiet for my taste, but it definitely looks like they go out of their way to provide either rest or recreation for their guests."

"That's for sure," DeMarco agreed.

They had been wandering over the estate for nearly two hours, leisurely, and had wound up here and now, standing on a low rise just behind the house, looking down on a huge and beautifully designed pool—currently covered for the coming winter—with what were clearly rock slides and waterfalls. There was a beautifully designed pool house nearby, and a small building at one end of the pool that clearly housed a swim-up bar, judging by the stone countertop jutting out from the closed building and over the edge of a section of the covered pool.

All around the entire area were flagstone paths,

meticulously maintained, that wound lazily through what was undoubtedly acres of a stunning garden in spring and summer. There were benches and chairs here and there for sitting, and tables with closed umbrellas scattered about.

Off to the right of the pool and at some distance were the tennis courts, also meticulously maintained, and in the distance straight out beyond the pool they could see what they had visited an hour or so before, which was a sprawling complex of stables, paddocks, and riding rings that was truly impressive.

"The whole place is impressive," Hollis conceded.

"You sound disgruntled," DeMarco noted as they turned in step and began making their way back toward the house.

"What, it doesn't strike you as strange? This place, in the middle of nowhere?"

"Not really. In today's bustling world, peace and quiet are at a premium, and the wealthy are always willing to pay for what they want. Besides, what else are you going to do with a place like this in these modern times with resident family having come down to only two people. Turn it into a museum or a hotel were probably the only real choices, and it's too far off the beaten track to attract many customers to a museum, even if it had more than antiques and extensive gardens to offer."

"Makes sense," she agreed.

DeMarco shrugged. "It also wouldn't surprise me if Alexander House hadn't hosted in past decades some impressive guest lists from all up and down the East Coast for society fund-raisers, political events, even gatherings of people who prefer to get together out of the public eye."

"Secret societies?" she asked, only half-seriously.

"Not in the conspiratorial sense. You can want to keep your business private without having some kind of creepy agenda."

"Says the man who was undercover in a very secretive and very creepy society."

"Well, that was a cult. Bit different."

He hadn't said much about that experience, and Hollis hadn't asked, assuming he'd share what he wanted when he was ready. She also assumed that since he'd been undercover for a very long time in an extremely dangerous situation, it could easily take a while before he was ready to talk about it.

Since Hollis had been there briefly, she at least knew how it had all ended, and that was enough for her.

As for the time he'd spent there, his assignment, she knew the facts of it, just as he undoubtedly knew the facts of her own . . . experience. But she doubted he'd picked up much about that telepathically, because the horrific details of what had triggered her psychic abilities were not something she thought about consciously, and they were details she tended to keep buried pretty deep.

According to Bishop, and he'd know.

"Hollis?"

With a sigh, she said, "I suppose you're right." Hollis glanced to her left, nearly stopped, then continued on. "But I wouldn't completely rule out secret societies."

"Why? Seeing spirits?"

"Oh, I've been seeing them all morning. And if what I'm seeing comes from over a hundred years of history . . . then something's definitely not right. There are a *lot* of spirits attached to this place, Reese. And that means a lot of people died here, or are or were connected to people here. At least, that's true if I understand the spirit realm at all."

"Can you tell the living from the dead now?"

"No, except for huge neon signs like clothing way, way out of fashion. But I imagine you would have commented more than once if you'd seen someone out here with us in the last couple of hours. I mean, I know you saw the maintenance people at the stables because we both spoke to them, so they were obviously alive, but . . . You didn't see people sitting in the gardens as we walked through, did you? Maybe a dozen people, plus as many maids and waiters serving them drinks and stuff, and that's not counting all the gardeners working at a discreet distance so as not to disturb anyone."

"No," DeMarco said. "I saw no one in the gardens."

"Yeah, that's what I thought. Or people swimming in the pool and being served on swim-up underwater seats at that counter?"

"Hollis, the pool is covered. The pool house and bar closed up."

"I know. When I looked at it just now, that's what I saw. But an hour or so ago when we walked past, the pool was open and a bunch of people were swimming. Even some kids, a few little ones. Going down the slides, splashing and laughing with their parents. People swimming laps. Sitting at the bar drinking out of glasses with little paper umbrellas. More laughing. I could hear them. I could smell the chlorine in the pool water."

DeMarco reached out and took her hand. "So you not only saw spirits, but parts of this place as they were . . . at another time."

"Apparently. There were flowers blooming, and some shrubbery, so it looked like late spring or summer. I have no idea if I was seeing this place during a single season, or just this place as all these spirits saw it in their living visits." She shook her head. "Almost like it all . . . blended together for me. A glimpse into Alexander House as a hotel. Except that some of the clothing I've seen marks at least some of these guests—or family—as being here during a time before the house was a hotel."

"You're sure?"

"Pretty sure, yeah."

"And it's not the kind of thing you've ever seen before?"

"*So* not. Until now, I just saw spirits, and they were definitely moving through our time, our dimension. This is different." She drew a breath and let it out slowly. "A new tool in my psychic bag of tricks. Oh, joy."

He stopped them, still yards short of the conservatory that served as one of the rear entrances to the sprawling house, and half turned so that he could look down at her gravely. "We will figure this out, you know."

"You think?"

"Of course. It's what we do."

Hollis managed a smile, though she felt it was a twisted

one. "Right. Right. I just . . . the more I see of this place, the more convinced I am that something is really wrong. That maybe something bad happened here."

"Do the people you see look injured? Upset?"

"No, I usually don't see wounds or injuries, thank God. It doesn't look like a horror movie to me, a fate the universe has spared me. So far." She drew a breath and let it out slowly. "I can see auras, when I concentrate, and those look normal enough. And these people . . . they look like they belong here. Going about their business. Relaxing, reading newspapers or books, strolling, talking. Most smile pleasantly as they walk past, or nod politely, so they see us, or at least me. Nobody looks anxious or worried or frightened. It's almost as if they don't know they're dead."

"You've encountered that before."

"Well . . . yeah, new spirits who were uncertain. Aware that something was wrong, something had changed, but either not ready or not able to accept that they had died. This . . . this is different."

"Why?"

"Because some of them have been here a long time, Reese. Those neon fashion signs I mentioned. It's more difficult to tell with the servants, because those uniforms apparently haven't changed very much, but the people . . . Family or guests, I don't know, probably both, and from their clothes we're talking about completely different eras. I saw one woman with a long skirt and bustle."

"Seriously?"

"Oh, yeah. And that one dates way, *way* back."

He turned his head to look out over the landscape behind the house, which, to him, was empty of visible people, then returned his gaze to Hollis. "Do the spirits themselves seem aware of any incongruity?"

"Because of all the different fashions? Not as far as I can tell. It's like I said, they all behave as if it's perfectly normal to be here and be . . . going through the motions." She opened her mouth, then closed it.

"But the unnaturalness of it is bothering you," DeMarco said.

Hollis didn't know if he'd guessed or read her, but she didn't much care. "You bet it does. I'd think it was just place memories, but like I said, these spirits are reacting to us, to each other. They're *here*. They're here and they believe it's normal for them to be here. A woman with a long skirt and bustle passes by a woman dressed like someone from the jazz age, and neither of them bats an eye? That's disconcerting enough. To me, at least."

"Maybe a costume party," he suggested.

She considered, then shook her head. "No, because then they'd be dressed up. Some of these people are dressed more formally than others, but most are in casual clothes. And no masks. Aren't there usually masks at fancy costume parties?"

"I would think so."

"So all these people from just about every decade going back to when this place was built, maybe even earlier, are still here. Long before it was a hotel. Long before modern modes of travel at least made it reasonable to visit this place for short periods of time."

"And?"

"And . . . how many people could have died in and around a private home that was not a hotel until about a decade ago? So many people from so many different eras? It doesn't make sense. Unless this place has experienced a hell of a lot of tragedy, then it just doesn't make sense."

"WELL, NO." ANNA Alexander looked anxious, which seemed to be her default expression. "There really haven't been any major tragic events here. I've lived in this house for more than thirty-five years, and my husband and Owen all their lives, of course. There's a book in the library about the history of the family, privately printed, if you'd like to see that. It goes back even before the house was built, when the family acquired all the land and lived a lot simpler here."

"We would definitely like to see the book," DeMarco said, then added, "but we won't find any tragic events in it?"

"Just the usual sort of thing you'd expect in a house this old, in a family going back so many generations. There have been deaths here, certainly. A few accidents back when the land was farmed and more livestock kept. Back when the flu took so many, it didn't spare this house, either the family or the servants. Other illnesses over the years. At least a couple of women I read of died in child-birth, and several children died young, of disease; both were common in those days."

She hesitated, then added, "A maid fell down one of the staircases and broke her neck, apparently tripping on a loose rug at the top. One daughter of the family committed suicide when her fiancé jilted her. And there were always rumors that Daniel's grandfather's first wife didn't actually run off with a salesman, but that he killed her and buried her somewhere about." Anna glanced around, almost as if she expected the possibly murdered wife to suddenly appear.

Hollis took a couple of steps and sat down in a chair.

They were in the cavernous room where they had first been brought the previous night, a room identified by the "hotel" map they had snagged in the foyer as the Grand Parlor. It was laid out with numerous seating groups scattered throughout the space, most of which managed to feel at least somewhat cozy despite the staggering size of the room, perhaps because of enormous potted plants and various screens and low display shelves used to delineate spaces. So family, visitors, or guests could find some semblance of privacy and quiet to read or talk.

Looking even more anxious, Anna sat down in the chair nearest the one Hollis occupied, while DeMarco moved silently to another chair in the grouping. A round table was at the center, perhaps intended for some board game or just refreshments.

"I know it sounds like a lot," Anna said, "but this *is* an old house, and a lot of people have lived here. Worked here. The family was much larger generations back, and in those days it wasn't uncommon for children to marry but not move far away, especially with so much land to work and stock to take care of then. First living in nearby cottages and then later here, when this house was built.

With all this room, privacy was never an issue, and it was pretty much intended to be a big family home. Some people did live their whole lives here, and died here. But most of that was just . . . living and dying. Not tragedies, usually, unless it was a child or someone else who went before their time."

Hollis leaned back with a sigh, and said to DeMarco, "I only had one question when we got here. Just one. I wanted to know about the light. So that the next time a spirit asked me, I'd know what to say. Now . . ."

"What's the matter?" Anna asked, clearly worried. "Have you—have you seen Daniel?"

"No. Sorry. That's his portrait out in the foyer, right? The one across from yours?"

"Yes. He had us both painted about ten years ago."

Shaking her head, Hollis said, "Sorry, I haven't seen him. Not yet, anyway."

"Then what's wrong?"

Hollis watched the older woman's hands twisting together in her lap, and for the first time she felt a pang of real worry. She had seen so many spirits; why *hadn't* she seen Daniel Alexander? Only because she hadn't been in the right place at the right moment?

"Hollis?" Anna sounded as anxious as she looked.

"Be honest," DeMarco advised Hollis.

Hollis had unconsciously begun chewing on a thumbnail and forced herself to stop. "Anna . . . I'm finding it really difficult to believe that no one, in the family or a guest, has ever reported anything paranormal here."

"Why?"

"Because there are spirits here. A lot of them. Inside the house, outside on the grounds. Pretty much everywhere. People who might have been guests or family. Certainly servants. From their clothing, people who lived more than a hundred years ago—and in just about all the decades since."

"And that's unusual?" Anna ventured, clearly at sea.

Hollis wanted to chew on her nail again but managed not to. "Well, yeah, it is. As a general rule, spirits tend to stay where they died, or in a place where they have family or other emotional ties. So seeing so many spirits from so much of the past, all gathered in one place, it's the sort of thing mediums experience in hospitals, in asylums and prisons, in really old hotels or other buildings with violent histories. Where people were murdered and committed suicide. Where bad things, negative things, happened a lot. Places that often housed horrible, tragic events like fires or explosions—events that killed a lot of people all at once."

"But you said . . . they were from different decades."

"Yeah, which is something I'd expect from an old hospital or old hotel, even if there hadn't been a major tragedy. Just people, as you said, living and dying. Over years, over decades. But this is the first time I've ever seen so many in a private home—or even part-time hotel. And there's something else I find really odd."

"What is it?"

Hollis considered a moment, then said, "Last night, when Jamie Bell appeared to me, she had a message for your brother-in-law. That's all, the only reason she'd stayed here. She knew she was dead, remembered how it happened, even had some awareness of how long ago it had been. She delivered her message and then she . . . went on. To whatever's next. That's—well, if anything can be called normal when you're discussing the paranormal, that is. That kind of experience for a medium. We concentrate, we open a kind of doorway, and if we connect, it's because there's someone on the other side with unfinished business. Someone who needs to do something or convey some kind of information before they can move on."

"And these other spirits you see aren't like that?"

"No. I'm not even sure if they know they're dead." She paused again, reading Anna's expression, and hastily said, "There's no reason to be afraid. Not of them. I mean, if they've been here as long as I think they have, and nobody's noticed, why would anything change now?"

"Well, you're here."

Hollis watched Owen Anderson emerge from the shadows beside the door and cross the room to them, wondering how long he'd been there listening. And why she hadn't realized he was there. "Yeah, I'm here. So?" She tried not to sound as belligerent as he made her feel.

Owen sat down in the fourth chair of the grouping. He didn't seem as openly distrustful as he had the evening before, but then, whatever he felt, little was showing on his impassive face. "So mediums open doors, you said. Doors to let in spirits." His tone was neutral.

"Doors. Not floodgates." She wished she didn't feel so damned prickly with him, but the man got on her nerves.

"Meaning all these spirits you say you see aren't spirits *you* let in?"

She thought he was taking a perverse pleasure in repeating the word "spirit" because every time he said it, it sounded . . .

"I would have known if I'd let them in," Hollis said firmly, not at all sure about that. "I don't know how much you heard just now, but in case you missed it, I think a lot of these spirits have been here a *long* time."

"Here, or on the other side of that door you opened?"

"IT'S NOT THAT I'm doubting you," Tony said.

Bishop looked at him.

"Okay, maybe a smidge. You just seem a little . . . rattled by whatever's going on in Tennessee. And that's not just unusual, it's as rare as hen's teeth. And unsettling."

"Surely you didn't think I was infallible, Tony."

"That's not the word I would have picked." Tony paused, then added, "But you've always been in control, or at least most of the time. Always the chess grandmaster, thinking six or eight moves ahead."

To that, Bishop merely responded, "I don't think of my agents or Haven operatives as pawns, I hope you realize that."

"That's not what I meant. Just that you . . . anticipate things. Or know about them before they happen. Maybe both. But with Tennessee—"

"All I said was that Callie should have checked in by now."

"Yeah, you said that. And you were frowning. I'm not

saying you never frown, but that was a worried frown if I've ever seen one. And you never worry."

"Maybe I just don't show it most of the time. I worry, Tony, believe me. Especially when something I don't recognize blocks me."

"Now, see, that's the part that worries *me*," Tony said. "That there's a Big Bad out there that you don't recognize. Which would make it new. And new is never good when we're talking about Big Bads."

"I don't know every evil that exists. No one does. We face things as they come, remember?"

"Well, I heard you tell Hollis something like that."

"It's the truth, and one you should recognize by now." Bishop shook his head. "Once events are set in motion, once people and their emotions are involved, all bets are off. Something even more true when you throw an unknown energy source into the mix."

"Hollis tell you that?"

"No."

Tony waited, then said, "What is going on down there? On both sides of that mountain?"

All Bishop said in response to that was, "Callie should have checked in by now. She really should have."

OWEN'S CHALLENGE STOPPED Hollis, but only for a moment. "Here. They behave as if they've always been here. They stroll in the gardens, and swim in the pool, and play tennis. Servants wait on them. They . . . walk through walls where there used to be doors."

That did, clearly, startle him. "What?"

"In the dining room, this morning, I watched a maid check the dishes on the sideboard and then disappear through the wall in that far corner. I assume there was once a door there. A second door into the kitchen hallway and the servants' quarters on this floor."

Owen frowned.

Anna, a bit pale, looked at him and said quietly, "Tell her."

"Anna—"

"Just tell her, Owen."

"Tell me what?" Hollis asked warily.

"She could have read the police report," Owen said to his sister-in-law.

"That wasn't in the report and you know it. Your father didn't want the others to know the truth. So he made sure Thomas was the only one. And we both know Thomas will take a lot of family secrets to his grave."

"He wasn't the only one of the servants who knew."

Owen shook his head. "No. Burton wouldn't have talked. No matter where he went, he wouldn't have talked. A man wouldn't talk about something like that. It reflected very badly on him."

"Tell me what?" Hollis repeated, louder this time.

Owen was still frowning, so it was Anna who met Hollis's gaze and said, "Earlier, when I told you about the maid who fell down the stairs—that was the official story. What really happened is that she hanged herself in what used to be the second doorway from the dining room to the kitchen hallway."

DeMarco, silent until then, said, "An odd place to commit suicide. Women tend to be more . . . private . . . than that. Unless it was to make some kind of a point?"

"She was pregnant," Owen said abruptly. "By a young man who was then the underbutler, and who denied being the father of her child. As soon as he opened his bedroom door the morning after we all learned about the situation, her body was the first thing he saw."

"'All' of you meaning—?"

Anna sighed. "Claudia—the maid—came to me in tears the night before, late. I hadn't been married to Daniel very long and wasn't really accustomed to having a maid. I didn't know what to do. Daniel came in and, even though Claudia seemed even more distraught, I told him."

Hollis murmured, "I'm sure that went over well."

Guiltily, Anna said, "I don't think Claudia forgave me for telling him. But I— Anyway, Daniel got Thomas, who was the only senior staff member still up, and they got Claudia back to her room quietly. Daniel told me that she wouldn't be turned out without a reference or anything dreadful like that, that he knew of homes for unwed mothers, that he'd make sure she was taken care of. And when she could work again, he'd make sure she was able to get a job."

"But not here," DeMarco said.

Anna lifted her chin a bit. "He reassured her as best he could. She wouldn't be abandoned, left alone to fend for herself and her child. She'd have the help she needed, as long as she needed it. And he told her that Burton—the young man—would certainly lose his job here. Thomas was going to tell him the next morning."

"But he saw Claudia first," Hollis said slowly. "So he also knew the truth about how she really died."

Anna said, "Thomas said he suggested that Burton, who seemed genuinely shaken, go outside for some air. He thought there'd be time enough later to tell Burton about losing his job if, indeed, that was still going to be the outcome."

Hollis lifted her brows. "With the pregnant girl out of the way and underbutlers at a premium, Burton might not have been fired?"

Owen grunted. "He would have. Might have been allowed to work a notice, but I don't believe my father would have allowed him to stay."

"Anyway," Anna said, "Thomas suggested that Burton take a walk and get himself under control while Thomas went to inform Mr. Alexander."

"Your father-in-law?"

"Yes."

"You called him—"

"Mr. Alexander, yes. My entire married life. He was . . . that sort."

Hollis shook off the tangent. "Okay, so Thomas went for Mr. Alexander, and once again he decided to fix things so nobody in the house looked bad."

Owen sent her a brief glare, but it was rather half-hearted.

Anna said, "He was very concerned that no scandal touch the family. It was his way, his conviction that such things could be harmful to the family and the business. And she was gone, took her own life, so what harm would it really do to call it an accident instead? A fall, perfectly understandable. They were able to—to cut her down and move her to the bottom of the stairs before any of the other servants were out of their rooms."

Evenly, DeMarco said, "And the ligature marks around her neck?"

Anna's hands twisted even more in her lap. "There . . . weren't really any marks. Her uniform had a high collar, you see. And she'd used a twisted bedsheet rather than a rope. The doctor Mr. Alexander called in said that a little bruising from a broken neck was natural, especially if she—if she died instantly, as he believed she had. He signed the death certificate."

"And the county sheriff accepted it," Hollis murmured. "Because how could it have been anything but an accident?" Before anyone could respond to the rhetorical question, she frowned and said, "Why did Mr. Alexander decide to close off that door?"

"He never said." Anna shrugged. "I doubt anyone ever asked."

"Even though it made the servants' job harder with just the one door to serve the dining room?"

"No one would have questioned him. Whatever was said belowstairs, I'm sure Thomas kept speculation to a minimum."

"I'm sure," DeMarco murmured.

"Belowstairs." Hollis shook her head. "I feel like I've wandered into *Masterpiece Theatre*."

"You're not alone," DeMarco told her.

"I suppose much of this does sound old-fashioned,"

Anna allowed, "but as long as Mr. Alexander was alive, things were done much as they had been for generations. The only real difference was that the emphasis on farming and livestock gave way to his various other business interests away from the property, from the land, and so he flew into Knoxville or Nashville two or three times a week."

"Flew?"

Owen said, "The company helicopter. Obviously, being this far out meant travel was more difficult." He shrugged. "It was a necessity rather than a convenience. After our father died, Daniel and I also flew to our offices at least a couple of times each week."

"And you still do?" Hollis asked.

With another shrug, Owen said, "It isn't so necessary now. Daniel and I were never as driven as our father was, so we gradually gave up controlling interests in most of the companies. I still attend board meetings and the like, but the day-to-day running of the businesses was turned over to others a long time ago."

Vaguely curious, Hollis asked, "Do you still use the helicopter?"

"When I need it, it's flown over from Knoxville. Or if Anna needs it, of course."

"I hate the thing," she murmured. "I'd much rather be driven, even if it does take a lot longer."

Hollis looked at her for a moment, then forced her mind back to the recently unveiled family secret. "So . . . nobody outside the family—and Thomas—ever knew that Claudia killed herself. But what about Burton? I suppose Mr. Alexander found a way to keep him quiet? I mean, probably not with the family a long time, like Thomas, so loyalty couldn't be counted on, especially since he was being fired. A nice severance package?"

She looked at DeMarco and said, "Can you believe we're having a conversation like this? In this day and age?"

"Not really," he replied, his gaze on Anna's still-writhing fingers.

Owen said, "Burton never came back. From his walk that morning. None of us ever saw him again."

TEN

Luther was still too shaken to say much on the way back to the cabin, but once they were there, he asked one of the many questions swirling around in his mind.

"It's Friday? You said it was Friday."

"It's Friday," she confirmed, using an antiseptic wipe from her first-aid kit to clean the almost invisible cut on her neck.

Almost invisible. To Luther, it looked like a murderous slash. And it could have been; that was what scared him. Callie had picked up his knife and carried it back here because he didn't want to touch it. He looked toward the door, where Cesar lay on his accustomed rug, watching Luther but without apparent malice or even visible tension.

The other three dogs, who had remained in the cabin during an outing whose purpose and destination was still a blank to Luther, were lying around the living area of the cabin, each on a thickly folded blanket or rug that served as a bed. They all looked completely calm and relaxed.

In fact, Lucy was snoring.

"What happened to Thursday?" Luther asked.

Callie frowned slightly and, finished with her neck, went to pour out two cups of coffee. She brought Luther's and set it on the coffee table in front of him, then sat down in the chair opposite him and sipped hers.

"Callie?"

"Well, I'm no doctor so I don't know the technical term, but my guess is that you experienced some kind of whiteout."

"I've never heard of that before."

She shrugged. "It's known to be a side effect of some drugs. And we've documented a few cases on the psychic end of things, apparently caused by exposure to energy, electrical and otherwise. It's the opposite of a blackout, in a sense. You walked through yesterday, and as far as I could tell, you were completely yourself. Acted normally. Spoke normally. Nothing to indicate you weren't completely here. Mind you, I had and still have my shields up; maybe I would have noticed something odd otherwise. Or maybe not."

"I don't remember anything."

"Yeah, that's what makes it a whiteout. To everyone around you, you're behaving normally. To you, it's like you dozed off sometime late Wednesday and slept all the way through Thursday and through this morning. What's the last thing you remember?"

He thought about it. "Lunch. Wednesday. We'd more or less arrived at a plan to stick close to the cabin for at least another day to give my leg a chance to heal. I thought we should call for backup and/or haul ass out of here. And you were going to contact Bishop. In fact, you started to contact him."

Callie sipped her coffee again. "Yeah, about that."

"What about it?"

"You don't remember?"

Luther concentrated, searching through maddening wisps of memory or knowledge. "You were . . . There was a shot I was supposed to give you if something went wrong when you contacted Bishop."

"Except that never happened."

"The shot?"

"Or any contact with Bishop."

Luther stared at her, then said, "Christ, I didn't do anything to hurt you *then*, did I?"

"You'd have more than a leg wound to worry about if you had. Cesar was watching, remember. And I hadn't given him a hold command."

"You told me . . . he'd react if something negative happened."

"Yeah. And he didn't. But when I dropped my shields to make contact with Bishop and Miranda, there was . . . definitely something wrong. Something out there. Almost but not quite pushing back. Not close exactly, but wherever it was, it was a kind of barrier preventing me from reaching out. It was like tuning in to a radio station but getting nothing except static. I couldn't get through."

"At all?"

"No. And the harder I tried to push through, the worse the static got. I decided I'd better back off and get my shields back up, so I did. And kept them up. When I opened my eyes, you were clearly worried and Cesar was calm. So whatever it was, he didn't sense it—or wasn't bothered by it. Maybe because whatever it was, it really wasn't *here*. I reached out—and it stopped me somewhere outside myself from reaching further."

Luther picked up his cup and took a long swallow, hoping the caffeine would help clear his head. It didn't. Much.

"Okay. I'm assuming nothing much happened Thursday. Yesterday."

"No. Cesar and I took the other dogs out a few times, but they didn't want to go very far from the cabin, so we didn't. He and I went out once alone, just to scout a bit farther. The rest of the time, you and I talked some. Cleaned our weapons. Swapped a few war stories."

Luther was sorry he had missed that. He had a strong hunch that Callie's "war stories" would be varied and fascinating.

Callie finished with a shrug, saying, "You were up on your feet by the afternoon, first using a makeshift crutch and then pretty much under your own steam. Even took a hot shower last night, and if you needed help, you didn't ask." She lifted her coffee cup in a slight salute. "So you do heal faster than the average bear."

He grunted. "So where were we headed? Before."

"My idea. In hindsight, not a good one. But among

other things, I was bothered by that blood I'd found, and that plus the dogs' fear of Jacoby made me curious. I wanted to find out if that negative energy around Jacoby's cabin—or around him—was closer than it had been before."

"I think we can safely say it was. We were no more than a few hundred yards from this cabin when . . . it . . . happened." Luther felt more than a little grim. "That crack in my shield?"

"I'm assuming that's why it targeted you, because mine was still up. I'm also assuming that during what happened out there, your memories of all the hours you lost were taken away from you. That's when it happened, I think. Just like the agents transporting Jacoby."

"I wonder if either of them turned into a raging maniac first," Luther muttered.

"Oh, you were too controlled to be a maniac." Callie's voice was utterly matter-of-fact. "I had my shields up, but I still got the sense that you were listening to something inside your own mind. Something very clearly telling you to cut my throat."

"Jesus, don't remind me."

She leaned forward, elbows on her knees, and gazed at him steadily. "Look, hard as it is, we have to go over this. You have to remember whatever you can, because we need to understand as much of this as possible. I can't contact Bishop and Miranda, and I'm not at all sure we should even attempt to hike down the mountain to town, not with that negative energy apparently expanding the way it is."

"What about your Jeep?"

"That's one of the other things that was bothering me. When I took Cesar out alone yesterday, one of the reasons was to check on the Jeep. All four tires have been slashed. It's not going anywhere."

"Jacoby? He was that close?"

"I don't know. No definitive evidence it was him. Generally speaking, people up here are respectful of vehicles, since you never know when your life might depend on one. But there's no way to know for sure it wasn't pure vandalism by some hunter or . . ."

"Or?"

"There are rumors of a few militia groups scattered about in these mountains. But I've never seen any sign of them up here, and I can't think of a reason why they'd target my Jeep."

"If they knew you were a fed, it'd be reason enough," Luther pointed out. "They have no love of the government, and no love of cops. Finding a federal cop parked in what they consider their own territory might at the very least cause them to leave some kind of warning."

"True. But that assumes they found out somehow. And I'd rather assume they don't have that kind of intelligence operations. Which is what our intelligence operations have told us." She smiled faintly. "Stop stalling. What do you remember, Luther? In those minutes before you . . . came back to yourself, what do you remember?"

"Blackness," he said almost involuntarily. "Like some goddamned alien ooze out of a horror movie inside my head, creeping over my mind, trying to smother it, take it over. And there were voices. Whispers, what seemed like hundreds of them, but all saying the same thing at the same time, almost a chant, all telling me—"

"To kill me."

"Yeah. To kill you. That I'd have . . . power. Power to do anything I wanted, more than I knew I could do . . ."

"If you killed me."

Don't. Don't let her stop you. Stop us. We have to do this. You know we do. It feels right, doesn't it? All the strength? All the power surging through you? Making you invincible? And it's all yours. You'll be able to do amazing things, Luther. You'll be able to do anything you want. Anything.

"Luther?"

He looked at her, shoving the stark memory of those seductive promises out of his mind. Hoping they were just memories. "Yeah. That I'd be invincible. If I killed you."

COLE JACOBY—OR, rather, the shell of that man who retained just enough awareness to know who and what he had been before—wiped his brow as he dug the shovel into the ground upright and more or less leaned against it.

He was tired. He didn't think he'd ever been so tired.

Just a bit more, Cole. Just a bit more, and then you can truly be part of us. You can be one of us.

"I buried her," he heard himself say sullenly. "What was left of her. All the pieces. Nobody'll ever find her up here." He didn't allow himself to think about what he had done. To her. And not because he didn't remember, but because he did.

Except it hadn't been him. It had been like . . . almost like watching a movie. Or being in a nightmare. Something had used his body, his hands, to do those terrible things.

Something that was taking him over, bit by bit.

Something that was going to win.

Because he hadn't the strength or will to stop it, even if he knew how to try, even if . . . Even if he still cared.

But he was mostly numb.

And mostly just no longer gave a damn.

Yes, you did well. And you felt stronger afterward, didn't you, Cole?

"I don't feel strong now."

It only lasts after you've become one with us. After that . . . after that, Cole, you'll be invincible. You'll have more power than you can even imagine. All the power you could ever desire.

He had the vague notion that there was something wrong with that offer, the dim understanding that if they . . . it . . . whatever . . . had to use him as a tool, just how powerful could they or it really be? But it was a fleeting thing, that question, gone almost as soon as it appeared, like a wisp of smoke.

"I never wanted power," he said. "Just money. Just enough money. I didn't need that . . . what you made me take. What you made it possible for me to take. I never needed that."

But we did, Cole. We needed it.

"If you have so much power, why do you need money?"

It takes money in your world. To buy . . . necessary things. To buy a safe place. To be left alone.

"I don't understand." He really didn't, but he also didn't really care.

You will. When the time comes, you'll understand all of it, Cole. Now spread brush over the grave so it won't be so obvious. And then go back to the cabin.

"So I can sleep?" he asked yearningly.

For a little while.

CALLIE LEANED BACK and sipped her coffee, frowning. "Well, that's interesting."

"Interesting? Jesus Christ, Callie."

"Well, it is. It's certainly not your average burst of negative energy. This thing definitely has a consciousness. More than one, from the sound of it. Which could explain its strength. And it likely would have been seductive to someone like Jacoby, who wouldn't have had the mental or emotional strength to resist as you did."

"I resisted? Because I had my knife to your throat, and that doesn't sound like resisting to me."

"I'm still alive. You resisted."

Luther really didn't want to talk about this but knew they had to, that she was right about that. "Did you help me, there at the end? To shove that energy out of my mind?"

"I was about to try, even though I didn't want to drop my shields, but you were able to do it alone."

"It felt . . . it almost felt like I had help."

"Not me. I don't know who else would have done it. Are you connected to anyone else? Linked? Psychically?"

"No."

Her brows rose slightly. "That sounded definite."

"It is. Probably like your unit, Haven operatives go through periodic tests and . . . challenges. To find our strengths and our limitations. Whatever may or may not have happened to change my abilities out here, until now I was a touch clairvoyant with a pretty strong shield. Our strongest telepaths had trouble reading me, and the other clairvoyants got nothing."

"What about empaths? What about Maggie?"

"Maggie says I protect my emotions, consciously or not, so she didn't probe. No other empath has tried."

Matter-of-fact, Callie said, "Probably because you're former military. Most with experiences like yours keep themselves pretty buttoned up emotionally."

"I suppose," he said, without saying anything more.

Callie didn't push. "Well, given that, it had to be your own strength that pushed that black negativity out of your mind."

Luther suddenly remembered her voice calling his name just before he shoved the blackness out, but he decided to keep that knowledge to himself, since he didn't quite know what to make of it.

"Maybe," he said. "Or maybe it was just a test. To see how far I could be pushed. How well I could be controlled. How can we really know either way? All we *can* know is that it got in. In me. And took control of my mind and body." He paused, then added, "I cannot begin to tell you how creepy and unsettling that is."

Callie didn't offer platitudes, just said, "And I can't understand how that feels—so far, at least. Honestly, I hope I never have firsthand knowledge. Though I can imagine, I think. Question is, what do we do about it? Maybe we *should* take the chance and hike down the mountain. Get you out of range of whatever it is, at least until we can get some backup on scene."

Luther considered. "How long would it take to reach town?"

"Well, given that we want to keep moving away from Jacoby's cabin and take the most direct route, that means we'll be covering some pretty rough terrain, straight down the mountain. You're still favoring your leg and need to; put too much strain on it too soon, and you won't be able to hike at all."

"What about the old logging roads you talked about?"

"They make the trip shorter—if you're in a vehicle. But it's not at all a direct route, and on foot following the roads would take twice as long as heading straight down the mountain."

"Okay, that makes sense. So how long?"

"Probably a few hours. Wouldn't want to start now; by the time we got ready and got out of here, it would mean night would catch us long before we reached town. Dunno about you, but I'd rather not either camp or hike out in the open at night, at least until we have a better handle on exactly what this energy is and whether it's still expanding."

"You won't get an argument on that. But it means giving Jacoby more time to do whatever it is he's doing."

"It's a risk. Stay or go, if he takes us out, there's nobody to warn either the town or our respective bosses and other law enforcement that Jacoby is a lot more than a simple bank robber and dangerous as hell."

"We just don't know *how* he's dangerous. Besides his guns, I mean."

"I'm less worried about his guns than I am the negative energy. And I still want to know as much as possible about that blood. Check it out more extensively to see if there's more, maybe a trail that maybe leads somewhere useful." *Even if she's already gone, don't I owe it to her to find her? Owe it to her family?*

"Callie, going back out there is *not* a good idea."

"I'm sure I've had better," she agreed. "But we need intel. Even before we leave this cabin, we need some idea of where that blood came from and where it leads, if anywhere. And we need to know *for sure* if the energy is centered on Jacoby or on the area around his cabin."

"Callie—"

"Look, I'll take Cesar and I'll keep my shields up. And my shields don't have a crack or a chink or any other vulnerability."

"As far as you know," Luther said grimly. "We can assume I was targeted because of a vulnerability, a chink in my shield, but we can't know that, not absolutely. There could have been some other reason, and maybe that didn't involve testing your shield. So we can't possibly be certain your shield has been tested and can withstand that energy."

"The whole point of being chosen for this," she reminded him, "is that I deal well with negative energy. My shield holds up against it, and sometimes I can even deflect it."

"But you admitted yourself this energy is unlike anything you've sensed before."

Callie shrugged. "Uncharted territory in some ways. We face that a lot in the SCU, and I'm guessing Haven operatives do as well."

He nodded reluctantly.

"So we get on with the job. Face what's in front of us, deal with it as best we can, and keep going." Callie shook her head. "I just . . . have to be sure there's not a victim somewhere up here being hurt." *Even if Cesar is sure. Even if I can't help her. I have to know.* "Before we leave. I couldn't live with myself if I found out later that I could have helped someone and didn't when I had the chance."

Luther finally voiced a possibility that had been bothering him. "And what if that blood was deliberately left to draw you out?" He lifted a hand when she would have spoken. "I know you said you thought Jacoby hadn't noticed you, wasn't aware of you as any kind of threat, but when we talked about that, it was in a slightly different context. The assumption that he was too busy struggling against what was trying to dominate him to bother worrying about you."

Callie sighed. "We didn't talk about something else being aware of me as a possible threat, because we didn't know for certain that it had a consciousness separate from Jacoby's. That negative energy."

"You believe it took my memories of more than a day." Luther kept his voice even with an effort. "A day with you. A day during which we talked about ourselves—and cleaned our weapons. And maybe knowledge I have, about Haven, about the SCU. It could have gotten that information even if it didn't take it. If that energy does have a consciousness with a plan, it knows exactly who we are. Both of us. And that means it knows we're both a threat."

COLE JACOBY THOUGHT at first that he was just slipping into sleep, and he was thankful because he was so, so tired.

When the blackness began to slide over his mind, the small inner self that still wanted to survive, that still wanted to be Cole Jacoby and alive, sensed the difference between this and other times. In all the other times, he had been allowed to rest, to sleep.

This time, he wasn't going to sleep.

He was going.

He was dying.

Not his body. His soul.

There was, fleetingly, the instinct to fight it, if only because he was afraid his soul was going to hell. But in his final conscious moments as Cole Jacoby, he realized that there was something far, far worse than hell.

There was being consumed by pure evil.

And as Cole Jacoby was swallowed up, there was only the shell evil would use, and his whisper added to the vast chorus of whispers that had all earned their place through the commission of horrifically evil acts.

And the vow of more to come.

LUTHER HAD DONE his best, but Callie, he discovered, had a quietly stubborn nature. She didn't argue with him, she merely got herself ready to go look for a trail, then left with Cesar.

Because she was a good agent, and she had to know.

Only the memory of his knife at her throat kept Luther from going with her. Whether she could withstand or deflect that negative energy might still be an open question, but *his* inability to do so had been proven.

Starkly.

Luther wasn't a man to pace, which was probably just as well for his healing leg. But in a quiet cabin where the only sounds were the grunts and snores of sleeping dogs and the occasional pop and crackle of the low fire, he had entirely too little to occupy his mind.

Which meant that he thought about why he was sitting here helpless to do his job while his partner—tacit partner, given the situation—was out there facing God only knew what kind of danger. At best, her shield would hold and she'd only be left possibly facing something that looked like Cole Jacoby but was pure evil and could use a gun with skill.

At worst, her shield would fail . . . and Luther had no idea what that black sludge of evil energy would do to her mind. He only knew what it had done to his.

To him.

Eternal minutes passed. An hour.

Even in the worst military situations he had faced, Luther had never known time to pass so slowly. To creep.

But his imagination didn't creep, it raced. And everything it showed him as a possibility scared the hell out of him.

Dammit, Callie, where are you?

THE BLOOD WAS gone.

Callie stood there staring down at it, frowning. No reason to clean blood off the ground, not way out here. So maybe an animal had gotten to it. No tracks, still, except those she had left herself, but—

She could feel it. Feel that strange, dark energy. Pressure, but more than that. Power. Hunger. Determination. Even with her shields up, she could sense it.

Need to go.

The one mental voice that could always reach her, even behind her shields.

Callie looked at her dog, her partner, and said quietly, "You still can't smell any kind of trail from here?" Out of long habit, she repeated the question silently, in her mind, because she had learned that Cesar understood that inner voice in a way he didn't completely understand her when she spoke aloud.

No trail. Bad. Bad smell. Bad feeling. Need to go.

"Do you hear anything?"

No. Ears hurt. Smell hurts. Need to go.

Callie didn't smell anything, and her ears didn't hurt—but she felt that pressure, same as before. It had to be what Cesar sensed as well. She gave up speaking aloud.

Cesar, if all you can smell is the bad smell, then how do you know we can't help her?

Smelled death. Before. She's dead.

And you're sure?

Sure. Need to go, Callie. Need to go now.

He didn't often use her name, and the level of worry it indicated made Callie want to reassure him. She leaned down a bit to touch him.

Something slammed into her with an odd whistling sound.

She looked down and saw something sticking out of her jacket. A stick of some kind. With something on the end . . . feathers? How odd.

Cesar grabbed the sleeve of her jacket and jerked her to the ground.

Callie heard another of those peculiar whistles, then a sort of thud, and saw an arrow sticking in the ground a few feet away. One matching the arrow stuck in her. It didn't take Cesar's urging to make her scramble awkwardly behind the cover of a thicket of brush to her right.

An arrow? The bastard has a bow and arrows?

Not uncommon for hunters to use compound bows, which could bring down even big game quickly and cleanly, but—

The shock of the sudden attack past, Callie felt the pain. Red-hot and paralyzing. It stole her breath, and made clear thought almost impossible. So it must have been instinct that made her peer in the direction of Jacoby's cabin, the direction the arrow had come from, to look for her attacker.

Need to go, Callie. Now.

"He could still be up there," she heard herself say, even as her gaze tracked up the slope, scanning, seeing nothing. At least, she thought she saw nothing. No one. But she was getting dizzy.

Gone. Black thing gone.

A bit fuzzily, Callie wondered if that was how Cesar saw whatever was left of Cole Jacoby. As just a black thing a canine mind could make no sense of.

Not that a human mind could make much sense of it either.

Go, Callie. Go now.

Taking care to remain behind the screen of the thicket, Callie sat as straight as she could, looking down at the arrow. It had gone in at an angle, since the bowman— Jacoby—had been on higher ground when he shot her. She didn't have to feel behind her to know that the end of the arrow was sticking out of her back somewhere near her shoulder blade. What she wasn't sure of was what kind of tip the arrow had. When she forced herself to try reaching behind to touch that tip, the wave of pain nearly made her throw up.

Callie.

"I have to pull it out," she heard herself mumble. "I know you aren't supposed to pull things out if they go into your chest or back, but . . . I won't be able to move with . . . both ends . . . of this thing . . . sticking out of me."

Get help? Luther?

"No time. I need . . . to get to him, Cesar. I need . . . back to the cabin. Let me—"

She grasped the shaft of the arrow with both hands, as firmly up against her body as she could manage. Then sucked in a deep breath—and pulled.

Everything burst crimson and then went dark.

Callie wasn't sure how long she had been out, but she woke to Cesar licking her face and whining, and in his mind was wordless urgency. She knew she had lost blood, maybe a lot, and her left shoulder was hurting like hell, but there was nothing she could do about either except get back to the cabin and Luther.

Using Cesar's sturdy, powerful body, she managed to lever herself upright, more or less. She had to pause without moving for a moment or maybe awhile, until the dizziness faded a bit. When she could finally focus, she found herself looking at the bloodstained arrow she had pulled out of her own body.

"New war story," she whispered.

Go, Callie. Go now.

"Yeah. Yeah . . . go now. Let's go, boy. Slow and easy."

There was nothing easy about it, but Callie hung on to her canine partner and just fought to stay on her feet and moving, allowing him to guide her.

TWO HOURS.

Unable to sit still a moment longer, Luther retrieved his weapon from the drawer by the couch and examined it.

Cleaned, definitely. And reloaded; if he remembered correctly, he'd had only about four rounds left in the clip when Callie had found him in the woods, his extra ammo lost along with all his other gear.

The clip was full.

Ah. They carried the same handgun, a Glock, and Callie had obviously provided him with ammo. He still didn't remember cleaning or reloading the weapon. Or the war stories. Dammit.

He replaced the clip and leaned forward to place the gun on the coffee table within easy reach, and it was only then that he realized the dogs were all awake.

And tense.

But they weren't looking at him. All three of them, still lying on their makeshift beds, were staring at the front door. Not growling, just staring. Just . . . waiting.

Luther found himself staring at the door, still leaning forward, his weapon still in his hand and ready.

Ready for—

He didn't know for what, but when the door swung wide open to admit Callie and Cesar, he felt only relief. For a moment.

Callie pushed the door shut, leaning back against it. She lifted a hand to push her hood away from her face, and he saw the blood on her fingers.

He was already on his feet and moving toward her when she spoke, her breathing labored enough to make the effort to speak clear.

"In the Marines. Did they teach you . . . assumption is the mother . . . of all fuck-ups?"

"I learned," he said.

About half a laugh escaped her. "I assumed I didn't need to worry . . . about anything but . . . the negative energy. Wrong . . . assumption."

Luther caught her before she could hit the floor.

ELEVEN

"It's Friday," Hollis said.

"I noticed," DeMarco said.

She glared at him for a moment, then dropped it and sighed. "I know. We'd be back at Quantico by now, or on the jet heading for a real case, if I could just do what I came to do and make contact with Daniel for Anna."

"I wonder."

"You do? Why?"

DeMarco stopped and stood looking around yet another wide hallway that was dark despite the lights *and* all the sheet-draped furniture; they were, with the permission of their hostess, exploring the wing of the house normally closed except when this was a hotel.

They had looked just about everywhere else for the spirit of Daniel Alexander, and Hollis had suggested this more out of desperation than any real hope of encountering the man's elusive self.

"Reese?"

"Is it the same here as everywhere else?"

"If you mean the spirits, yes. Not that many, but during the day in a hallway of bedrooms and suites, I wouldn't expect many."

"Anybody stand out?"

Hollis looked around, by now more baffled than creeped out by what she saw. "Not really. Mostly maids cleaning the rooms. More than you'd see in your average luxury hotel in a single hallway, but I imagine part of the extra-deluxe service here is not walking into your room at two in the afternoon and discovering the maid hasn't gotten there yet."

DeMarco didn't frown often, but he did then. "Like everywhere else, from different times?"

She took a closer look. "Yeah, I think so. Wait— definitely. The maid uniforms stayed pretty much the same over the years, apparently, but the hemlines go up and down, and so do the sleeves and collars."

Apparently musing aloud, DeMarco said, "Lots of servants. Lots of guests. Lots of family members you've matched to various portraits and photos Anna let us go through. But no Daniel."

"Yeah, I don't get it. He should be here. He lived his whole life here. He died here. Where else would he be?"

"Maybe he moved on."

"I wish I believed that. I'd tell Anna and we could get out of here. But . . . I don't think so, Reese."

"Why not?" He was looking at her now, intently.

"I don't know. Just a feeling. Sometimes I think if I only turned my head fast enough, I'd see him."

"As if he's deliberately staying out of your sight line?"

It was Hollis's turn to frown. "Maybe. But . . . Why would he?"

"Maybe that's what we should be asking ourselves. Not why you're seeing so many spirits, but why you aren't seeing the one you're looking for."

She resisted the urge to clutch at her hair. "Jeez, that sounds like a cosmic riddle. I hate riddles. They're like those math problems with two trains leaving a station."

"You didn't like the trains, I take it."

"Kept seeing them crash. No matter how I worked the math, my trains always crashed into each other." Hollis stared at her partner and added, "You're trying not to laugh."

"Sorry."

"Crashing trains aren't funny. People and animals die."

DeMarco blinked. "Animals?"

"Circus trains. My trains are always circus trains."

He cleared his throat, but his question still sounded a bit unsteady. "Why?"

"I don't know. They just are." Hollis refused to laugh, even though she was beginning to feel the need to.

"So in your math problems, the imaginary trains are circus trains."

"Yes."

"Your way of making the exercise interesting?"

"I guess." She thought about it. "It means more to get it right."

"So the people and animals don't die?"

"Well, it wouldn't mean as much with freight cars. A mess, I suppose, and maybe fire or a chemical spill or something like that." She thought about it some more and felt a flicker of concern. "Yeah, I wouldn't want a chemical spill. Almost as bad as circus cars."

"Bad enough." DeMarco cleared his throat again. "You're really tired, aren't you?"

She actually had to think about *that*, which pretty much answered his question. "Yeah. Yeah, I am. Why am I? Other than walking around the place and talking, it's not like I've done anything to get tired. And God knows I've eaten enough for fuel."

"Opening a door for spirits takes a lot out of you."

"But I haven't," Hollis said slowly, only then realizing. "Not since the other night with Jamie Bell and her message to Owen. Not since . . . Brooke warned me to be careful."

"All these spirits, and you never opened the door once?"

She shook her head. "No. I mean . . . they were here already. I felt them almost from the first, and after Jamie, after the next morning, they were all around me, and I could see them."

"After you opened the door for Jamie."

Again, slowly this time, Hollis shook her head. "I didn't consciously open the door for her. I was irritated by Owen, and—and she was just there."

"You weren't in control."

"No." Hollis had lost all desire to laugh.

"But you were tired afterward." He paused, then added, "Drained, really. Much more so than usual for you. I thought it was just the long travel day topped off by Owen's attitude, and then Jamie Bell. That the combination took more out of you than usual."

"I thought so too."

Reese took her hand and turned to retrace their steps to the main part of the house. "I think we need to call Bishop," he said.

Hollis was surprised. "It's not like you to want to check with the boss about anything short of a crisis," she said.

"I'm beginning to think we're in the middle of one," he said, rather grim now.

"Because I see all these spirits?"

"Because you aren't in control—and see all the spirits. Dammit. I was so busy thinking about what you were seeing that I missed the signs *I* should have been seeing."

"Signs of what?"

"Signs of a vortex."

"THEY'RE RARE," BISHOP said. "Are you sure?"

"It's the only thing that makes any kind of sense," DeMarco replied.

The phone in the foyer had no speaker, and there was no extension nearby; Hollis was sitting on the foyer table, both because she was tired and because she was better able to comfortably share the phone's handset with her partner.

"Spirits everywhere, Bishop," she told their unit chief. "I didn't let them in. Even trying to contact Daniel

Alexander, I haven't really been doing anything except . . . looking for him in the crowd. I didn't realize that's what I was doing until Reese made me see."

DeMarco said, "Old house, remote location, down in a valley with a hell of a lot of granite all around us, and at least a dozen old mine shafts in the area, radiating out like spokes on a wheel. Some on the maps and some not. The family's been here a long time, much longer than this house, and the history they had printed mentions that before the house was built, there was almost a small town here. Even had a church at the other end of the valley, complete with graveyard."

"The church isn't there now?"

"No. Gone before this house was built. There's Internet access via a satellite dish, so I was able to do a search, even if it was slow as hell. Seems there was a very wet winter followed by an unusually rainy spring one year, and the result was one hell of a mudslide. In fact, witnesses reported that it looked like half the mountain slid down into the valley. Trees, boulders, everything. Took out the church, covered the graveyard in mud and debris so deep no one even suggested they try to uncover the graves. Before the mudslide, this valley was a mile longer than it is now."

Hollis said, "But it was so long ago you can't really see any evidence of a mudslide. I mean, a geologist probably could, but not us. There are trees growing down at that end of the valley, big ones. Well, I mean, over a hundred years . . . mighty oaks can grow." She felt more than saw DeMarco give her a look, and added to Bishop, "But isn't a vortex some kind of whirlpool?"

"In water, yes. In this case, it would be a whirlpool of energy. Spiritual energy."

"And nobody saw all the spirits until I got here? But I didn't *do* anything, seriously."

"You're a powerful medium, Hollis. You see auras. You can heal. And if what Reese described is accurate, you can do what only one other psychic I've ever known can do: look into time.[6] See pieces of the past, maybe the future as well. All that indicates tremendous power. And that power is attracting what was spiritual energy that was probably a lot more diffuse, unfocused, before you arrived."

Hollis began to rub her forehead. She had a headache. "Please don't tell me I'm precognitive. That's one psychic tool I definitely do not want."

"No, this is something else entirely."

"What is it?"

Bishop sounded unusually tense. "It doesn't really have a name. Hollis, you're . . . rewriting the book when it comes to psychic development. All I know for sure is that, given the right place, the right physical conditions, and the right circumstances, your presence alone could become a focal point for energies. And not just spiritual energies, but other kinds as well."

Hollis was almost afraid to ask.

She *was* afraid to ask.

DeMarco did it. "For instance?"

---

6 *Whisper of Evil*

"That depends on what's on the other side of the vortex. Hollis, these spirits have auras?"

"When I concentrate and look for them, yeah. Why?"

"Auras that vary in intensity and color? As they do with living people?"

She had to think about that, and it made her head hurt more. "Um . . . now that you mention it, I didn't see a whole lot of variety. And the glow was . . . fainter."

"Colors?"

"Dark. And . . . not really colors. I mean, not black, but just . . . dark. I thought it was just the house, but even outside, when I saw them, the auras were dark. What the hell does that mean?" Even as she asked, Hollis had the strong suspicion that Bishop knew these answers, had been expecting the questions, and knew a hell of a lot more about what was going on than he had so far revealed.

Which was something she should have been used to by now.

"It means we're leaving," DeMarco said.

"No," Bishop told them, "that's the last thing you should do."

Oh, yeah, he knows stuff. Dammit.

"Bishop, she's getting weaker. Just in the last hour, I've almost *seen* the energy draining from her."

"Isn't that wrong?" Hollis asked, pushing her mad aside for later and trying her best to think clearly. "I mean, if I'm at the center of this, shouldn't I be getting stronger?"

"You didn't open the door, Hollis. Right now, all that energy is rushing around you. Pulling at you. You aren't in control."

"That's what Reese said."

"And it's what you have to change."

"Brooke said to be careful."

And then vanished. I thought she was going to help. Why isn't she helping?

"She was right. This energy is very powerful, and you'll feel the pull of it trying to draw you toward the center, more and more, especially once you start. You'll need an anchor, a lifeline, and that's Reese. You know the drill: physical contact, and be very sure that isn't broken. For the duration, Hollis."

She thought fleetingly of the possibility of more nights spent here, from now on with the necessity of constant physical contact between her and DeMarco.

A kind of shotgun wedding.

Oh, great, that's just great. Can't I do anything *in my life normally?*

Bishop asked, "Where do you see the most spirits?"

Hollis hauled her wayward thoughts back into line and realized she really didn't have to think about that. "Inside the house. Outside, close to the house. The farther away, the fewer spirits. Out at the barn complex, I didn't see any. At least, I don't think I did."

"Fewer spirits upstairs than on the main floor?"

"Now that I think about it, yes."

"You haven't been in the basement?"

"No," DeMarco answered. "It's a huge house; we haven't explored the basement or the attic."

"The center of the vortex is likely to be below ground level, so I'm guessing the basement. There aren't only mine shafts in the area, there are unexplored caves as well, and some of them run for miles underground, originally formed by prehistoric rivers. They would provide a natural geological opening for that side of the vortex, and a physical channel for the energy as it moves. The true center has to be somewhere in the basement, and I'm betting you'll find either a sunken place in the basement floor or else an actual door, perhaps leading down into a cave the builders or original owners had a use for."

"Bishop—"

"You'll need to stay away from the center of the vortex when you open the first doors; it's what's draining your energy now."

"Wait, I have to open and then close more than one door?"

"It's necessary to divert some of the energy and weaken the vortex before you close the final door. There are five specific doorways. North, south, east, and west. Then center. Center *has* to be the last one you face, and that one you don't try to open wider. That one you have to close. And seal."

"What? Bishop, this whole thing sounds—"

"Hollis, with everything you've seen, everything you've experienced, why does this seem so unbelievable to you?"

She didn't know. She really didn't.

"I'm just tired. Tell me what to do so I can fix that, will you?"

With uncharacteristic promptness, Bishop told her exactly what she had to do.

LUTHER WASN'T SURE how badly Callie was wounded until he got her quilted jacket off, and by then the small hole just below her left collarbone wasn't terribly reassuring, because he knew she had lost a lot of blood; there was an exit wound almost identical to the entrance wound in her back, slightly lower than the entrance wound, which he automatically noted as evidence that the shooter had been on higher ground—or on his feet when Callie had been crouched or kneeling, something like that.

He pushed all that aside for the moment, because Callie was his first priority, and he was not happy that she had been forced to use far too many of her first-aid supplies earlier patching *him* up.

He used a clean bath towel, folded over her shoulder, using both hands to put pressure on the entrance and exit wounds and stanch the bleeding.

"Through and through," she murmured. "At least you won't have to dig for a bullet."

"Lucky you." His voice was grim. "What the hell happened?"

"Wrong assumption, remember?" She was watching him, half lying on the couch, slightly propped up as he had been only a few days before. Her jacket was lying in a heap on the floor nearby, and he had exposed the wound in her shoulder by simply tearing her sweatshirt open from the collar down her arm and through the left wristband.

"I didn't hear any gunshots," he said.

"That's because . . . the bastard didn't use a gun. He used a bow. Probably a compound bow, to have so much power. And an arrow with a . . . blunt end. Forget what they're called. Meant to go all the way through game animals, like deer or elk. Pierce vital organs without doing . . . much damage to the hide."

"Jesus. What, he used up all his ammo shooting at me?"

"Maybe so. Doubt he expected to do much shooting if . . . the plan was to lay low. Hell, maybe I just caught him starting out on a hunting trip." She sucked in a breath, the first real sign of pain, then said, "Hey, when you get me to stop bleeding like a stuck pig . . . get Cesar cleaned up, will you? He just about carried . . . me back here."

Luther glanced over his shoulder to see the Rottweiler sitting near Callie's jacket, his gaze intent on his mistress—whose blood definitely stained his normally glossy coat. The other three dogs were still and quiet, not quite as tense as before, but not relaxed.

Probably the smell of blood, he thought.

"I will, don't worry. Just try to stay still."

"He tried to warn me," she murmured. "Cesar. He was bothered, but didn't . . . seem to know why. Just anxious. Wanted to come back here. But I had to see that blood again. And . . . you were right. That's where . . . the bastard had me in his sights. I didn't see him. Cesar was worried and . . . I sort of leaned over just a bit to touch him. That's when I got hit. If I'd been standing straight . . ."

The arrow probably would have gone through her heart.

"No warning shot this time," Luther said. "He meant to kill you."

"Yeah."

"What about the energy?"

"I could feel it. I'm almost positive . . . it's in him. Maybe *is* him. Whatever he is now."

"You felt it through your shield?"

Callie nodded. "Pressure. And something dark. Weird to feel something . . . dark. But that's how it felt. I pulled the arrow out . . . knew it hadn't hit anything . . . vital. And hard to stay . . . low and move with the damned thing . . . sticking through me. I held on to Cesar and . . . stayed low. Let him guide me. Hell . . . almost carry me."

"Do you think Jacoby followed you?"

"I think he's not done. Better get me patched up as soon as you can."

"He's not going to put an arrow through this cabin," Luther said, with a nod toward walls constructed of actual logs. "Only two small windows, and those are curtained, plus blocked from most angles by the roof over the porch. No shot."

"He could burn us out," Callie said. "If all he wanted was the two of us dead. But . . . that's not what he wants. What it wants."

"You sensed more even with your shield up?"

"Yeah. Hunger. For strength, for power. Negative energy takes. Remember? It takes. This thing takes. More than memories."

"Callie—"

"Your abilities have more power than you know,

Luther. But he knows. *It* knows. It got a taste earlier. And it wants more."

"More?"

"Its plan. Its end game. I don't know what that is, but I know there's a goal. And it needs your strength and power to reach that goal."

The memory of coming back to himself holding a knife to Callie's throat was enough to spur Luther, but all he said was, "Listen, I know some rough-and-ready first-aid, but nothing close to your skills. All I want to do is get the bleeding stopped, pack the wound and bandage it securely, do what we can to ward off shock, and get you to a real doctor as fast as I possibly can."

She leaned her head back against the pillow. "It's a long hike off this mountain."

"It's a shorter one to Jacoby's cabin. And his truck."

"If there's any reason in that thing, any ability to think about tactics—and with a goal it *has* to have that—it'll know. I'm wounded, you're not fully recovered, and Jacoby is probably the one who disabled my Jeep, before he totally lost control. Before the dark energy became so . . . palpable. I think he could have gotten that close without us knowing. Without even Cesar knowing." She caught her breath, clearly in pain, then added, "It's narrowed our options."

"And maybe set a trap. Yeah, the thought had occurred." He checked her wounds, still bleeding but sluggishly now. Time to do what he could to dress the wound so that Callie could be moved. It made his stomach drop to realize he could do something to make her condition even worse, but he had been on too many battlefields not to be a realist.

Do the best you can and move on. Survive.

Still watching him, Callie said, "Either way, we'll have to get past him. Or go through him."

"I'm not picky."

"He got in your head before. What makes you think he won't do it again the first chance he gets?"

"Because this time I have an edge," Luther said.

"What?"

"This time, I know what he can do. And I'm ready for him."

"DO YOU UNDERSTAND?" Bishop asked.

It was DeMarco who replied, his voice *almost* as impassive as it usually was with most people. "We understand, Bishop."

"Not so sure I do." Hollis's voice was fainter over the speaker in the conference room, as if she were a bit farther away from the phone on their end. "I mean, concentrating on closing a door the way I concentrate on opening one, I get. I think. I visualize an actual door, and then see myself opening it. Or closing it. But I don't understand why the four points have to be opened and then closed before we can do what we're supposed to at the center. Just to release some energy and then narrow access to it all?"

"In part. You also need to replenish your own energy, and once you're away from the center and can channel some energy from the other doorways, you'll accomplish two goals. Closing down everything but the center, and gaining enough strength to seal the vortex permanently," Bishop replied.

"Am I going to hate this?"

Before Bishop could answer, DeMarco said, "Channeling so much energy when her abilities are unstable? Bishop, have you lost your mind?"

"If I'm right, it could go a long way toward stabilizing Hollis's abilities, which is an opportunity she's never had before now."

"And if you're wrong?"

"I'm not. Hollis, you have to be at the center of the vortex, and for you to be effective that vortex has to be a manageable size, not spread out over thirty acres or more."

"Okay, but . . . Where is the energy coming *from*, Bishop? I know Reese talked about the geography of this place, but isn't a vortex a bit like a black hole? Not with gravity but, like you said, basically a huge doorway. I mean, it has two sides, right? We have energy swirling here, but at the center it has to be going somewhere or coming from somewhere else. Doesn't it? Oh, shit, don't tell me it goes through Diana's gray time."

Considering the tension and even urgency he had uncharacteristically used at the beginning of this phone call, Bishop's voice was calm now. "No, this is a different kind of doorway. Geography helped form it on both ends. And for decades, maybe for centuries, it remained stable. On your side, spirits not ready to move on, or too weak to completely fight the natural pull of the vortex to remain there, stayed. Held hostage by a force they had no way to fight."

"And on the other side?" DeMarco asked.

"It's all about balance. The other side is negative energy, dark energy. And for a long time it was confined to a very small area."

"Until?" DeMarco's voice held the tone of a man who intended to get his questions answered.

"Just as on your side of the vortex, the right—or wrong—person arrived at a certain location with a certain set of abilities. He was drawn there unconsciously, long before now. Led there. He thought it would be a safe haven for later, when he knew he'd need one. Only his mind is too weak to fight what he found waiting there for him when he returned, was already open and receptive to the dark energy, and now it's got him. It's got a vessel, and a need to grow stronger, and to do that it needs to produce more dark energy."

"How?" Hollis asked, not sure she wanted to know.

"The only way negative energy can be produced. By evil acts."

LUTHER HAD WONDERED absently whether Jacoby's dogs would be willing to leave the cabin, especially if they had run from whatever now completely ruled their former master. But when he had Callie on the litter that was harnessed to Cesar, the dogs rose from their beds and came to join them near the front door.

"Easy, guys," Callie murmured. "Just stick close."

"Think they understand you?"

"I know they do." Still pale but curiously serene, she

looked up at him with an odd little smile. "It's one of my things."

Somehow, that didn't surprise him. "So you're a true dog whisperer, able to communicate with them on a psychic level?"

"Not just dogs," she said. "Some other animals too. Clearest with Cesar after years of practice. Luther, Cole Jacoby is gone, and the thing that looks like him is very, very powerful. You're a new telepath with a cracked shield, and it wants your power. Just how do you expect to be able to get past him? Because I trust you don't mean to fight him?"

Luther checked his weapon for about the third time, stalling because he still wasn't at all sure how he would be able to do anything to fight all the negative energy surrounding what had been Cole Jacoby. He wasn't even sure he could shield his own mind from the negative effects of being anywhere near it—except that he had never before in his life felt anything as powerful as the absolute determination to make damned sure he couldn't be used to hurt Callie in any way.

Not again.

And just to help guard against that, both his big hunting knife and her gun were within her easy reach on the litter. He didn't dare give up his own gun, but the promise that he would *only* use it against Jacoby was like a mantra in his mind.

When he finally holstered his weapon and looked at her, he was saved from having to reply at all.

She was staring straight ahead at the still-closed door,

her very dark eyes oddly fixed, a tiny frown between her brows.

Luther wasn't exactly sure how he knew that to pull her focus would be a mistake, but it was another thing he was absolutely certain of. So he merely waited, watching her, noting without really thinking about it that all the dogs were watching her as well, clearly not disturbed but intent.

It felt to him like forever but was probably no more than two or three minutes before she blinked and shook her head, as if throwing off a dizzy spell of some kind.

"Son of a bitch," she muttered. "I wonder how long he's known he could do that if he had to."

"Do what?" Luther asked. "And who?"

"Reach me telepathically—with my shields up." Her tone was even, but there was an edge to it. "Bishop."

"What, he got through just now?"

"Yeah."

"And?"

Callie checked her watch, tapped it with a frown and cursed absently, since it was clearly stopped, then said calmly, "We need to wait about five minutes before we head out."

"Why?"

"Because I'm told whatever's controlling Jacoby is about to be distracted in a very big way. And should give us a window to get to his Jeep and get the hell off this mountain."

"What kind of distraction?"

"The kind only Bishop could orchestrate."

TWELVE

A Jeep borrowed from someone at the stables had been sent to the house, requested by a clearly baffled but polite Anna Alexander, and DeMarco didn't speak until he and Hollis were in it and were heading, by compass, toward the north side of the property.

"Feeling better?" he asked then.

Hollis looked down at their linked fingers, then ahead at what was basically a wall of forest looming as they neared. "The farther we get from the house, the less weak and shaky I feel. It's easier to concentrate now, to focus. And it looks deserted out here."

"It *is* deserted."

"I mean no spirits."

"Yeah, I was reasonably sure you meant that. No living people, either. A few horses to our west, but since this is a pasture, I'd expect that."

Hollis honestly wasn't sure if he was trying to be funny, but given what she knew of him, she decided not.

"Remember what Bishop said," DeMarco reminded her. "Concentrate ahead of us, at the edge of the woods. The Jeep's compass says we're heading due north."

"I'm staring, but so far I don't see anything," she said. "Hey, did you get the feeling Bishop was expecting something like this?"

"No," DeMarco said. "I got the feeling he was expecting *exactly* this."

Hollis had to force herself not to glance at him so she wouldn't break focus, but something in his voice told her Bishop was going to have some explaining to do when all this was over.

Always assuming, of course, that even DeMarco was able to . . . persuade . . . Bishop to explain himself.

Which really wasn't at all likely.

"So you think this is one of his master plans?"

"Don't you? I'd bet anything you like on the probability that he has another team on the other side of the vortex. Probably as much in the dark as we were."

Hollis winced. "Where the negative energy is? I'm guessing that is not a pleasant or safe place to be. Man, I wonder who drew the short straw for that assignment."

"Somebody who didn't know what they were walking into."

She hesitated, still staring ahead of them at the forest, but was driven to say, "Listen, I get as pissed at Bishop as any of us when he does this sort of thing, but there's always a method to his silence. He puts the right people in the right places at the right times. He'd never leave any of us in danger without multiple backup plans, and you know it."

"One of these days he's going to go too far. That's all I'm saying."

"Let's talk about it later," she suggested. "Because . . . there. I see something. Keep going straight."

"How far?" he asked, slowing the vehicle.

"Bishop said the electronics in the Jeep could be affected, so stop at least twenty yards out from the trees. What I'm seeing is to the right of that really big oak tree."

DeMarco continued on for another minute or so, then stopped the Jeep. He used his left hand to put the vehicle in park and turn off the engine, since his right hand was securely holding Hollis's left.

"Close enough?"

"Yeah, I think so."

"What do you see?" All DeMarco could see were trees.

"There's a funny kind of shimmer in the air beside that tree. Almost like an aura, but with nothing visible at the center." She kept her gaze on what Bishop had told them would be a doorway. "Damn, he was even right about the color. It's silvery, but shot through with dark streaks."

DeMarco looked at the stopwatch hanging from the rearview mirror, something also borrowed from the stables. "Almost time. It'll probably be easier for you to climb over the console than for me to."

"I'm afraid to look away even for a second," she confessed. "If I lose the doorway, I have a horrible feeling this whole thing falls apart. And if there's a team on the other side of the vortex, I'm guessing they need me to do my job in the worst way."

"Don't think about that. Don't worry about saving other asses Bishop put on the line. Whatever happens, this is on him."

"And I thought *I* was pissed," she murmured.

"Like I said, he's gone too far. Okay, since this is a nice working Jeep without a top, just stand up, and you should be able to almost step over the console."

Hollis wasn't at all sure about that, but she followed his instructions and managed not to make a sound of surprise when he somehow got his free arm around her to help her across the console and out of the Jeep. Without at all breaking her focus.

"You're sort of handy to have around," she noted lightly, still intent on that shimmering doorway.

"I try." He paused, then added, "If we start walking now, we should be about three feet away from that tree with about a minute to spare."

Suddenly even more nervous, Hollis said, "I know we have to start at a specific time, and I know we have to be at the fifth and final door at a specific time—and there's a lot of driving and distance in between, even assuming I can do this as quickly as Bishop believes I can. Hell, even assuming I can do it at all."

"All you have to do is follow your instincts. I won't let go of you no matter what." He began to lead her forward. "Just concentrate on opening the door, hold it open for one minute, then, when I tell you it's time, concentrate on closing it."

"I hope the clock in your head is a good one, because I can't judge time when I'm dealing with normal spiritual energy, much less something like this shit."

"The clock in my head is accurate to the second," he said calmly. "I'll let you know when to close the door."

"Okay." Hollis stopped suddenly. "Close enough. I hope. Jesus, that thing is . . . I've never seen anything like it."

"Get ready," DeMarco said. "On one, open the door. Five . . . four . . . three . . . two . . . one."

Hollis was never sure how she could do what she could do, but in that instant, she just did what she was told.

She opened the door.

The shimmering halo she stared at seemed to pulse, then grew larger until it was a good seven or eight feet top to bottom, and at least four feet wide. And its center was no longer empty, but swirled with every color imaginable. Swirled, sparkled, crackled—and then all the colors shot out toward Hollis.

She had no time to brace herself, and afterward confessed that there had probably been no way to do that anyway. It was like being hit with a blast of hot air, except that it tingled and tickled and stung and stroked, all in the same timeless moment. It washed over her and through her, and she felt the power of it somehow join with her own strength, increase it, felt her doubts and uncertainties fading and a new and startling clarity surround her.

"Get ready to close the door, Hollis."

It was almost an intrusion, that voice, and for a heartbeat she considered ignoring it. But her new clarity of mind told her that was a dangerous thought, a deceptive thought, and she concentrated instead on preparing to close the door she had opened.

"Five . . . four . . . three . . . two . . . one. *Now*."

With a confidence and ease that surprised her, Hollis closed the door.

The shimmery halo returned, shrank, and, as she watched it, shrank to only a glowing point no larger than an orange. Then vanished.

"Hollis?"

Hollis took a step back, abruptly keenly aware of her fingers linked with DeMarco's, of a connection that was much stronger now, even as she absorbed all the other new sensations.

Strength such as she had never felt in her life. Power she knew with absolute certainty she could tap into as she had never done before. And that strange, compelling clarity of mind and even of vision; she could literally *see* more clearly than she ever had before.

"Wow," she murmured. "And that's just the first door."

"No time to bask," DeMarco said, leading her toward their borrowed Jeep so they could hurry to the preselected eastern point of the giant compass they had superimposed over the property surrounding Alexander House.

East. The second door.

Again, that would take them some distance out from the house and the more manicured gardens, not pasture this time but still far enough away that Hollis couldn't see a spirit or possible spirit for at least a hundred yards.

"I wasn't basking," she protested. "I was . . . marveling. Did you *see* that? I mean, was it visible?"

"I saw your aura," he said, matter-of-fact. "Sort of silvery. Here, back over the console. Remember, we don't break the link now until after the final door is opened and closed. And from this point on we have to hurry if we have a hope of closing the vortex."

"Silvery?" Hollis did as he suggested, nimbly scooting across the Jeep's center gear console and into the passenger seat. "Interesting."

"Why?" He got the Jeep started and headed for the nearest pasture gate, so they could continue moving toward their eastern compass point, their path a wide circle around Alexander House.

She hesitated, then said, "It's just that your aura looks like that when your primal sense kicks in. The one that warns you when a gun or other weapon is pointed your way."

"So maybe you're tapping into something primal," he said after a moment.

"Or all that energy is changing me. Again." She thought about it, then shrugged. "Well, it feels like a good thing. So far, anyway. No nosebleed, no headache, and I don't feel the least bit tired. Energy to spare. I almost wish Bishop hadn't told me I'll need all the strength I gain at the four points in order to open and close the final door."

"I'm glad he warned you. It's out of character for him, but I'm glad he did it."

"I wonder why," Hollis muttered, suddenly uneasy. "He doesn't act out of character often, but when he does, it's usually as good as a giant red warning flag of trouble."

"A warning of something worse he didn't warn us about?"

Hollis untangled that in her head. "Yes. Maybe. Just . . . let's hurry and do this."

"Hold on," DeMarco told her, meaning it literally as he pushed the Jeep's speed over the uneven pasture terrain.

They couldn't break the link even for a second.

Not until it was over.

AT FIRST, LUTHER thought that the woods around the cabin were just unusually quiet; he couldn't even hear birds singing, which was odd, and even odder was the muffling sense that made him want to yawn widely, as if to equalize pressure in his ears. Then he realized, abruptly, that it wasn't the woods or anything in him. It was Callie.

Cesar stopped even before he did, halting the litter no more than thirty yards from the cabin. He didn't seem disturbed, nor did the three dogs following the litter closely. They simply looked at Luther and waited.

Luther looked at Callie. "What're you—"

With only a faint thread of strain in her voice, Callie said, "Bishop said I could do this. And what Bishop says we can do, even if we've never done it before, we find we can do."

"Are you shielding me?" he demanded.

"Sort of. Patching the crack in your shield and . . . making the whole thing stronger."

"Bishop told you to do that? In your condition? Goddammit, Callie, that's crazy."

"Jacoby is about to be . . . really distracted. And while he's distracted, we have to slip past him to that truck."

"Callie, I don't need—"

"It's not just for you. He's . . . already sensing us. I'm just trying to . . . make him work for it. We have to distract him on this side. For just a little while longer. It's important."

Luther swore under his breath and bent to give her a handkerchief. "Your nose is bleeding. Callie—"

She held the cloth to her nose, but her voice remained clear and calm. "We'll argue . . . about this later. Remember my condition. Weakened. Not sure how long I can keep this up."

"Jesus. Is your insane boss trying to get you killed?"

A ghost of a laugh escaped her. "Never. Or you. We're just trying to fix . . . something that could destroy . . . more than we could imagine."

"According to Bishop."

"Well, he's usually right, especially . . . about . . . stuff like this."

"I think he has you all hypnotized into believing that."

"Can't hypnotize a psychic. You know that. We need to move. Now. And you might want . . . to make sure I stay conscious. Not sure I can hold this on automatic."

Luther swore again, this time not so quietly, but turned away from Callie and walked beside Cesar as the powerful dog resumed pulling the litter carrying his mistress, and the silent group of man, woman, and dogs moved deeper into the forest toward the cabin rented by what had once been a man named Cole Jacoby.

And was now something so dark and twisted there was only one word to describe it.

Evil.

HOLLIS AND DEMARCO were out of the Jeep and walking toward the third compass point, south, a point that fell between the stable complex and the extensive "rear" gardens of Alexander House, when Hollis stopped abruptly and half turned to look behind them.

"Oh, wow," she murmured. "Creepy. Very creepy."

With the minutes counting down in his head, DeMarco turned to look as well, but all he saw was the slightly winding flagstone path that allowed the more athletic of guests to walk from the house to the stables, through the gardens that would be beautiful in spring and summer. Beyond that lay the covered pool and surrounding recreation areas, deserted to his eye, and beyond those the house itself.

DeMarco saw nothing unusual or out of place.

"What?"

Hollis cleared her throat. "They're . . . all looking this way. The spirits. In the gardens, around the pool, at the tables. Everywhere I can see. They're all just . . . standing there. Looking this way. Watching us."

DeMarco imagined that would look creepy. "Are they moving toward us?"

"No. Just facing this way. Like they're waiting. To attack. Like a zombie apocalypse. Man, I've gotta stop watching horror movies."

"Why would you?" DeMarco asked as he got them moving again toward the third compass point. "You basically live in one."

"Don't remind me. Okay, concentrating . . . This is getting easier. I see the doorway."

"Same as the first two?"

"Pretty much."

"Okay. Soon as we get close enough, stop and do your thing."

"How close are we on time?"

"We should hurry," DeMarco answered calmly. "We're not even sure exactly where in the basement we'll find the final doorway, so we need to reserve some time for that."

Hollis stopped. "Here. About three feet away."

He saw nothing but didn't let that bother him. "Go ahead. I'll know when it's open if your aura becomes visible again. But say it's open anyway, in case this doorway is different."

Hollis focused, concentrated. And just as he watched her aura flare brightly around her and felt the now-familiar warmth from their clasped hands creep up his arm, she said, "Open."

DeMarco automatically kept time in his head, watching her aura pulse with power, the steely sheen intensify in her once-blue eyes.

It hadn't faded away after the second doorway had been closed.

He hadn't told her about that.

Consequences. There are always consequences. Maybe Bishop's right and this will stabilize her brain so there are no more surprise psychic abilities. Maybe some of us will be able to stop holding our breath for fear the next new ability will be too much for her.

And maybe this will only make things worse.

Calmly, he said, "And . . . five . . . four . . ."

Maybe channeling so much energy will destroy her.

". . . three . . . two . . ."

Why the hell don't I stop this?

". . . one."

"Closed," Hollis said. She turned her head and looked up at him with a faint smile. "And on to door number four."

He turned and led her briskly back toward the Jeep. "How do you feel now?"

"Like I could run a marathon without breathing hard. Jesus, it's weird. This feeling. I think I could be a superhero. Seriously."

"You'd hate the tights."

"I could have a cape. I've always wanted to swirl a cape."

"Pictures of you on the news, on YouTube. People asking for autographs. You'd hate it."

"I don't know. It has its appeal."

He knew she wasn't serious.

But her eyes were even more metallic, and he didn't know what that meant, whether it was a good thing or a bad one.

CALLIE WAS SO focused on projecting her shield outward and maintaining its strength, so determined to safely deflect away whatever negative energy might be directed at any of them, she almost missed something else.

But Cesar didn't. They were just over halfway to Jacoby's cabin when he stopped, turned his head toward the slope above them, and whined softly. And, as usual, Callie heard his voice clearly in her mind.

Girl. Near.

Since she was facing back the way they'd come, more or less, Callie could see that Jacoby's dogs also reacted, though in their case it was a matter of tucked tails and visible uneasiness. Whatever canine thoughts they had were too unfocused for her to pick up, but Cesar's mind-voice remained clear and steady.

Pieces. Cut her up. Grave.

It was almost impossible to keep her focus as coldness rushed through Callie, but she hung on grimly to the only means she had of protecting all of them.

"What is it?" Luther asked, stepping back so he could see her face. "It's not like I'm leading him, but I'm assuming Cesar wouldn't have stopped without good reason."

Callie had sensed more than seen or heard Luther's determination to walk steadily even though his leg must have been giving him hell. She had also sensed his wired alertness and the frustration he struggled to hide at not being a hundred percent in a situation this deadly.

"Callie?"

She drew a breath, fighting to keep her focus. And to weigh her words carefully, because if Luther became too distracted here and now the consequences could be disastrous for more than just them. "Cesar is very good at finding things. Bombs. Drugs. Bodies."

Luther looked at Cesar, then turned his own head to look up the mountain slope above them. "Bodies. Are you saying Jacoby has killed someone?"

"We didn't get this far before. Cesar and me. I mean the last time. Since we found the blood. I didn't tell you because there was nothing we could do about it, but I trust him more than a blood test kit. That blood was human. Female. And the girl it came from . . . is buried somewhere upslope. Cut up in pieces."

THIRTEEN

The western compass point was reached, and this time Hollis found the doorway hovering just in front of a very tall granite boulder.

"Got it," she told her partner.

His rather coldly handsome face was, as it was much of the time, impassive, even enigmatic, but Hollis had been conscious even through her concentration on the doorways of his anxiety.

He was worried about her.

As they got out of the Jeep quickly without breaking physical contact, this particular art mastered by now, she briefly considered and then rejected bringing up the subject.

No time.

Besides, she was reasonably sure she knew why he was concerned. She had turned herself into a conduit to channel and even absorb raw energy—and much of it was dark energy.

She wasn't sure he knew that, though he might by now suspect as much. Bishop hadn't described it so, had in fact stated that the negative energy was on the other side of the doorways, the other side of the vortex, but Hollis had been a medium long enough to know that even the strongest mediums had little control over what came through an open doorway.

Bishop most certainly knew that.

Bishop had told her to open and then close these doorways. To channel the energy, releasing most, retaining some. And he had sent her and DeMarco here knowing this was the end game. He hadn't explained his reasons for choosing her over more powerful mediums in the unit, other than to say that this could help "seal" her abilities just as she was closing and sealing these doorways.

He'd said this might fix her.

Not in those terms, of course, but Hollis got it. She knew DeMarco got it as well. Maybe he even believed it, or had. Until he saw visible evidence of the energy she was channeling and absorbing into herself. Until he got some notion of the magnitude of the power.

But he still didn't know just how much of that energy was dark.

And even though Hollis had recognized it with the first doorway and that sly urging to ignore her partner's voice calling on her to close the door, she hadn't told him about it.

That hadn't been anything of her, that voice. It had

been the energy. It had been the evil. And she was strong enough to resist it.

They were approaching the fourth door, and even though Hollis knew there was no time for a discussion, she also knew that there was a danger in allowing DeMarco to even begin to question what they were doing.

It struck her only then, and forcibly, that she was aware of what he was feeling—and it was a one-way connection.

He wasn't reading her.

At all.

She wasn't broadcasting. Her energy contained? New energy providing a kind of shield for her? There was no time to find out for sure.

Pushing that aside to deal with later, if necessary, she said calmly, "It's not that this will fix me, you know."

"What?" He almost stopped them.

But Hollis kept steadily approaching the fourth door.

"Why Bishop sent us here. Sent me, knowing this is what I'd have to do. It's not about fixing me."

"It's about closing this vortex." There was, in his voice, something of the tension and anxiety she felt in him. And the awareness that there was no time to fully discuss this. For which he blamed Bishop.

Oh, Bishop, so many people are going to be pissed at you the next time you see them.

"Closing the vortex, certainly. But there's a reason he wanted it to be me. And it isn't about fixing me."

"You're not broken." His voice roughened on those words, then steadied. "Then why you?"

"He knew it couldn't corrupt me."

"What?"

"The dark energy. The evil."

DeMarco did stop them then. He stared at her, and even though she could literally hear the seconds ticking away in his mind, he made time to say, "Dark energy. If it's dark, why does it . . . why does your aura sparkle? You said the spirits here had dark auras, but yours isn't. I can see it now. I watch it while you channel the energy. It's bright. It's light, not dark."

"What you see is what I'm releasing. Like . . . dirty water through a filter. I'm the filter. It goes in dark and comes out light."

He stared at her, frowning. "If you're the filter, what happens to you?"

"I told you. I'm stronger. More powerful."

"But if that's from dark energy—"

"That's why Bishop sent me. Dark energy, evil, can't corrupt me, Reese. I've already faced it. And survived it. Years ago. Evil did its best to destroy me, and it failed."

He drew a quick breath and let it out more slowly. "Are you saying evil only gets one shot?"

"I'm saying evil can only win if it deceives. If it hides behind something we aren't afraid of. It can't do that with me. I smelled the brimstone. I heard its voice. I saw its face. Not with these eyes, but with this mind, this understanding." She saw something in his almost impassive face, and felt more.

"Hollis—"

"It's all right, you know. That these eyes have changed. That they look so different right now. Maybe they'll . . .

unnerve other people if they stay this way even after we're done here, but for the first time, they feel like my eyes. Not the eyes of a stranger. I can *see*, Reese, as well as or better than I ever have. I hope I keep that at the end of the day. I really do. Even if the cost is eyes that look like shiny dimes."

"You feel they look that way?"

"I know they do. For now, at least. Maybe forever. And I don't mind at all."

After a moment, he nodded, and they continued the remaining few yards toward the fourth doorway.

"Tinted contact lenses," he said.

"That could work," she agreed.

"You're sure you can handle this?"

"Absolutely. And, you know, it might just fix me. Ultimately."

"You aren't broken."

"A debate for another day."

"There's no debate. You aren't broken."

Hollis stopped just about three feet from the fourth doorway. She felt herself smiling. "Okay. Ready?"

"Have at it."

LUTHER WAS CLEARLY disturbed by the knowledge that Jacoby—or the dark energy controlling him—had committed murder, especially given the brutal disposal of the body. But he was also clearly anxious to get Callie safely into the hands of a doctor as soon as possible.

"How many times has he killed?"

Callie shook her head. "I have no way of knowing that, though given how long he's been up here, I can't believe he had enough time to kill more than once." *It was the torture that fed the evil, and torture takes time.*

But she didn't say that out loud.

"When it's all over and Jacoby is dead or in custody, we'll make sure this whole mountainside is searched. For her. For the place where she was held and hurt. And for any others he may have killed."

"There's no time," Luther said, mostly under his breath.

"I know. We need to go." She looked at her watch. "It's being distracted now. Being given something else to think about. Besides us. We need to take advantage of that. We need to keep moving. Cesar knows where we're going. And he'll take the most direct route possible and still avoid the cabin."

"You're sure he—it—is in the cabin?"

Callie drew a breath, trying to ignore the increasing pain of her wound. Ignoring the weakness. "All I can tell you for certain is that the dark energy that was trying to touch us not long after we left my cabin isn't trying right now. But that doesn't mean it won't again."

After a moment, Luther turned and began walking again, even as Cesar continued. Jacoby's dogs followed the litter closely, almost stepping on each other's paws they were so close. Silent and still visibly anxious.

"Stop trying to protect me," Luther said suddenly, his

voice low. "I can see what it's taking out of you. You need to conserve your strength, Callie."

All too aware that she was weakening fast, she replied, "You know what it can do."

Luther paused briefly and then continued walking, this time beside the litter. "Believe me, I remember. But I don't believe it could control me like that again. Not like that."

"Why not?"

"Maybe because I'd recognize the trick this time."

"And would you?"

"Yes."

Callie bit back a sound of pain as the litter moved over a rougher patch of ground and she was jostled a bit.

Sorry.

It's okay. Just keep going, Cesar.

"What if you don't recognize it?" she asked Luther.

"I will. Just stop trying to shield me." He hesitated, then added, "But if I *do* get taken over again, do us both a favor and shoot me. I'd rather die on this mountain than live knowing I hurt you. Or worse."

Callie knew very well that he wasn't being dramatic or even especially heroic. He *was* the kind of man to whom losing control of his own actions would be a special kind of hell, as would harming an innocent.

She responded by saying calmly, "Well, the thing is, if I shoot you, it's probable neither one of us will make it off this mountain alive. Cesar can't drive, and by the time we get there, *if* we get there, I won't be in any condition to myself. So let's not let evil win this time, huh? I'll try to keep a patch on that crack in your shield, but the rest is up to you."

Luther nodded, but he was also frowning. "That may be the best thing I can use to protect my own mind," he said. "The knowledge that losing control of it dooms all of us."

Callie opened her mouth to say something, but then paused as she became aware of a distant dark flicker.

"Luther—"

"I know. It may be distracted, but us escaping isn't part of its plan. I can almost see it reaching for us."

"Stay aware of that. It can only get in by deception."

"You might have mentioned that sooner."

Callie almost laughed. "Sorry. A recent realization, I'm afraid. This is not a kind of evil I've faced before, but . . . it's always a trick. How evil takes hold. How it attacks and controls the unwilling." She realized it was getting harder to breathe, but tried to ignore that. "Evil . . . is deception. It can't be stared in the face, its real face. Except by someone . . . who understands . . . what it is."

"Callie?"

Her eyes were nearly closed. "Even . . . when I . . . sleep. My shield. Even when I sleep. It protects me. But not anyone else. Not you."

"Dammit, Callie."

Her eyelids flickered, and she sent a last glance up at him, murmuring, "It doesn't want me. I'm weak. I can't do anything . . . for it. Except . . . distract you. Don't be distracted. Know it for what it . . . is. Stare it . . . in the face."

Luther knew she was out. And he also knew that just like her attempt to patch the crack in his shield, his attempt to patch up her wound had ultimately failed.

She was losing blood; if he couldn't get her off this mountain very, very soon, she'd die.

. . . or you can help her along. That's the best thing to do, you know that. You don't want her to suffer. Or . . . do you?

Completely aware of the voice in his mind, Luther said calmly to Callie's dog, "Cesar, keep going. No matter what. Take her to the truck." He had no idea if the dog could possibly understand, but added anyway, "And if I don't come soon, find a way to save her. Get her off this mountain."

Still moving, the Rottweiler turned his head and looked back at Luther, then continued moving, faster now.

She'll be better off. And so will you. I promise.

Luther recognized where they were by now, and knew how close they were to the cabin.

"Get her to the truck," he repeated to the dog, and then he set off in the direction of the cabin.

Straight to the cabin.

HOLLIS GOT OUT of the Jeep near the front door of Alexander House, hardly even aware of coming out the driver's side, her hand still locked with DeMarco's. She was looking around and, as they started for the door, said, "*Really* creepy now. Definitely the zombie apocalypse. There must be two dozen spirits out here, all watching us. No expression. No movements. Just watching us."

"What about their auras?"

She hesitated for just a moment, concentrating, then shook her head. "I can't see their auras. A flicker of color here and there, but nothing complete."

"Color?"

"Yeah."

"Then maybe this is working. You may have channeled away enough of the negative energy to almost free them from this place."

"You think that's why their auras were all dark? It wasn't their energy at all, but the negative energy holding them here?"

"As good an explanation as any other," he said.

"It's good enough for me."

They didn't ring the bell but went straight in, surprising Anna Alexander at the bottom of the stairs in the huge foyer.

"Were you successful?" she asked, clearly still baffled by their earlier request for a Jeep and a stopwatch, not to mention a compass.

"Ask us in half an hour or so," Hollis told her. "Which way to the basement, Anna?"

Even more baffled, the older woman replied, "It's—the door is off the kitchen hallway near the main storage room for this floor."

"Is it locked?" DeMarco asked.

"No, of course not."

They left her there without another word, and it wasn't until they'd nearly reached the hallway they needed that Hollis said absently, "Bet she's wishing she hadn't invited us to stay. We're weird houseguests, you can tell that's what she's thinking."

"I have no idea what she's thinking," DeMarco said. "I haven't been able to read her or Owen."

"Really?"

"Not all that surprising. Even with a seventy-five percent success rate, that still leaves a lot of people who aren't on my frequency."

"Huh."

"Is that bothering you for some reason?"

"We'll talk about it later," Hollis said. "There—is that the door we're looking for?"

It was. And in a few short minutes, they found themselves standing in an enormous but low-ceilinged basement filled with the clutter of generations, its only virtue being that the lighting was excellent for a basement.

Almost too good.

"Picture frames," Hollis said. "Old picture frames and broken furniture, and trunks filled with God knows what. Why do people save stuff like that? I mean, donate it if it's usable and scrap it if it isn't. Why do people hang on to stuff?"

"Beats me. But never mind the stuff. Bishop said you should be able to see this doorway clearest of all. Let's try to find the center of this space."

"We're running out of time, aren't we?"

"Yes," DeMarco replied.

Hollis looked at the cluttered space with a feeling of helplessness she didn't like. At all. "You've got a better sense of direction than I do," she told her partner. "Given the compass points, where we found the doorways, where would the center of the compass fall?"

He hesitated for only a few seconds, then began leading Hollis through the maze of Alexander family stuff. "This way. I think."

There was a lot of stuff. And the path they had to take toward the center of the enormous space was a winding one.

In the end, they nearly fell through the doorway.

"Whoa!" Hollis held on to DeMarco's hand with both of hers, halting him abruptly. "One more step and you'd be in the thing. It's right there."

They both looked down at the concrete floor. DeMarco saw a large, odd sort of dimple in the concrete. Hollis saw their fifth and final doorway.

DeMarco said, "I'm betting there's some sort of hollow underneath that. Didn't Bishop say there was likely a cave connecting this side of the vortex with the other side?"

"Yeah. And he was nicely evasive about just where the other side of the vortex is. Bet he knows, and probably to the inch."

"We'll deal with Bishop later," DeMarco said, something in his voice indicating that he had plans along those lines. "For now, this thing has to be sealed. He said it would be the hardest one by far. The one doorway that wants to stay open."

"How are we on time?"

"If you can get it opened and then closed again in the next five minutes, we should be good. After that point, Bishop said the other side of the vortex would probably be opened, and then it can never be closed."

"But no pressure," Hollis muttered.

Instead of standing beside her this time, DeMarco stepped behind her, shifting their hands without losing contact so that his left and right hands held hers. Their fingers laced together.

"Go for it," DeMarco said.

THE VOICE IN his head was still talking to him, but Luther wasn't paying enough attention to even know what it was saying. He was too busy circling the cabin slowly, gun drawn, frowning at the other sounds he heard.

It took him several minutes to find a doorway to the cellar, open, and he went down the rough, packed-dirt steps without hesitation.

What he saw was surreal, a scene out of some nightmarish movie or book. Candles of all shapes and sizes were placed all around the periphery of the storage space, on old, raw wooden shelves that still held an occasional dust-coated canning jar or rotting basket or mildewed box that had once held the necessities of life on the side of a mountain.

Candles flickering, lighting the space with odd, jerky move-ments.

Or maybe that was just him.

He was digging.

The hole was in the center of the space, only about two feet deep and twice that across, with dirt mounded around half of it. He stood in the hole, pounding a pick-axe three times, four—and then laying it aside and picking up a shovel. Prodding and scooping the loosened dirt, tossing it on the mound already accumulated.

He didn't even seem to realize that Luther was there.

At the foot of the steps, his gun trained on what had been Cole Jacoby, Luther just watched for a few minutes.

Kill him. Go ahead. Do it. You know you want to. He shot Callie, didn't he? And doesn't he deserve to die for that? You're a soldier, you know it's the truth.

Ah. So that sly, sneaky voice was back. Luther wondered how on earth it had ever managed to control his mind. But he knew. It had been able to do that because he hadn't known what he was fighting.

Now he did.

"Should I call you Jacoby?" he asked over the sounds of digging. "Or did you stop being him a long time ago?"

He hadn't really expected an answer. Then the man in the hole turned, and Luther found himself gazing at his own face.

FOURTEEN

Hollis wasn't at all sure the rushing sound wasn't in her own head until DeMarco practically yelled in her ear.

"Is it my imagination, or is something trying to pull you in this time?"

"Hang on," she yelled back, without taking her eyes off the darkly shimmering doorway. "Whatever's on the other side is desperate to stop me doing this. It's pushing energy too fast."

She really thought it would overwhelm her for what seemed like an endless moment of time, but DeMarco held on to her, an anchor and lifeline, and she didn't hesitate to pour every bit of her own physical strength into the strangely instinctive process of filtering and redirecting dark energy.

Every black fragment or filament of energy that was flung at her was grabbed, cleaned of its darkness somehow by her own positive energy filter, and then channeled back through the doorway.

The rushing sound was so loud because at this doorway alone energy was going both ways simultaneously.

Hollis could hear, around the edges of her mind, the panicked whispers that grew louder and eventually began to keen in misery, but the rushing of energy simply overwhelmed them—not Hollis.

It seemed to last forever, and then there was an abrupt instant of utter stillness and quiet, a quiet so loud it hurt the ears. Hollis wanted to yawn widely to clear her ears, but before she could even begin that automatic action, the stillness was shattered by what sounded to her like a gunshot.

As she watched, the sparkling doorway below her shrank until it was the size of a pumpkin, and then the size of a grapefruit, and then only a spark the size of a cherry.

Obviously, I'm hungry. When did I last eat?

The cherry-sized spark made a soft but sharp *pop*, and then it vanished.

Completely.

The vortex was closed and sealed. Hollis wasn't at all sure how she knew that, but she did.

"Did I hear a gunshot?" DeMarco wanted to know.

She unlaced the fingers of one set of hands so she could turn to face him, pleased when he made no attempt to release her other hand. "I thought I heard one. Interesting. Did you hear the quiet little pop there at the end?"

DeMarco shook his head. "No, I just felt you relax."

Almost idly, she said, "I wonder if that shot was real."

"Do you care?"

"Just curious. Mostly because I have no idea how all this worked." She stared at him for a moment, then said, "Will it sound really anticlimactic if I say I'm hungry?"

"Not to me. Are you really okay otherwise? No weakness or dizziness or anything?"

She considered, then shrugged. "No, I feel fine. Better than fine, really."

"Ready-to-run-a-marathon fine?"

Not without a certain pang of regret, she said, "No, most of that extra energy and strength seems to be gone. I just feel oddly like I've had a relaxing vacation—and at the same time would really like a nap. After I eat a big plateful of something good."

"So you're back to normal."

"I guess. How about the eyes?"

He smiled slightly as he gazed into the eyes. "Blue. But not the same blue they were before."

She really wanted a mirror right then. "Oh. Well, then, I guess we're done here. At least with this part of the trip. The part I expect Bishop was most concerned with."

"Leaving—?"

"Hopefully passing on a message from Daniel to Anna. Assuming I can contact him now."

"Because when the vortex was closed—"

"—other doors seem to have closed along with it. At least, I'm not feeling all the spiritual energy I was before. Let's get out of here. I want to find out if all those spirits really were able to leave this place."

LUTHER WAS FROZEN for an instant, but then he recognized a final, desperate attempt to trick him, and as easily as that he was looking at the haggard face of Cole Jacoby rather than his own.

For at least a minute, he felt sorry for Jacoby.

Until he remembered that was only the shell that used to be a man. A bank robber who, somewhere along the way, opened by accident a door he should never have found, and lost more than his soul in the process.

A heartbeat later, everything happened fast.

Jacoby dropped the shovel and reached for the pickaxe, swinging it above his head, his face transformed from haggard to almost indescribably evil as he lunged toward Luther.

It was a small space.

Luther fired and hit Jacoby squarely in the chest.

Even as close as they were, the bullet didn't slam him backward as so dramatically depicted in the movies and on TV. The evil face turned to one of infinite surprise, and then Jacoby simply dropped in a boneless heap to the musty earth of the cellar.

Luther waited a cautious moment during which he could have sworn he could hear, somewhere distant, a river rushing. Then he eased forward and checked for a pulse.

Jacoby's skin was cold and clammy, and there was no pulse.

Is there even a law against shooting a dead man?

There was no time to linger and wonder. Luther turned and hurried up the earthen steps, then shouted Cesar's name, heard a deep-throated bark in response, and ran toward it.

The truck was there, parked at the end of what might have been a kind of dirt road, its rear end toward the cabin to aid in unloading supplies. And beside it stood Cesar and the litter, with Jacoby's three dogs sitting nearby. The only one who was clearly tense and anxious was Cesar, who whined loudly.

Luther holstered his weapon and bent to check Callie. To his immense relief, he found a pulse, but it was faint, and the pallor of her skin told him she was still losing blood.

Without wasting another moment, he checked the door of the truck, finding it unlocked and the keys under the mat as Callie had expected them to be, because that was usual on the mountain. An oddly trusting thing, but a rugged vehicle up here really could make the difference between survival and death.

Luther was as careful as he could be and still moved quickly to get Callie out of the litter and onto the backseat of the Jeep and secured as well as possible against what was sure to be a bumpy ride to town.

Assuming he could find town.

He unfastened Cesar from the litter's harness, then went to open the hatchback of the truck and whistle Jacoby's dogs in, an implicit command they obeyed with every sign of joy.

When he shut the hatchback and returned to the driver's-side door, which was still open, he was surprised not to find Cesar inside the vehicle. Instead, the Rottweiler was standing a couple of yards in front of the Jeep, on the sad excuse for a road.

"Cesar, c'mon, boy. We have to go."

The dog barked, then turned and moved another yard or two down the road, pausing to look back at the man.

The message was clear. Night was approaching. Cesar knew the way to town. Left to his own navigation, Luther didn't doubt he could wander around in these mountains for days.

Callie didn't have days.

He got in the truck and started the engine, muttering under his breath, "Christ, I hope I'm not wrong about this."

Then he put it in gear and began following the Rottweiler.

HOLLIS STOOD OUTSIDE the conservatory and gazed down over the gardens and pool. And smiled.

"No spirits?" DeMarco guessed.

"No spirits. Though I sort of wish I'd been able to see them go. Can't help wondering if they just popped out of existence like the energy cherry in the basement."

DeMarco took her hand and began leading her back toward the house. "You need food," he said.

Hollis didn't argue, and only a few minutes later they were enjoying what a cheerful maid referred to as "a little something before dinner."

"They do know how to spoil you here," Hollis observed.

"Oh, yeah."

"I wonder where Anna and Owen are."

"I asked while you were off washing your hands. Thomas said with great dignity that they would see us at our convenience in the Grand Parlor. I can almost see Owen tapping his foot."

Hollis winced, took a drink of very sweet iced tea, and said, "I suppose an objective observer could say we've sort of taken advantage of their hospitality. I mean, bent on fixing Bishop's vortex rather than spending more time trying to contact Daniel."

DeMarco looked thoughtful, but when he spoke, it was to say, "I say we keep on calling it Bishop's vortex. No—Bishop's Vortex. In caps. And talk about it a lot when he's around."

"You really are pissed at him."

"You could say."

"Come on, it all ended okay."

"On this side of the vortex. We don't yet know what happened on the other side."

Hollis frowned. "Yeah. I'd forgotten. I hope nobody got hurt over there. Wherever there *is*. I mean, there was something that sounded a lot like a gunshot."

"I'd suggest we call Bishop and ask, but part of me doesn't want to give him the satisfaction."

"You two boys need to learn to play nice."

He eyed her. "You're just as annoyed as I am."

"Yes, but I plan to be adult about it. I'm going to look Bishop square in the eye—and then kick him in the shin."

DeMarco smiled, but then sighed. "We both know he's never going to change. Still, I plan to have a few words with him about this little trip."

"Oh, so do I. But in the meantime, we probably should go and talk to Anna and Owen. Since we've been racing all around their property all afternoon and yelling at each other in their basement. They might be curious."

"You think?"

"Sarcasm doesn't suit you," she told him severely.

He followed her away from the table and out of the dining room, saying merely, "If you think you cornered the market on sarcasm, think again. By the way, what do you think of your new eyes?"

She glanced back over her shoulder at him out of eyes that were still blue, but definitely changed. "I could get used to them, I think," she said. "Sort of waiting to find out whether I get to keep the clarity of vision. I definitely like that."

DeMarco might have responded to that, but Thomas was before them suddenly, opening the doors to the Grand Parlor, expressionless and yet somehow conveying disapproval.

Feeling a bit sheepish, Hollis led the way into the room and to the seating group nearest the door, where Owen made a halfhearted effort to rise from his comfortable chair. There was a silver tray on the table at the center of the grouping holding the remains of coffee and pastries, and on the other side of the table, Anna sat with her customary almost-rigid posture.

Hollis took the third seat of the four, and as DeMarco

took the last chair, she said to their host and hostess, "We're really sorry about today. All the rushing around and . . . Well, we're sorry. But I *can* tell you that it wasn't exactly useless activity."

"Did you see Daniel?" Anna asked eagerly.

"Well . . . no." Hollis bit her bottom lip, then said, "We found a way to release the other spirits here."

"All of them?" Owen asked dryly.

Hollis had expected more direct scorn, so her answer was less sharp than it might have been. "Look, I don't expect you to believe me, but they were trapped here. A lot of souls, being prevented from going on to wherever they were supposed to go next. This was sort of a natural . . . The geography of this valley was—"

She decided to give it up.

"Never mind. Anna, I hope the reason I haven't been able to contact Daniel before now was because it was like looking for a needle in a pile of needles. The others are gone now, as far as I can tell. So maybe I can contact Daniel. But I can't promise success. Reese and I don't want to trespass on your hospitality any longer, though, so we'll drive back to town tomorrow. If you do want me to keep trying to contact Daniel, I'm willing. But we should stay in town."

"Vending machines," DeMarco murmured. "No wireless Internet. Oddly low, lumpy beds."

Even Owen smiled. "Being the only motel in Devil's Gap, the Horizon doesn't have to try very hard."

"It doesn't try at all." Hollis cleared her throat. "We've been extremely comfortable here. Extremely. But I haven't been able to deliver what you asked of me, Anna, and the Horizon will be fine until I do. It's only fair. That—"

She stared past Anna, watching a tall, distinguished-looking man walk around a giant potted palm and come to stand just behind Anna's right shoulder. He was smiling.

He was Daniel Alexander.

"Or," Hollis said, after a brief glance down at the gooseflesh on her arm, "maybe we'll just go home tomorrow."

Anna looked frozen. "He . . . he's here?"

"Standing right behind you." To the spirit, she said, "Where have you been? I think every spirit in the state was here, except for you."

Calmly, he said, "Miss Templeton, if you had contacted me immediately, you and your partner wouldn't have remained here long enough to do what you needed to do."

"That's why you stayed out of sight?"

"It seemed best."

Anna looked over her shoulder, then desperately at Hollis. "He's speaking to you?"

"Sorry, sorry. Yes, he's speaking." Hollis sometimes forgot she was the only one in the room hearing and seeing what she was hearing and seeing. But then she glanced at DeMarco—and saw that his slightly widened eyes were fixed on the spirit.

"You see him too," she said slowly.

"A fun new toy," DeMarco said slowly. "My turn, I guess."

"About time." Hollis looked back at Anna, shoving yet

another thing aside to be dealt with later. "He said he stayed out of sight because he knew we were here to do something else. Freeing the other spirits." There was really no reason to mention the vortex, she decided.

"My brother didn't believe in ghosts," Owen said rather harshly.

Still calm, Daniel offered a message, which Hollis relayed, trying not to laugh. "He said to tell you that when you're up to your ass in alligators, it's a little difficult to remember that your main objective was to drain the swamp."

Owen actually paled. "That—was on a poster in my bedroom when we were kids."

"So he said. And no offense, Owen, but Anna's been waiting a long time to talk to Daniel, so . . ."

He remained silent, his gaze scanning the area all around his sister-in-law's chair.

Anna whispered, "I need to know it's him."

Hollis watched that distinguished face soften as he looked down at his widow, and she really, really wished Anna could see what she saw.

Daniel said, "The message I promised to give her is simple. This is no trick, no deception, no con. I am the love of her life, as she is the love of mine. I am always with her, and I always will be. She carries me wherever she goes, not because of my wedding ring, but because I will never wish to be anywhere but at her side."

Hollis repeated the message carefully, sentence by sentence. And when she finished, she saw Anna relax for the first time. Saw a look of peace and contentment soften her face.

The older woman hooked a finger inside the high neckline of her dress and pulled out a fine chain that was always hidden inside her clothing. Hanging on the chain was a man's wide gold wedding band.

"Thank you," she said to Hollis.

"My pleasure." Hollis looked up at Daniel. "If I could give her the gift of seeing you, hearing your voice, I would."

"I know. But you gave her peace, Miss—Hollis. You gave her peace. Thank you for that."

"I'm glad I could help."

"Tell her I want her to enjoy her life. To travel, make new friends, whatever makes her happy. We'll be together again when it's time."

"I'll tell her."

He bowed his head slightly, looked down at his widow with another of those loving smiles, then slowly faded away.

"No light," Hollis said to DeMarco. "You see now why I find all this a little bit confusing. Sometimes a light, sometimes not."

"I don't think he's going anywhere." DeMarco looked at Anna with a slight smile. "He really is always with you. But he wants you to be happy and enjoy your life. Stop running around looking for psychics to tell you what you've always known."

"You're tampering with the text," Hollis muttered.

DeMarco sent her a look but continued to smile at Anna. She returned the smile, then got to her feet, keeping the two men seated with a curiously elegant gesture.

"I think I'll go to my rooms and rest a bit before dinner. It's been a . . . very eventful day. I'll see you all later."

When the door closed behind her, Owen sighed rather heavily. "Well, at least now maybe she'll be content. I can thank you for that, and with all sincerity."

Hollis eyed him. "You're welcome. Still not convinced I really saw Jamie Bell?"

His expression didn't change. "I think . . . the message got through. And like my sister-in-law, I can at least know a kind of peace."

She shrugged. "Well, I'll take that. I'm not out to convince the world I'm a genuine medium, Owen. And we have enjoyed your hospitality. Thank you."

"Don't mention it." He got to his feet, adding, "I think I'll go make a few calls before dinner. See you then."

Hollis watched the door close behind *him*, and then said to DeMarco, "Isn't it fun, being a medium?"

With more expression on his face than was usual for him, he replied, "So far, not loving it. Unnerving."

"Yeah, well, just wait until—" She watched as Brooke suddenly appeared, and she almost laughed as, out of the corner of her eye, she saw her partner start in surprise.

"Where have *you* been?" she demanded. "I thought you were going to help me learn about being a medium."

"I've been near all the time," Brooke said, rather absently. "You were doing fine, you didn't need my help."

"I might," DeMarco muttered.

Brooke looked at him, then at Hollis. "You're going to enjoy this, aren't you?"

"Bet your ass." Hollis saw DeMarco shift a bit and said

to him, "Trust me, she may look like a kid, but she's older than both of us."

"I really am," Brooke said to him. Then she frowned and added, "I'm sorry. You're remembering the Brooke I was. At the Church."

Hollis half closed her eyes. "Damn, I'd forgotten that. Sorry, Reese."

"Unnerving," he said to her, eyeing Brooke. "I didn't know her, really, just to see her. Still . . ."

Brooke waved a hand, her gesture as curiously elegant as Anna's had been. "Stop feeling guilty about that. And talking about me as if I weren't here."

"Excuse me," DeMarco murmured.

Brisk now, Brooke said, "Because we have other things to talk about."

"Such as?" Hollis asked politely.

"Well, two things. Bishop's on his way. And then there's the money."

"What money?"

"The nearly ten million dollars that Owen Alexander has been hiding for Anna's younger half brother. The half brother who hadn't known she existed until he stumbled on the information while he was bored and researching his own past. So many people can't resist using the Net to see what's been printed or written about them. He uncovered more than he expected to find."

"Brooke," Hollis began, not even sure what she was going to ask.

"And discovered even more when he came here looking for her. And found Owen instead."

FIFTEEN

Callie had drifted in and out for some time she couldn't measure. Sometimes painful things were being done to her. Sometimes voices talked over her, one of them rather harsh and impatient. And sometimes there was just peace broken only by mechanical-sounding clicks and whirs and beeps.

And an occasional soft whine that was familiar.

She had no idea how long she'd been out of it, and she was a bit fuzzy on the events that had occurred before she had lost consciousness.

I was shot. By an arrow. Because I was dumb, mostly. Luther . . . patched me up as best he could. And then . . . I was on the litter? Long way to . . . Jacoby's cabin. I think. What then? Don't remember.

When she finally forced open her eyes, the first thing she realized was that Cesar was lying beside her on the bed. The hospital bed. He was mostly alongside her legs, which put his big head at just about her hip level.

The whine she had recognized was him. Worried about her.

She moved her hand, finding just enough energy to lift it and place it on the broad head of her anxious dog.

"Hey, boy."

Scare me. Don't.

"Sorry." She saw the IV taped to her hand and frowned a little, her gaze following the tubing up to a bag of clear liquid.

"So you're finally back with us. Don't ever scare me like that again."

Callie turned her head and saw Luther sitting in a chair on the other side of the bed. His face was calm, but . . . haggard. Weary.

Beyond him, to her surprise, she saw squeezed into a corner a long couch with a rather loud print fabric, and on it in a pile were Jacoby's three dogs, sound asleep.

She returned her gaze to Luther, brows lifting in a mute question.

"They bend the rules in small-town clinics," he told her. "Cesar wasn't about to leave you, which nobody here decided to argue about, though he stopped himself outside the operating room and waited there patiently until they wheeled you out. And the other three decided the same, or followed his lead. Whichever. Point is, they're allowed. Besides, there's only one other patient here at the moment, recovering from an appendectomy, and she's at the other end of the building. We moved that god-awful couch in from the waiting room so the dogs would have a place to nap. Rugs are frowned upon, apparently, as tripping hazards."

He paused, then said, "The docs here approved your work on me, just so you know. Other than a fresh bandage, I was good to go. Your wound was a bit trickier, because as it turned out, that arrow nicked an artery. That's why you lost so much blood. But they were able to repair the tear and replace at least some of the blood you lost. You can probably walk out of here in a couple of days."

Callie absorbed that. Now that she was awake, she felt surprisingly well, so apparently the long sleep had done her good.

"Here." He was holding a glass with a straw in front of her. "Some water. Your throat is probably too dry to try talking."

She sipped the water, feeling her indeed dry and slightly sore throat relax. After that, she was able to ask the question uppermost in her mind, even if a bit huskily.

"Jacoby?"

"Dead." Without going into details about that, Luther continued in a slightly wry voice. "While the docs were working on you, I talked to the sheriff. Despite what you said, it appears he's enjoying the unusual excitement in his town, even with retirement looming. Said it was the most interesting his job had ever been, and he only wished he'd known what was happening sooner. Mind you, he doesn't have to be up on the mountain with the feds and search teams who've been at it since dawn, and he did show the requisite sober regret for the girl even if she wasn't a local, but—"

"They found her?"

"Yeah, a couple of hours ago. Just as you said, in a shallow grave, and . . . dismembered. Well, actually cut into smaller pieces. No local or even regional missing girl or woman matching the general description of her face, hair and eye color. They're comparing that info to missing-person reports, female, all up and down the Blue Ridge and into adjoining states, but it's a long list. In the meantime, they'll run her fingerprints, try to match dental records or, failing that, DNA. I'm told it could take weeks, though the feds sent everything to their lab and say it should be quicker than that, at least if her prints or DNA are on file. In the meantime, there's an army up on the mountain, some looking for more bodies nobody wants to find, and some looking for the stolen money everybody wants to find. And a few still processing the section of mine shaft Jacoby used for his torture chamber; it's a couple hundred yards higher up from his cabin. I got a description from one of the feds, and that's all I want. Don't need to see the place.

"It's late morning on Saturday, if you're wondering. We got here last night, almost entirely thanks to Cesar. He ran in front of the truck, showing me the way through that insane tangle of old mining and logging roads. Without his help, we'd still be up there on the mountain. And you'd likely be dead. The docs here told me if we'd gotten to the clinic even an hour later, you likely wouldn't have made it."

Callie absorbed all *that*, her hand resting on Cesar's head, fingers absently pulling gently on his silky ears.

Thanks, pal.

Happy.

Luther cocked his head, looking back and forth from her to her dog. "You two really do communicate. Telepathically?"

"Something like that. Picking up on it?"

"I think so." He was cautious. "I'm still getting used to this stuff, but there've been a few times since yesterday I caught what seemed to be a word or two, and it didn't seem . . . like a person."

"No, his thoughts are different. Partly emotional. Sometimes concepts more than words. With other dogs, like Jacoby's three, it's almost entirely emotion, and really unfocused. They haven't worked with a telepath the way Cesar's worked with me his whole life. He's learned to use words to express his thoughts and emotions. They don't know how to do that. At least, not yet."

"Planning on working with them, are you?"

"Maybe. Probably. Though I'm not sure about the details. I travel a lot. Cesar travels with me, but four dogs traveling with me would probably be a bit much."

"Well, I had a feeling you'd want to find them a safe home. I called Maggie at Haven. There are already several dogs, at the main house and throughout the compound. Most are pets of operatives or employees; some belong to Maggie and John. Big place, kind people, lots of acreage on which to safely run if that's what they like. Maggie said they're welcome."

He paused, then added, "And you'd be welcome to visit them as often as you like. Work with them yourself, or teach one or two Haven operatives how to do it."

"Like you?"

Luther met her gaze, his own a little amused and something else. "Haven has plenty of telepaths, and so does the SCU. But telepaths who can communicate with animals . . . Let's just say that opens up interesting possibilities. After witnessing firsthand the sort of things Cesar can do, the kind of help he can offer in dangerous situations—because guiding me off the mountain was his idea, not mine—I'm fairly anxious to learn more about those interesting possibilities."

Callie nodded slowly, thoughtfully. "I imagine Bishop would give me time to spend at Haven so we could explore those possibilities. I mean, bound to be helpful to have more investigative tools for the toolbox."

"That was my thinking."

"I imagine we can work something out."

It was Luther's turn to nod, gravely. "For the sake of psychic research if nothing else."

"Absolutely."

Flirting? Cesar wanted to know.

Callie was momentarily startled, since it wasn't a word or even a concept that she had worked on with her dog. But she supposed it was certainly possible he had picked up the concept on his own. Because he was a very smart dog, and he was acutely observant when it came to the subtleties of human behavior.

Not subtle.

She stared at her relaxed dog for a moment, gazing into calm brown eyes, then returned her attention to Luther as he laughed.

"No, not subtle at all. I suppose we can work on that. Or just not bother."

"It's been less than a week," she pointed out.

"It's been a lifetime. Two lifetimes. You have to admit, a lot was packed into the last few days. You saved my life. Cesar and I saved yours. I think there's a Chinese proverb or something about a saved life belonging to you. So, in our case—"

"Don't you dare," Callie said, trying not to laugh.

"It's a three-way," he said with unexpected and rather beguiling humor. "Though that can stay just between us. Assuming Cesar gets it and agrees to keep it to himself."

Agree. Cesar closed his eyes with a sigh, able to relax at last and get some sleep, tuning out the humans who, at their cores, were utterly certain they were his guardians and not the other way around.

Amusing creatures, humans.

BISHOP EMERGED FROM the mine shaft's narrow door—the door put into place and heavily barred decades ago when this shaft had been closed—and Tony didn't have to ask; whatever he'd seen inside had been bad. The scar on the left side of Bishop's face, usually almost invisible, was pale in contrast to his tan, and a sure sign of emotional turmoil that was otherwise hidden.

Since this was not, technically, their investigation, or at least not one Tony had been involved in, he had elected to remain outside and had been watching searchers, some with cadaver dogs, combing the mountain slope all around the mine shaft.

Now, as their unit chief joined him, Tony merely asked, "Do you think they'll find more bodies?"

Bishop shook his head once. "I don't think there was time. Cole Jacoby wasn't a killer, and this wasn't about killing. I doubt he was even consciously aware of doing what he did. Judging by what was found in the shaft, the girl was a hiker. She made two bad mistakes; she went hiking alone and she went hiking in this area. She was a victim of opportunity, almost dropped in Jacoby's lap."

"If it wasn't about killing—"

"It was about increasing the level of negative energy he was able to channel."

"So he—or, rather, it—could open this side of the vortex?"

"Yeah."

Tony thought about it. "So weren't you taking a chance having Hollis on the other side of the vortex? I mean, I get that you believed only a powerful medium could have closed that end, and in such a way as to get rid of a lot of the dark energy, but with her there it was a certainty that she'd draw even more energy to gather all around her."

"It was a chance we had to take."

"You were counting on Callie and Luther being able to keep Jacoby distracted just long enough."

"Something like that."

Tony eyed him. "You knew both of them would be wounded." It really wasn't a question.

"Some things have to happen just the way they happen."

"So whoever you and Haven sent here was going to get hurt?"

"Callie and Luther needed to be here."

Too accustomed to uninformative replies, Tony sighed and said, "Well, both teams got the job done. But didn't Maggie warn you that Luther might not be all that pleased by how things went down?"

"Luther met Callie." Bishop turned and began to head back down the slope. "Let's go, Tony."

"It sounds like a line in a song," Tony complained, following him. "Luther met Callie. That had to happen too, huh?"

"It had to happen here."

"You going to tell them that?"

"Of course not."

Since the slope was treacherous in places, Tony concentrated on not falling on his ass, not speaking again until they reached their Jeep, parked on one of the old logging roads.

"I still don't get where the money ties in to everything," he complained as he climbed in the passenger side. "It was awfully convenient that Jacoby stumbled on both sides of a vortex."

Bishop started the Jeep and guided it through the crowd of other vehicles, then turned toward town, as usual finding his way easily despite the confusing network of dirt roads and sometimes hardly more than paths crisscrossing each other.

"Boss?"

After a moment, Bishop said, "Energy affects most of us, you know that. In an inexperienced or latent psychic, the right kind of energy can guide or even control the psychic on an unconscious level."

"He was being controlled all along?"

"I doubt that Jacoby was anywhere near powerful enough himself to have stolen time and memories from two agents."

"And before that?"

"The seeds were probably planted before he was caught, and likely even before the robbery. It was far too ambitious a heist for him based on his history and known skills. And there were too many little glitches in the building's security systems that helped him pull it off."

"Glitches caused by energy?"

"No way to prove it, but I'm guessing yes."

"But that would mean there was energy involved long before he put the two agents out."

"Yes. He suffered a head injury during a fairly brief prison stay when he was quite a bit younger."

"And head injuries often turn latents into active psychics."

Bishop nodded. "He might never have been aware of the change in him. But since it probably started in prison, it's virtually certain that the first energy he was exposed to as an active psychic was negative energy."

"Yeah, I remember Callie talking about how negative the energy is in prisons. Worse than just about any other place, she said."

"And strong. I doubt Jacoby could have resisted, even if he'd known what was happening to him."

Tony thought about that, hanging on as the Jeep bumped its way over the rough logging road. "So it was no coincidence that Jacoby just happened to rent a cabin built literally on top of one end of an energy vortex."

"There are no coincidences. The dark energy was already in him when a bored prisoner looked up information on himself and discovered a half sister he hadn't known about."

"He had Internet access in prison?"

"At that point, he was a nonviolent offender. He had Internet access with a guard looking over his shoulder. A guard with no way of knowing that the family research Jacoby was engaged in could produce anything dangerous."

"Okay. And then?"

"He researched his half sister, then the Alexander family she'd married into. Read about Alexander House. When he got out of prison that time, he actually stayed there. But neither Anna nor her brother-in-law were in residence."

"And we know all this how?"

Not exactly answering, Bishop said, "We'll find his name in the guest registry; he stayed at the hotel for a week nearly two years ago."

"Long before the bank robbery."

"Yes. And on that trip to Alexander House, he passed through Devil's Gap, it being the closest town to the hotel."

Tony waited a moment, then asked, "And?"

"And he was drawn here, to this mountain."

"Why?"

"That head injury in prison. He was already doing things he couldn't have logically explained. Going to Alexander House to meet the sister he hadn't known existed was probably one of the last real decisions or choices he actually made with a clear mind. Ironic."

"Because—?"

"Because that was the beginning of the end for Jacoby. The end probably would have come eventually, since he was bound to land back in jail at some point and again be surrounded by dark energy. But visiting Alexander House, and then coming to this mountain, sealed his fate."

Tony didn't find that at all melodramatic, which rather surprised him. "He wasn't strong enough to fight it, I gather."

"No. We both know evil, Tony; it's insidious, especially if you don't know it's . . . lurking. By the time he realized, if he even did, it was far too late for him to regain control."

"So it was something else in him, that evil, that wanted him at the cabin?"

"On one side of a natural but very powerful energy vortex."

Tony remained silent this time until, to his relief, a logging road finally spilled them out onto a real, if winding, blacktop road. Then he spoke slowly. "Correct me if I'm wrong, but Jacoby being controlled like that, being lured so specifically, implies that the energy was . . .

had . . . a consciousness long before Alexander House or Devil's Gap, or that cabin back there."

Bishop was silent.

So Tony tried again. "Or maybe . . . was being used by a consciousness, at least in the beginning. Before any dark energy at the mouth of a vortex could come out and play. Maybe by a single human mind."

"Not so sure about the human part," Bishop said finally.

"Wait a minute—this was done by a person?"

"You heard the sheriff. Not counting the victim, there were only three people up here this last week. Callie, Luther, and Jacoby. All were affected by the energy of the vortex, but only Jacoby was being controlled by it."

"So . . . whoever it was, whoever started everything, they weren't on the mountain."

"No."

"Do you know who it was?"

"I have my suspicions."

Suspicions Tony knew Bishop would keep to himself until he was certain of his facts. Despite the truth that his agents and operatives were more often than not left in the dark about certain facts of their investigations, Bishop virtually always knew more than he shared.

And sometimes that was a lot.

"The point," Bishop said, "is that we won this round."

"There'll be another?" Tony asked warily.

The Jeep rounded a curve and came suddenly upon the rather odd little town called Devil's Gap, and as Bishop drove down the single main street toward the town's single medical clinic, he said, "One thing I've learned is that sometimes an enemy can haunt you for a long time."

HOLLIS WAS THOROUGHLY exasperated. "He has the jet. And could certainly get a chopper from the airport. Why the hell didn't he get here last night?"

"Brooke didn't say he would," DeMarco reminded her calmly. "She just said he was on his way."

"And is he coming by way of California? From a starting point of somewhere near Boston?"

"I have no idea."

She glared at him. "Why are you so calm? Yesterday you were pissed at him."

"I'm still pissed. But also very curious. For one thing, even you admitted that it wasn't *like* a spirit to offer such very specific information as Brooke did about the money. Nor is it usual for a spirit to then warn us to keep quiet about it until Bishop got here."

"Yeah, that part of it is seriously annoying. Especially after she pointed the finger at Owen. I could barely look at him last night, and I'm glad we haven't seen him yet today." She frowned. "Are you packed?"

"Yeah, same as you." He leaned in the doorway to his bedroom and watched her pacing their shared sitting room. "And I imagine our hosts are wondering why we haven't left yet."

"Probably haven't left their own bedrooms. I don't think we've ever seen them before ten, have we?"

"No, neither one seems to be an early riser."

"But it's nearly ten now, right?" Like most SCU agents, Hollis couldn't wear a watch. In fact, if she got too close and most certainly if she touched it, she could stop a clock. Easily.

DeMarco was the rare SCU agent who could wear a watch. But this morning, when he looked at the one on his wrist, she knew that had changed.

"Stopped on you, huh?"

"Yeah." He didn't sound either surprised or annoyed, merely matter-of-fact. "But the clock in my head is still working; it's quarter to ten."

"Okay. I say we take our bags and head downstairs. If Bishop isn't here by the time we get the car loaded, we can damned well either confront Owen or start looking for the money ourselves."

"We only have Brooke's word for it that Anna even *has* a half brother. I couldn't find any trace of that information last night, remember."

Gloomy, she said, "Yeah, but you also couldn't get very deeply into the genealogy stuff, not with the Internet connections here. Besides, Bishop knew. You heard it in his voice when we called him, just like I did. He was just evasive enough to let it show. What I can't figure out is what's up with all the weird secrecy. This *kind* of secrecy, I should say. And the delay. Can *you* remember a case where he put his agents on hold until he got there himself?"

"That's not exactly what he's doing."

"Because this wasn't supposed to be a case? He knew

it was a case when he sent us here. Whether he knew for sure *when* he sent us might be open for debate, but I'm betting one thing he was certain of was that he needed two teams in specific places to accomplish whatever his goal was. He knew about the vortex. Maybe he needed us here to confirm it, and to help close it, but he knew about it."

"And the money?"

Hollis was frowning. "Did Bishop know Owen has it? I don't know, maybe. He's got such a damned Machiavellian mind it's sure as hell possible. And it's going to get him into trouble one day. Serious trouble."

"Most of us seem to be in agreement on that point."

She sighed. "Yeah, I know. Come on, let's go downstairs. I can't stand just waiting around without doing anything."

"You won't get an argument."

SIXTEEN

The timing was perfect. Hollis and DeMarco reached the bottom of the stairs just as Thomas was admitting Bishop—and Tony Harte.

"I had to come along," he said to his fellow team members. "Still trying to get it all worked out in my head."

"Join the club," Hollis said with some feeling. But she was too professional to air her grievances in front of the stately butler, so all she added, to him, was, "Thomas, could you please tell Anna and Owen that we'd like to speak to them before we leave? We'll wait in the parlor."

"Of course, miss."

Tony stared after him, then raised his brows at Hollis. "Seriously?"

"Yeah, he's from another age. This way." She led them all into the Grand Parlor and closed the door behind them.

But it was DeMarco who spoke first. "Who did you tell him you were?" he asked Bishop. "I'm guessing the truth might spook Owen, to say the least."

"I spoke to Mrs. Alexander earlier this morning and told her there was a family matter I needed to discuss with her. From what you've said about Owen Alexander, I expect he'll join us out of curiosity."

"Probably," DeMarco agreed.

Hollis was looking at her boss through narrowed eyes. "I take it your morning has been busy?"

Bishop smiled faintly. "The other side of the vortex."

Dammit, he has a way of taking the wind out of my sails. She wondered how many of her fellow agents had read that thought, but her tone was milder when she said, "I hope nobody was hurt. We thought we heard a gunshot just before the last door was sealed."

"Callie Davis was wounded, though not with a gun. She's fine, recovering in the clinic in Devil's Gap."

Hollis blinked. "We were that close?"

"With the town and half a mountain between you, yes." He briefly explained that Callie had been informally teamed with a Haven operative, who had also been wounded by Cole Jacoby.

And that Luther Brinkman had shot and killed Jacoby.

"Jacoby the bank robber? Jacoby who was Anna's half brother?" Hollis wanted to know.

"Yes. But half siblings separated by a lot of years and distance; the two families were never blended. As far as I can tell, Anna never even met Cole Jacoby when they were kids. She's probably forgotten he ever existed."

"If she even knew," DeMarco offered.

Bishop nodded. "Entirely possible. But Jacoby knew; when we looked more closely at his history, we found he'd done research a couple of years ago. And came here, looking for Mrs. Alexander."

"She wasn't here?" Hollis guessed.

"No. But he had the chance to explore the place. It was after the biggest robbery of his life that he returned here, believing this would be a safe place to stash the money. But since she again wasn't here at the time, and since Owen Alexander appears to have made some sort of deal with Jacoby, I doubt he would have told her about the visit."

Tony looked at Hollis, again with lifted brows. "Is Alexander the sort of man who'd be willing to hide nearly ten million dollars in stolen currency?"

"I wouldn't have said so." She frowned. "Unless he was lying to us, he more or less relinquished control of the family business but stayed on the board of directors. Not really the actions of an ambitious or greedy man, right? No sign either he or his sister-in-law was in financial trouble. And no signs of criminal leanings in his background. Other than one bad mistake he made as a kid and has been haunted by ever since, he appears to have walked the straight and narrow."

She briefly explained about Jamie Bell.

"Well, if you ask me," Tony said, "the only possible explanation is—"

The door opened to admit Anna, followed closely by Owen.

Under her breath, Hollis said to Tony, "Your timing sucks."

"Or not," he said.

Hollis didn't get a chance to respond to that, distracted by the introductions.

Anna, the perfect hostess, led the way to one of the larger seating groups in the room so everyone could sit down, though she was clearly somewhat bewildered.

"I'm afraid I don't understand how all of you are connected? Mr. Bishop said this was about a family matter?"

Distracted again, this time by the odd idea of Bishop being a mister rather than an agent, Hollis almost missed his response to Anna.

"It's Agent Bishop, Mrs. Alexander. I'm with the FBI."

Owen scowled at him. "ID?"

Bishop produced his credentials, seemingly unmoved by the way Owen very intently studied them before passing them back to him.

"What does the FBI want with Anna?" he demanded of Bishop. "It *was* her you asked to see, wasn't it?"

Pleasantly, Bishop answered, "Because this concerns her family, Mr. Alexander. Ma'am, were you aware you had a younger half brother?"

Rather blankly, she said, "A brother? No, I had no idea. My parents divorced when I was very young, and he—my father was—"

Bishop helped her out. "He was abusive and your mother was granted a restraining order against him. Shortly after that, he moved to the West Coast and never contacted you or your mother again."

"It was a long time ago," Anna said slowly. "He never hit me, and I think my mother recognized what he was quickly enough and was strong enough that leaving him was easy for her. She remarried. My stepfather, who legally adopted me, was always kind—and then eventually I met and married Daniel. I haven't thought of my biological father in decades. He married again?"

Bishop nodded. "To a woman who didn't recognize what he was quickly enough, or wasn't strong enough to leave him when she did. He abused both her and their son, though Cole Jacoby was still young when his father was killed in a bar fight."

Anna blinked. "A bar fight. I see. And—and my brother?"

"Became a petty criminal who did time in prison, and eventually graduated to bank robberies," Bishop told her calmly. "Which is where the FBI enters the picture. Ma'am, your half brother was killed yesterday, not very far from here. Shot in self-defense by a private investigator who had tracked him up into the mountains."

Anna looked completely disconcerted, which Hollis could well understand. It had to be upsetting to learn of the existence of a half brother and be told of his life of crime and his death, all within the space of a few short moments.

"He's dead?" Owen Alexander looked briefly almost as disconcerted as his sister-in-law, but then his face settled into its customary unrevealing expression.

Bishop looked at him and smiled. It could be many things, that smile of his, but when he directed it at Owen, it was curiously dangerous. "He's dead, Mr. Alexander. So, of course, we've come for the money."

There was a long, long silence. Hollis allowed her gaze to roam from face to face. Tony and DeMarco were watchful; Anna was still obviously bewildered, Owen's face was stonelike, and Bishop . . . Well, he was Bishop, giving away nothing of his thoughts or feelings.

Before Owen could say anything, Bishop went on, his tone still calm, even pleasant, but with steel around the edges. "Months ago, Cole Jacoby came here, looking for the half sister his research had uncovered. It had taken him time to discover who she was and where she was, but he had time on his hands then, so he found out about her. And about the Alexander family she married into. About Alexander House, where he actually stayed for a time, just another hotel guest.

"But Cole Jacoby was less interested in establishing family relations than he was in finding a safe place he could turn to if he needed one. This remote place seemed an excellent potential hideaway or safe house. So he . . . banked that information for future need. When he robbed a bank and got away with ten million dollars rather than the considerably smaller amounts that had kept him off the national radar, he knew law enforcement agencies and officials all up and down the eastern part of the country would search for him, and search hard. He knew he'd be caught, and sooner rather than later. So he needed a place to hide the money."

Owen opened his mouth, but Bishop continued in that calm, relentless voice.

"I don't know what sort of deal he offered, or why you accepted it, but I can make a few educated guesses. You disliked business, disliked turning your home into a hotel for half the year, but you always enjoyed the good life, so those were necessary evils. Then Jacoby showed up, with millions he'd stolen, and he told you he'd split the money with you, if only you'd keep it hidden until he returned— or until the statute of limitations was up. It seemed a good deal to you. A few years of patience living as you always had, and then a windfall that would allow you to live as you liked, without being tied to a business or a home that was no longer really yours."

"I want a lawyer," Owen said, then spoiled the very smart demand by adding impatiently, "You can't prove any of that. There's no one here who will testify that anyone named Jacoby ever visited this house."

In an aside to her partner, Hollis murmured, "More family secrets Thomas will take to his grave?"

"Probably," he agreed just as quietly.

"And," Owen added, "even if you have a warrant to search the place, you aren't going to find stolen millions here."

Bishop smiled again. "Just because it wasn't in the original plans for the house doesn't mean we don't know about the false panel in your closet, Mr. Alexander. Hiding a space large enough to house all that cash."

Owen went white. "You can't— How do you—"

Hollis couldn't resist. "That's the thing about spirits, Owen. They tend to know all our secrets. Especially the dangerous ones. And the spirit of a girl you never knew in life knows all about that false panel, how to open it, and what it hides. And she was happy to share the information. Her name was Brooke, by the way.

"Gotcha," Tony said.

EPILOGUE

It wasn't until considerably later, on the jet heading back to Quantico, that Tony said to Bishop, "You're not going to tell who you suspected of possibly being behind all this, or at least the start of it, are you?"

"The keyword is *suspected*, Tony." Since Hollis and DeMarco were near the back of the jet talking, Bishop's voice was quiet.

"Okay, I get that you might not have proof. But, Boss, if there's yet another enemy out there, shouldn't we all know who it is?"

"All I have is a hunch." Bishop turned his head and gazed out the window of the jet, at the serenity of white clouds. "If and when I have more than that, I'll share."

"Will you?"

"Yes."

For some reason, that bothered Tony. A lot.

"Not exactly usual for you," he said slowly. "Sharing that sort of info, I mean. I know I asked, but . . ."

"If I'm right," Bishop said, "he'll make another move. And sooner rather than later. I think this one just . . . got away from him. Out of his control. Because he didn't know about the vortex."

"He planned to use Jacoby because he just wanted the money?"

"Needed it."

"To come after us?"

Bishop nodded silently.

Slowly, Tony said, "And he's a strong enough psychic to control another mind? Jacoby's mind, at least in the beginning?"

"Yes."

"But who could do that?" When his question was met with silence, Tony tried again. "An old enemy or a new one?"

"Both."

"How is that possible?"

"I told you, Tony. Some enemies can haunt you. Some enemies can haunt you for a very long time."

HAVEN OPERATIVE AND SPECIAL CRIMES UNIT AGENT BIOS

CALLIE DAVIS, FBI SPECIAL CRIMES UNIT

Job: Special Agent

Adept: *Telepath*. Also possesses the ability to recognize, shield against, and even repel negative energy.

Appearances: *Hostage*

LUTHER BRINKMAN, HAVEN SPECIAL INVESTIGATOR

Job: Private investigator

Adept: *Clairvoyant* with psychometric abilities

Appearances: *Hostage*

JOHN GARRETT, COFOUNDER OF HAVEN

Job: Oversees the organizational duties of running Haven and makes certain all equipment, information, and assets are ready when his people require them.

Adept: He is not psychic but possesses a unique understanding of those who are.

Appearances: *Touching Evil, Blood Dreams, Blood Sins, Blood Ties, Haven, Hostage*

MAGGIE GARRETT, COFOUNDER OF HAVEN

Job: Maggie handles the operatives and investigators who work for Haven, overseeing their training and, even more, monitoring their emotional and psychic welfare, both at base and when they're in the field.

Adept: An exceptionally powerful empath/healer, Maggie has the ability to literally absorb into herself the emotional and even physical pain of other people, in a sense speeding up their healing processes and helping them to cope with extreme trauma. The act of doing so requires that she give of herself, give her own energy and strength to the person she's helping.

Appearances: *Touching Evil, Blood Dreams, Blood Sins, Blood Ties, Haven, Hostage*

NOAH BISHOP, FBI SPECIAL CRIMES UNIT

Job: Unit Chief, profiler, pilot, sharpshooter, and trained in martial arts

Adept: An exceptionally powerful touch-telepath, he also shares with his wife a strong precognitive ability, the deep emotional link between them making them, together, far exceed the limits of the scale developed by the FBI to measure psychic talents. Also possesses an "ancillary" ability of enhanced senses (hearing, sight, scent), which he has trained other agents to use as well. Whether present in the flesh or not, Bishop always knows what's going on with his agents in the field. Always.

Appearances: *Stealing Shadows, Hiding in the Shadows, Out of the Shadows, Touching Evil, Whisper of Evil, Sense of Evil, Hunting Fear, Chill of Fear, Sleeping with Fear, Blood Dreams, Blood Sins, Blood Ties, Haven, Hostage*

HOLLIS TEMPLETON, FBI SPECIAL CRIMES UNIT

Job: Special Agent, profiler-in-training

Adept: *Medium.* Perhaps because of the extreme trauma of Hollis's psychic awakening (see *Touching Evil*), her abilities evolve and change much more rapidly than those of many other agents and operatives. Even as she struggles to cope with her mediumistic abilities, each investigation in which she's involved seems to bring about another "fun new toy" for the agent.

Appearances: *Touching Evil, Sense of Evil, Blood Dreams, Blood Sins, Blood Ties, Haven, Hostage*

REESE DEMARCO, FBI SPECIAL CRIMES UNIT

Job: Special Agent, pilot, military-trained sniper; has specialized in the past in deep-cover assignments, some long-term

Adept: An "open" telepath, he is able to read a wide range of people. He possesses an apparently unique double shield, which sometimes contains the unusually high amount of sheer energy he produces. He also possesses something Bishop has dubbed a "primal ability": he always knows when a gun is pointed at or near him, or if other imminent danger threatens.

Appearances: *Blood Sins, Blood Ties, Haven, and Hostage*

TONY HARTE, FBI SPECIAL CRIMES UNIT

Job: Special Agent, profiler

Adept: Telepath. Not especially strong, but able to pick up vibes from people, particularly emotions.

Appearances: *Out of the Shadows, Touching Evil, Whisper of Evil, Sense of Evil, Hunting Fear, Chill of Fear, Blood Dreams, Blood Sins, Blood Ties, Haven, Hostage*

PSYCHIC TERMS AND ABILITIES

(As Classified/Defined by Bishop's Team and by Haven)

Adept: The general term used to label any functional psychic; the specific ability is much more specialized.

Clairvoyance: The ability to know things, to pick up bits of information, seemingly out of thin air.

Dream-projecting: The ability to enter another's dreams.

Dream-walking: The ability to invite/draw others into one's own dreams.

Empath: One who experiences the emotions of others, often up to and including physical pain and injuries.

Healing: The ability to heal injuries to one's self or others, often but not always ancillary to mediumistic abilities.

Healing Empathy: The ability to not only feel but also heal the pain/injury of another.

Latent: The term used to describe unawakened or inactive abilities, as well as to describe a psychic not yet aware of being psychic.

Mediumistic: The term used to describe a person who has the ability to communicate with the dead.

Precognition: The ability of a person (a seer or precog) to correctly predict future events.

Psychometric: The ability to pick up impressions or information from touching objects.

Regenerative: The ability to heal one's own injuries/illnesses, even those considered by medical experts to be lethal or fatal. (A classification unique to one SCU operative and considered separate from a healer's abilities.)

Spider Sense: The ability to enhance one's normal senses (sight, hearing, smell) through concentration and the focusing of one's own mental and physical energy.

Telekinesis: The ability to move objects with the mind.

Telepathic mind control: The ability to influence/control others through mental focus and effort. An extremely rare ability.

Telepathy (touch and non-touch or open): The ability to pick up thoughts from others. Some telepaths only receive, while others have the ability to send thoughts. A few are capable of both, usually due to an emotional connection with the other person.

UNNAMED ABILITIES INCLUDE:

The ability to see into time, to view events in the past, present, and future without being or having been there physically while the events transpired.

The ability to see the aura of another person's energy field.

The ability to channel energy usefully as a defensive or offensive tool or weapon.

KEEP READING FOR AN EXCERPT FROM
THE NEXT BISHOP / SPECIAL CRIMES UNIT
NOVEL FROM KAY HOOPER

HAUNTED

AVAILABLE SEPTEMBER 2014
FROM BERKLEY BOOKS

PROLOGUE

Cathy . . . Be careful, Cathy . . .

He's watching you.

She woke with a start and in a state of uneasiness she couldn't explain to herself, not at all certain if that whisper had come from a nightmare she couldn't even remember. She didn't, after all, have that pounding-heart terror one of her rare nightmares inevitably left her with. Her small apartment was quiet, peaceful. Since she lived just outside the downtown area and three floors up, there were no traffic noises or anything else to disturb her sleep.

But her alarm lacked fifteen minutes before it was due to go off, and it was unusual for her to wake before. In fact, she was known to hit the snooze button at least twice before dragging herself out of bed just about every morning.

Except this chilly winter morning.

Cathy Simmons went ahead and got up, shutting off

the alarm so it wouldn't go off while she was in the shower. But instead of going straight to the shower, as was her habit, she first went around her apartment checking the locked door, the closed and locked windows. Peering outside uncertainly.

Nothing seemed out of the ordinary.

Nothing *was* out of the ordinary.

The apartment was warm, but she felt cold.

And she didn't know why.

Just need a shower, that's all.

She wasn't in danger. Nobody was in danger. The murder the previous week was just . . . well, just finally Sociable's turn to have something bad happen. That's what it was. Everybody said so. Just a weird and unsettling thing, probably a stranger passing through, and most certainly gone now. No threat to anybody else.

That was what everybody was saying.

Though the sheriff had been awfully quiet about it . . .

Frowning a little, Cathy turned on the coffeemaker, left ready the night before, then went to take her morning shower.

She had lived in Sociable forever. Or, at least, it felt that way. Twenty-four years. She had taken her first steps here. Had fallen out of the big oak tree behind her family home and broken her arm at the age of twelve. Had gone to grammar and high school here. Had received her first kiss and a lot more here—from a boy who had bolted for college right after graduation without so much as a backward glance at the "girlfriend" two grades behind him.

And with no scholarship prospects or family money, and since she was unwilling to go into debt when she'd had no definite career plans anyway, Cathy herself had graduated high school with decent but not stellar grades and attended the community college off the highway one town over, close enough to drive there and back every day.

Reluctantly she had taken business courses because she'd had nothing better in mind, and had afterward landed a teller job at the Hollow Creek Bank. It paid well enough to keep her comfortable if not affluent financially, and it wasn't difficult. But it also hadn't exactly put her on a desired career path.

She still didn't know what that might be.

Working at the bank for more than three years now, she had the uneasy suspicion that there wasn't going to be a career, just a job that was okay. Maybe marriage and kids, but no likely prospects had turned up. And since she knew the relatively few eligible men in town—a population that seldom changed—too well and too long to believe a candidate lurked somewhere on the fringes of her social life, that really left only guys passing through or newcomers to the area.

Guys passing through . . . Well, that was just never a good idea.

And she could count on her fingers the newcomers to the area in recent years, several male but all married or clearly involved with or interested in someone else.

Glum, Cathy got out of the shower and dried off, then

wrapped the towel around herself and reached up absently to wipe the steam off the mirror over her sink.

That was when she saw it. The message.

Letters, clear as anything, as if a steady finger had traced them on the fogged mirror just seconds before.

Time's up, Cathy.

ONE

Deacon James had grown up in a small town, so he didn't exactly feel out of place when he followed the winding mountain road out of fairly dense forest and rather suddenly into the three-block-long downtown area of Sociable, Georgia.

North Georgia.

Remote North Georgia.

And the town seemed to cling to the mountainside, a unique but surely impractical place on which to site a town.

It looked the way many small mountain towns looked, with the "major" local businesses on the relative flat of Main Street while smaller businesses as well as a scattering of Victorian homes and a few startlingly contemporary ones on climbing side streets appeared to perch precariously behind and above.

Probably have a hell of a view.

It was a one-side downtown; across the street was a fairly wide strip of well-kept grass striped with the occasional neat and carefully graveled path leading down a gentle but boulder-strewn slope to a wide and apparently shallow mountain stream which, given its location, almost seemed even more than the town itself to defy gravity and sense.

The town had clearly taken advantage of what could only be used as a recreation area, providing scattered attractive shelters with picnic tables beneath, benches, and the aforementioned well-kept paths, as well as at least two comfortably wide footbridges across the stream. There was even what looked like a small park with swings for the kids and a big jungle gym with an attractive wrought-iron fence with a gate for safety around the play area.

But there wasn't much else on that side of Main Street, because there wasn't a whole lot of room.

Beyond, on the other side of the stream, were a few smallish trees on an even more narrow strip of grass, a couple of benches facing the spectacular view from an as-close-as-you'd-want-to-get perspective, planting beds covered with mulch hinting at flowers to come in the spring—and then, bordered by a different and stronger wrought-iron fence to prevent a tragic slip, a pretty sheer drop to the bottom of the valley at least three hundred yards below. The valley that stretched out for miles and seemed to be mostly pasture dotted with cows and horses, a few fields obviously farmed, and widely scattered older homes holding the people that farmed them.

With the mountains ringing the valley, it really did present an extremely attractive view, and no doubt a pleasant place to live for many reasons, among them the absence of any industry producing pollution of the air or groundwater, and a population small enough that most knew each other but not so small that there was nothing better to do than to nose into each other's business.

Still. It was an odd place to put a town, Deacon thought, but he had seen odder, especially along the Blue Ridge with its old mountains and old towns that had sprung up generations ago around now defunct mining or trading, or to serve the many farmers in the valley—where the land was too valuable a resource to waste on businesses and official buildings that could easily perch on the mountainside above.

Well, not *easily*. But from a practical standpoint, if farming and ranching served the local economy well enough, sensibly.

Deacon knew that many towns like Sociable pretty much depended on a local-driven economy supplemented by seasonal tourism sparked by this or that "festival" or other annual draw besides the scenery. Most such small towns, in these difficult economic times, struggled to remain viable, and most watched the younger generations move away after high school because there was so little to offer them in the way of a career or even a good, steady job that wouldn't keep them in a small office or behind a counter for the rest of their lives.

But it appeared that Sociable was doing all right for itself, or at least all right enough that all the buildings

Deacon could see on Main Street appeared to be attractive and occupied, at least surviving if not thriving. He couldn't see a single vacant building, at least along the main drag. And there had to be some money about; he had passed both a high school and a middle school on the drive in, both newish and sprawling buildings less than five miles from downtown.

He'd passed a couple of car dealerships too. And churches. Several churches.

And there was one church downtown, perched high above Main Street, its whiteness and slender steeple almost shining in the afternoon light. Maybe watching over the town and valley below.

Maybe.

There was a bed-and-breakfast literally at each end of downtown, with a well-kept and attractive building housing a three-story hotel smack in the middle. There were numerous stores, at least three restaurants, a couple of banks. A sheriff's office apparently shared a fairly large building with the town post office and courthouse, and he could see at the far end of Main Street what looked like a fire station. There were two doctors' offices visible, a pawnshop that looked less seedy than many, a bookstore, and two different coffee shops, one chain and one local.

He wondered idly which got the most business; it was difficult to tell at first glance.

Deacon parked in front of the first of the coffee shops he came to, mildly surprised to find no parking meters. He got out and closed the car door without bothering to lock it; his luggage was in the trunk, and Sociable really didn't look like the sort of town where cars were jacked right off Main Street.

In least not in broad daylight.

He stretched absently, a bit stiff after the long drive, and looked around with casual interest for a few moments. There was a fair amount of activity in the area on this Tuesday despite the February chill in the air, and as far as he could tell, no one paid him any special attention.

Not really a booming tourist town, Sociable, but the scenery and small-town charm did bring enough visitors that the arrival of one more caused no particular notice.

Even now.

Which, Deacon thought, was a bit surprising. The people he saw went about their business, their expressions preoccupied but not especially tense or uneasy. When two met in passing, they appeared to exchange casual greetings, but no one lingered to talk.

He would have expected that.

Then again, what he was seeing might very well be the citizens of Sociable being uneasy and on edge. Maybe they generally did stop and talk to each other, get coffee, shoot the breeze, discuss local events.

Like murder.

Deacon frowned a bit, but decided to get out of the chilly air while he considered the matter. He went into the coffee shop, which he found to be typical of most he'd been in: small tables with minimalist chairs, a long banquette along one wall with evenly spaced tables in front of it, and in one rear corner a tall counter with glass cases showcasing various sandwiches and pastries. A drop to a lower counter on either end, where a customer ordered and then picked up said order.

There were signs advertising free Wi-Fi, and at least two customers sipped coffee or tea as they worked at laptops, while two others appeared to be reading on tablets. There were even three independent "stations" just past the banquette with laptops set up for customer use.

A pleasant young woman took Deacon's order, and since it was a no-frills black coffee and a large wedge of apple pie, he was able to carry both to a table in the other back corner in only a couple of minutes.

He settled into his chair and sipped the coffee, which wasn't bad. He sampled the pie, which was excellent.

And he watched, without being obvious about it.

More customers trickled in and out over the next half hour. Some came for coffee and left with their ubiquitous paper cups and preoccupied expressions; a few lingered to chat with the staff behind the counter, which included several young women and only one young man.

A couple sat enjoying coffee, pastries, and a quiet conversation, clearly in no hurry to leave.

A woman with a laptop arrived to get coffee and settle down to work, or check her email or social media sites, or surf the Net, or whatever she was doing. A teenager showed up, bought what he and the staff laughingly referred to as "milk with a little coffee," and then went to one of the provided laptops and settled down to what looked like an online game.

Just as outside, no one appeared tense or on edge. In fact, the occasional chats at the counter erupted more than once into quiet laughter, and the staff behind the counter appeared unfailingly cheerful.

Okay, just two murders. So maybe that's not so unusual. Nothing worth talking about, for most people. So what if this town hadn't had a murder in decades until less than two weeks ago, and has had two since then. Maybe Melanie's wrong in believing it's bigger than murder, worse than murder.

Maybe . . . it's just Melanie.

Wouldn't be the first time, right?

MELANIE JAMES HAD worked at the Hollow Creek Bank for more than three years, and she liked her job. The bank truly was a "hometown" sort of place and had been for at least three generations, its canny local investors and managers both smart and skilled enough to keep it prospering even during the periodic economic downturns of the state and even the country.

And since Sociable was a small town where neighbor still helped neighbor and most had very strong work ethics, being the loan officer for the bank seldom involved unpleasant duties such as turning down a request for a loan, whether personal or business.

"It's just for the rest of the winter," John David Matthews was saying in his laconic, matter-of-fact voice. "Got some fine stock to sell in the spring and over the summer months."

"You've always been a good credit risk, John David," Melanie told him with a smile as she gave the paperwork a final check. "Hey, how is that pinto mare coming along?"

"My daughter's training her, says she's smart and good-natured. No vices. You still interested in her?"

"Definitely. I've been saying for the last year that I wanted to have a good riding horse, mostly for weekend trail rides." It was a favorite activity among several of her friends, enjoyable because the area was crisscrossed with miles of mountain trails.

"The pinto would be a good choice."

"For a Sunday rider?"

He smiled. "I'd say. Sophie trains with kindness and takes her time; her horses always seem to take on her own sweet nature. With a pasture to run in when you aren't riding, the pinto's bound to be a calm mount."

"Good. Maybe I'll come see her this weekend, if it's okay."

"'Course it's okay. I'll tell Sophie you're still interested. You can call the house and let her know if you do decide to come."

"Great, I'll do that. And you be thinking of a price, okay? I'd be boarding her with you, of course." Her downtown apartment was nice, but hardly boasted stable or pasture. And John David provided fine care at a reasonable price for any animals boarded with him.

His rugged face appeared mildly pleased, which for him was as good as a broad grin; boarding fees and guided trail rides made up most of his income from fall to spring, so a prospective new boarder was welcome news. As was the strong possibility of a horse sold.

Still, being a practical man, he said, "You know you can always borrow a horse if you want to ride. Don't have to have the expenses of buying and boarding."

Melanie gathered up the signed paperwork into a neat stack and smiled at him. "Little girls dream of owning their own horses one day. I did. Now I can actually do it. And I've got my eye on that pinto, John David."

"Consider her reserved."

"Thanks. Now—here are your copies of everything, and here's your check. Always a pleasure doing business with you." The words were conventional, but her tone made them friendly and personal.

"Thank you, ma'am." He smiled as he rose, and they shook hands before he headed out into the bank to deposit his check.

Melanie rechecked to make sure all the paperwork she needed was in his file, then closed it, and for a few moments gazed down at the folder on her blotter without really seeing it.

Good job. Good town. Good people. She had friends. She had dates when she wanted them. She had a nice home she enjoyed, and money enough to live well.

It was a good life.

Or, at least . . . it had been.

The cold knot in the pit of her stomach was never very far from her awareness now. Because something was very, very wrong in Sociable. Something . . . unnatural. And she was afraid that meant at least one person in her life wasn't at all who or what she believed them to be. In fact, she was almost certain that was the case.

Not a stranger, Trinity had said, eyeing Melanie calmly. No evidence of that, and plenty going the other way.

Someone in Sociable was a murderer.

A horribly vicious murderer whose crimes defied understanding and even—almost—defied belief.

It's not natural, what happened. It's not . . . normal. Somebody gets mad and somebody else gets dead. Somebody gets greedy and somebody else gets dead. Simple motives for simple, stupid crimes, mostly obvious right from the start. That's what Deacon says. And he's right. That's the way it works. But this . . .

This was definitely not simple, and if the killer was stupid, he or she was hiding it well.

Even with no experience investigating murder in Sociable, Trinity was no fool, and probably better trained to handle the unlikely than most small-town sheriffs. And she wouldn't hesitate to arrest even a friend if the evidence warranted it.

She was giving Melanie the benefit of the doubt.

For now, at least.

Melanie had so far gotten only a few odd looks from some of her fellow citizens, but she knew it was early days yet. And that with every day that passed without the killer being unmasked, let alone caught, she would get more and more of those looks. As time went on and the very air grew thicker and thicker with tension, with anxiety, people would look for a focus for their suspicion and fear.

She was a relative newcomer to the town. And even if they didn't know for sure, people would imagine . . .

motives. From the reasonable to the irrational, there were bound to be motives.

Hell, she could think of a few herself.

Which explained her panicked call to Deacon.

Melanie wasn't exactly having second thoughts about that, except that she hated feeling this need for . . . somebody on her side. Somebody who knew her too well to believe . . . even reasonable motives.

Someone who knew she was not a murderer.